I0534937

# SHADOWS
## -
# OUTSIDER

by

THOMAS D. RUDD

To Kathy,
God threw away the mold when he made you.
Love you forever.

To Britt and Jo-Jo,
The best daughter-in-laws in the world,
Love ya!

To Will, Evie, and Micah,
The best grandbabies in the world
Love, love, and love.

Copyright © 2025 by Thomas D. Rudd
All rights reserved.

No part of this book may be reproduced, stored in a retrieval
system, or transmitted in any form or by any means,
electronic, mechanical, photocopying, recording, or
otherwise, without the prior written permission of the
publisher, except for the use of brief quotations in a book
review.

This is a work of fiction. Names, characters, places, and
incidents either are products of the author's imagination or
are used fictitiously. Any resemblance to actual events,
locales, or persons, living or dead, is entirely coincidental.

Independently published.

Paperback ISBN: 978-1-966939-02-3

For inquiries, contact: dachieftdr1701@hotmail.com.

Printed in the United States of America.

All rights reserved.

Special thanks to Muhammed Waqas for his tremendous
artwork.

# TABLE OF CONTENTS

PREVIOUSLY ON SHADOWS...

The first time I saw a Shadow, I thought I was imagining things. Turns out, I wasn't.

It's funny how life can change in an instant. One day, you're just a kid—the heir to an organized crime syndicate. The next, you're in Witness Protection because your father— who, surprise, surprise, decided his son was a liability— wants you dead.

Not exactly a normal life.

But Havenwood? Havenwood wasn't normal either.

At first, it just seemed... off. Too quiet. Too still. The kind of town where the houses looked normal, but you could feel something watching. And I was right.

It wasn't just the town. It was the people.

My mom and I barely survived my father's purge of my grandfather's old crew before WITSEC dropped us into the hands of two U.S. Marshals—Bell and Taylor. It didn't help much. Turns out Taylor was working for my father the whole time. She shot Bell a few months in, right before everything went to hell.

Then there was our neighbor, Bryan Jensen—a man with more ghosts in the closet, literally, than he had time for. A guy who kept to himself, whose past had burned him worse than anything I could imagine. He lost his family once, but Havenwood? Havenwood didn't let the dead stay gone.

Neither did his wife, Ashley.

Turns out Havenwood—or Haven in the Woods—was the secret home to a centuries-old Coven of witches. And Ashley?

1

She was their ruler in all but name, feared even by the things that went bump in the night. The Coven called her 'The Huntress', and if the stories were true, she'd been hunting for a very, very long time.

But even she had a past. One that tied her to Bryan. And, more importantly, to their daughter.

Brianne.

That's where things got complicated. Because from the moment I met Brianne, something changed. I couldn't explain it. It was like I had known her forever. Like she was supposed to be a part of me.

She wasn't just a girl. She was a ghost.

She was mine. And I was hers.

That didn't sit too well with Ashley, who—despite being The Huntress—was also a ghost. Don't worry... I know it's complicated, but I'll explain later.

Anyway, the deeper I dug into Havenwood's secrets, the worse things got.

The Shadows—things that shouldn't exist, things that fed on fear—were drawn to me. And they weren't the only ones.

The Custodians—Coven members embedded in society—were watching.

Ed Jones—their leader, who just happened to have it bad for Ashley... and Bryan—was waiting.

And my father, Alexi Sokoloff, came looking for me.

But he wasn't expecting Bryan.

Bryan didn't hesitate. He ended it.

Alexi Sokoloff was dead.

But that didn't mean we were safe.

Havenwood still had its monsters. And some of them wore human faces.

In the end, we survived. But we didn't escape. Not really.

Ashley was still out there. The Custodians weren't finished.

And Ed Jones... well, it turns out he had plans of his own.

And Bryan? Bryan did what he always did. He adapted. He fought back. He became exactly what the town feared. And what it needed.

A Witch Hunter.

Now? A new life? A fresh start? Maybe. Someday.

But the past? The past doesn't let go.

Jones is still out there. Watching. Planning.

And as much as I want to believe we left the troubles of Havenwood behind... I know better.

Because Havenwood never really lets you go...

## PROLOGUE: VENGEANCE AWAKENED

A single, bare bulb hung from the low ceiling, casting a sickly yellow light that swung slightly, disturbed by the violence that had erupted moments before. The ceiling, a patchwork of rough, weathered wood beams and exposed stone, bore the weight of centuries, with cracks running like veins through the mortar. Where the bulb swayed, it cast shifting shadows above, flickering across the uneven surface like dark, jittering tendrils. Dusty cobwebs clung stubbornly to the beams, shivering with each subtle draft slipping in through unseen crevices in the ancient stone.

Bryan Jensen, his ragged hair and stubble-covered face battered and bloodied, slumped in the heavy, wooden chair at the room's center, his wrists bound tightly to the armrests with a coarse rope that bit deep into his skin. His once-strong frame seemed shrunken, each labored breath hitching in his chest, becoming shallower with each passing moment. His face, once set in determined lines, was barely recognizable—bruised, swollen, and streaked with blood that trickled from cuts along his cheekbones and brow. His dark hair, matted and slick with blood and sweat, clung to his forehead, his head hanging to one side. His eyes drifted in and out of the dim glow of awareness as though reluctant to release the final spark of life clinging to his battered body.

As the chill seeped deeper into the walls, Bryan's final breath left him in a shuddering release. For a brief moment, silence reigned as if the house itself held its breath, waiting for his end to settle. The shelves lining the basement's walls were filled with tools, crates, and storage boxes—each now marked with dark, drying blood, transformed into grim relics of the horrors that had unfolded in this room. Shadows lingered in the corners, shifting with the bulb's dim movements, casting sinister shapes across the cold, unyielding stone walls. The basement's chill seemed to crawl through the walls, creeping into Bryan's bones, growing colder as the life slipped from his body.

Then, the temperature dropped sharply. An unnatural chill crept through the ancient stones, frost edging over the walls like a living beast inching closer to Bryan's slumped form. The bulb's yellow glow dimmed. Shadows stretched longer, deepening the sense of foreboding.

And then, in the thickened darkness, a presence stirred.

Bryan's deceased wife, Ashley, a striking woman in her early thirties, her ghostly ethereal figure, emerged from the shadows, a spectral glow illuminating her ghostly form as she drifted toward Bryan, her gaze softening with both love and fury as she took in the broken, bloodied man before her. Her dark hair, deep as midnight, cascaded in gentle waves around her shoulders, framing a face both haunting and beautiful. In death, she was just as captivating, her deep brown eyes gleaming with an intense, otherworldly light. She appeared as if time had preserved her last living expression—a fierce determination mixed with sorrow, beauty marred by tragedy.

Spectral fingers reached out to gently brush his face, ghostly and cool against his battered skin. They lingered over the bruises and cuts with a tenderness that defied the nightmare around them. Ashley's touch sank deep, stirring a faint, fragile spark within him, reminding him of a life that felt both infinitely distant and painfully close. She looked upon him with a gaze that seemed to transcend time and memory—a gaze that promised love, vengeance, and a final reckoning.

But as she reached him, Ashley's gaze shifted to the far side of the basement. There, slumped and mutilated in a growing pool of blood, lay the body of Bryan's last tormentor, Nicholai, a cruel and sadistic henchman of Alexi Sokoloff. Her wrath had painted the room—blood sprayed across the walls, torn fragments of flesh and entrails scattered like grisly confetti. The man's face was frozen in a mask of terror, twisted and torn as if he'd encountered a horror beyond comprehension.

With a ferocity that had transcended the boundary between the living and the dead, she had torn him apart, leaving him sprawled in a grotesque tableau of punishment. Her vengeance had been swift, brutal, and final—a declaration that no one would harm her husband and walk away.

Bryan's final breath slipped from him like a fading ember, as though even in death, he resisted surrendering entirely. The darkness pulsed, thickening as if alive, wrapping around him. Frost spread along the walls, creeping inward with Ashley's arrival, the air crackling with a strange energy that seeped into his veins.

"No, my love," she murmured, her voice resonating with a power that transcended the physical world. "You're not done yet. We're not done yet."

Ashley's form descended upon him, melding with him, her essence intertwining with his. A bone-deep chill laced through his veins, filling him with a cold fire that reignited his last spark of life. Her spectral eyes flicked to the nearby tool bench, where a rag and a handgun—likely used by his tormentor earlier—rested amid the clutter. With an almost imperceptible wave of her hand, the rag slid across the bench, carried by an unseen force, wrapping itself securely around the weapon. The gun hovered for a moment before settling into Bryan's mangled, three-fingered hand, the cloth binding it tightly to his grip, ensuring it would remain in place despite his trembling.

His body twitched—a spasm in his fingers, a jerk in his leg—before the convulsions grew. His head snapped back in a silent scream as her will poured through him, binding him to her. Bones cracked and aligned, wounds closed, and color returned to his pallid skin, grotesquely mending under her spectral influence.

Bryan—no, Ashley, within Bryan—pushed up from the chair, the ropes once binding him snapped as if made out of thin air, his limbs trembling yet driven by a force that defied his injuries. His mangled hand, now securely wrapped with the cloth and gripping the gun, lifted with eerie steadiness. As he staggered past the chair, he barely glanced at the lifeless body of Alexi's lieutenant, a twisted reminder of the horror Ashley had ended in her rage.

His eyes snapped open, no longer warm brown but black as coal, radiating a bottomless darkness. Bryan's chest heaved with a deep, ragged breath, his body rising with an impossible strength.

Bryan—Ashley, within Bryan—stood tall, her presence radiating through him, commanding the shadows around them. She looked down at the lifeless body, her lips curling into a sinister smile. Crossing the threshold into the cool night air, her vengeance was absolute, propelling Bryan

7

forward with her unyielding purpose—a shared fury that would stop at nothing to exact justice for all they had lost.

***

The forest loomed dark and silent, the air cold and thick as Bryan forced one foot in front of the other. Each step felt like a battle against his own body, his breath coming in ragged gasps. Blood trickled down his arm, staining the ground as he staggered, the weight of Ashley's presence both guiding him and draining him.

Bryan could feel Ashley's presence slipping, her hold weakening as his strength ebbed. But he pressed on, his mind focused on making it to the house at the end of the path. Anna and Riley were there, caught in Alexi's twisted game.

Anna, his reluctant neighbor, had stepped into his world out of sheer necessity and, in doing so, had unknowingly pulled him back toward humanity. Earlier tonight, she had realized the weight of her own feelings—realized that she'd fallen in love with the mysterious man next door. For months, Bryan had remained a shadow in her life, a quiet, brooding presence that seemed untouchable. Now, she understood why. And yet, despite her growing affection, she still didn't know the full truth of who—or what—he really was.

Then there was Riley. Just ten years old, the boy was terrified but brave in a way that struck Bryan deeply. Tonight, Bryan had placed an impossible weight on Riley's young shoulders: the task of leading his mother to safety. In doing so, he had admitted something he had never voiced before—a simple, heartfelt truth: If I ever had a son, I'd want him to be like you.

Neither Anna nor Riley had been prepared for what they'd discovered about Bryan. The enigmatic man who had once been nothing more than a distant neighbor was now their only hope of survival. And as Bryan fought his way through Alexi's cruel game, every step was a desperate promise to himself: He wouldn't fail them. Not this time. He had to reach them—no matter the cost.

The dim light of the house glimmered faintly ahead, and Bryan stumbled through the darkened woods, each step feeling heavier than the last. Ancient trees loomed around him, their twisted branches clawing at the air as if to ensnare him. Thick fog coiled at his ankles, curling up from the damp forest floor, making the path nearly impossible to see. Silence pressed in close, broken only by his labored breathing and the faint creak of branches in the night.

Ahead, Ashley's ancestral home, decaying and decrepit, emerged from the shadows, half-swallowed by overgrown thistle bushes and crawling vines. Its narrow windows glared out, unblinking, as if the house itself waited. Roof gables and arches cast jagged silhouettes against the moonlit sky, silent witnesses to the tragedies written into its walls.

He stumbled up the crumbling steps, each one groaning under his weight as he leaned against the rotting railing. The wood, damp and splintered from years of neglect, shivered beneath his hand. With a trembling grasp, he reached for the door handle, the thick wood cold under his fingers as he pushed it open.

The door creaked, and oppressive darkness pressed in. Inside, the air was thick with rot, mildew, and the heavy scent of forgotten memories. Dust coated every surface, visible in the faint glow from a narrow hallway stretching forward. Shadows pooled in the corners, dense and suffocating, pressing in around him with a watchful, almost predatory intent.

Bryan's gaze drifted up the staircase, rising toward the upper floor. The handrails, once intricate and polished, were thick with grime. Each step creaked underfoot, the sound resonating through the silence as though the house itself protested his intrusion.

From above, a faint, muffled scream pierced the stillness, followed by the ominous crack of splintering wood. Bryan froze mid-step, his fingers tightening around the railing. Dust sifted down from the ceiling, and then, with a resounding thud, a massive shape hurtled down, crashing into the floor just above him.

For an instant, Bryan caught a glimpse of Dimitri—Alexi's towering lieutenant—falling from above, his body tumbling down along with a cascade of rotting wood and dust. Shadows obscured his face, but Bryan could make out the smear of fresh blood on his knuckles and the sweat glistening on his brow. The thug hit the floor with a sickening crash that rattled the house's decrepit frame. Then, with a loud crack, Dimitri's weight drove him through the floor again, splintering the wood beneath him.

The room was filled with swirling debris and the choking scent of ancient dust, mixing with a sharp, metallic tang—the unmistakable smell of blood. Bryan stepped back, shielding his face as particles drifted around him, thickening the already stifling air. Somewhere below, there was a final, grotesque thud as Dimitri's body impaled itself on something jagged in the basement. The silence that followed was dense, broken only by the unsettling creaks of the house settling once more.

Bryan forced himself to move, his heart pounding as he made his way to the room where he knew Anna and Riley were. Light seeped faintly out of the open hallway, illuminating the swirling dust and making it seem as though the house itself was breathing with evil intent. He took a steadying breath, bracing himself for what awaited him beyond.

The silence returned, thick and oppressive, as though the house had swallowed him whole.

Bryan climbed the final steps, his legs trembling, and entered a narrow corridor lined with decaying portraits of Ashley's long-dead ancestors. Their painted eyes were dark and cold, and their resemblance to Ashley was unmistakable in the solemn expressions and watchful gaze that seemed to follow him with every movement. The walls seemed to pulse with eerie energy. The flickering light cast twisted shadows that shifted and moved on their own.

At last, he reached the room where Anna and Riley had made their desperate stand. The door was open, revealing a space once overtaken by decay. The ceiling arched above him, casting the room in an oppressive gloom. Dusty, torn drapes hung over tall, narrow windows, blocking the faint moonlight and leaving the space in nearly impenetrable darkness. Cobwebs stretched across the room's corners, which sagged slightly, weighed down by neglect.

In the dim light, Alexi, the ruthless, cold-blooded human manifestation of a 'wolf in wolf's clothing,' turned, his face frozen in a smug grin as he recognized Bryan—or thought he did. The man's dark suit was immaculate, but the blood on his knuckles and the satisfaction in his eyes revealed his pleasure in the violence he had wrought. Alexi's gaze met Bryan's, momentarily confused by the void in Bryan's soulless, coal-black eyes.

And now, here he was, standing in the doorway, gripping Nicholai's gun, determination etched on his battered face.

Anna's breath hitched as she stared into Bryan's black, soulless eyes. His presence filled the room, but it was wrong—terribly wrong.

A single word came, low and guttural, Ashley's voice blending with Bryan's, carrying a chilling finality that sliced through the air. "Boom."

The pistol roared, and the back of Soloff's head erupted outward in a violent spray of blood, hair, and slivers of bone. His body collapsed, leaving a trail of crimson as it crumpled to the floor.

Pale as a ghost, Bryan collapsed, his back against the wall, sliding down. Anna and Riley rushed to his side.

"No, no, no... stay with me... stay with me," Anna pleaded, pulling Bryan to her chest. Her voice quivered with fear and desperation. She looked at Riley. "Go for help, hurry!" Riley, his eyes wide with terror, reacted instantly, sprinting out of the room.

Bryan's eyes, unfocused, stared blankly ahead. His eyelids fluttered closed as he slowly went limp.

"Come on, Bryan, come on." Anna sobbed, clutching him tighter. "Stay—stay with me. Please, God, please help him," she whispered desperately, looking up as if seeking divine intervention.

In that moment, Bryan's eyes snapped open—black as coal. Anna gasped, pulling back as his hand snagged her wrist with a grip that was too intense, too cold.

A swirling, jet-black mist began to drift out of Bryan's eyes, ears, nose, and mouth... his pores. It gathered and drifted off, stopping over the gaping, jagged hole that, like the house's maw, had swallowed Dmitri. Anna, still holding Bryan, watched as Ashley's ghostly form took shape, flickering between horror and beauty.

Ashley stepped forward and knelt beside Bryan, her form shifting with each breath. Her focus was on Anna, her eyes flickering red with a cold, calculated hatred.

"You have no idea how much I loathe you," Ashley whispered, her voice dripping with venom.

Ashley's monstrous hand shifted to a gentle caress, her touch unnervingly tender.

"His last thoughts should've been of me and our child, not you and yours," she said, her form flickering between monstrous and beautiful. "Fear not. My love for him outweighs my hatred for you."

The room grew cooler as Ashley's form shifted entirely to beauty, her gaze softening as she looked at Anna. Several tense seconds passed, and then her gaze softened.

"Do you love him?" Ashley asked, her voice a mix of sorrow and resignation.

"Yes," Anna whispered, tears streaming down her face.

"Would you die for him?" Ashley's voice was barely audible, a quiet plea for understanding.

"Yes," Anna and Riley, who silently stepped into the room, his race for help forgotten, answered in unison, their voices trembling with emotion.

Ashley's form snapped back to its monstrous state, her gaze locking onto Riley, who had just entered the room. Tears streamed down Riley's face as he stood in the doorway, clutching the amulet Bryan had given him. Ashley's monstrous form softened as Riley approached, his small hand trembling as he extended the amulet toward her.

"Please, take this," Riley whispered, his voice quivering with fear. "Take it or take me... please... just don't take him."

Ashley's monstrous hand reached out but faltered. Her gaze softened, and the glow of the amulet reflected in her eyes. As she hesitated, a faint glow appeared behind her—a more petite, delicate figure bathed in soft light. It was Brianne, semi-transparent and barely visible.

Brianne, Bryan's dead daughter's ghostly figure, lost at the tender age of eight, hovered just behind Ashley, her form flickering like a fragile candle in the wind. She embodied innocence, a stark contrast to the darkness that consumed Ashley. Her wide, sad eyes bore into Ashley's monstrous form, silently pleading.

Ashley turned, her gaze shifting from Riley to Brianne. The monstrous rage that had twisted her features softened, hatred dimming as she looked upon her daughter. For a moment, the two specters seemed to communicate without words, a silent exchange resonating deep within the room.

"Please, Momma." Brianne's voice was soft, almost a whisper, but it cut through the tension like a knife. "Let him go. He's suffered enough... We've suffered enough."

Ashley's monstrous form trembled, the dark energy crackling with conflicting emotions. She turned back to Bryan, her gaze filled with pain and sorrow.

"But I love him..."

"I love him, too," Brianne said gently, her eyes filled with understanding. "But you have to let him go. It's time."

Ashley's eyes glistened with unshed tears. She looked at Bryan, her monstrous features softening until she was once again the beautiful woman she had once been. She knelt beside him, reaching out to touch his cold, pale cheek.

"Bryan," she whispered, her voice full of love and resignation. "I'm sorry... I'm so sorry."

Bryan's body convulsed one final time, the darkness pouring out like black mist, swirling before it was drawn into the abyss. His eyes fluttered closed, his breathing shallow but steady. The room grew still, its tension loosening.

Ashley's ethereal form now radiated beauty, the monstrous darkness gone. She turned to Anna, her expression one of sad acceptance.

"Take care of him," she said softly, her voice carrying a weight of finality. "He'll need you now... more than ever."

Anna nodded, tears streaming down her face. "I will. I promise."

With one last look at Bryan, Ashley turned to Brianne. The two spirits exchanged a loving glance, then began to fade, dissolving into the soft light that filled the room.

As they disappeared, the amulet in Riley's hand glowed brighter, its light washing over the room, purging it of the lingering darkness. The oppressive atmosphere lifted, and for the first time in what felt like an eternity, the house was silent and peaceful.

Anna held Bryan close, her heart pounding as she watched the light envelop them. Riley moved closer, his small hand resting on Bryan's arm as the supernatural traces faded away.

"Is it over?" Riley whispered, his voice trembling.

Anna looked down at Bryan. He was alive, breathing—but different.

A shadow still clung to him, deep in his eyes.

She wanted to tell Riley yes. She wanted to believe it. Instead, she pulled him close and whispered, "For now."

*** 

Outside, the night lay in an uneasy stillness. The house stood in silence as if holding its breath. The thistle bushes, once writhing with unseen malice, had curled inward, brittle and lifeless.

16

And yet, something remained.

Far beyond the clearing, where the trees swallowed the moonlight, something moved. The wind stirred, carrying with it a whisper—low and hungry, an echo of a presence that had never truly left.

The war wasn't over.

It had barely begun.

## CHAPTER 1 - THE NIGHT UNFOLDS

Riley stumbled through the woods, his feet pounding the ground as he reached the clearing where the flashing lights of emergency vehicles cast an eerie glow over the trees. He barely registered the chaotic scene around him as he ran toward the waiting arms of the SWAT team, shouting for help.

Lucas, a paramedic, moved swiftly, calling out to his team, and within seconds, they were charging into the woods, a line of dark figures against the tangled forest.

Minutes later, they emerged, Bryan's body strapped to a stretcher, his face pale, his right hand gruesomely bound with a blood-soaked rag that barely concealed the missing fingers. Blood seeped steadily from the wound, leaving a trail on the ground as they rushed him to the ambulance.

Anna clung to his side, her expression fierce as she held his remaining fingers, her touch as gentle as it was desperate. Her fingers traced his knuckles, silently willing him to stay tethered to life, to her. Riley watched, his heart pounding as they loaded Bryan into the ambulance, his mother climbing in after him, her gaze never leaving his face, the bloodied cloth covering what was left of his right hand a sickening reminder of the price Bryan had paid to keep them safe.

The doors slammed shut, and the sirens blared, slicing through the night as the ambulance tore down the road, racing toward the hospital. Riley stood watching, his heart heavy yet filled with fragile hope. As he was led to another ambulance, he closed his eyes, whispering a silent prayer for

Bryan, for his family, for a new beginning amid the darkness they had endured.

As the ambulance sped down the road, a figure stepped from the edge of the gathering crowd, his face cast in shadow.

Ed Jones, a member of the Havenwood town council, tall, dark, and handsome, watched the flashing lights recede into the night, a cold smirk twisting his lips. To the townspeople, he was a figure of respect, part of the town's fabric—a quiet man with old ties to the Coven. But in his eyes flickered something dark, something dangerous, an ancient anger that had been simmering for far too long.

He hadn't forgotten Ashley's rejection, the insult of her choosing an Outsider over him. Her ghost might be gone, but Bryan still lived—barely. That Outsider, the one who had stolen what was promised to him. His gaze lingered down the road, his fingers flexing at his side, the weight of old spells and unspoken oaths humming in his blood.

And as the crowd began to disperse, Jones' expression darkened, the glint of vengeance and unfinished business simmering beneath his polished, outward calm.

Jones had watched from a distance as the SWAT team and emergency personnel swarmed around what was once Ashley's ancestral home. His eyes narrowed, taking in the chaos with grim satisfaction.

From his shadowed vantage point, he saw them loading Bryan's broken form onto a stretcher, Anna clinging to him with desperate tenacity, her hand still clutching his even as they guided him into the ambulance. Pitiful, he thought, lips twisting in a slight sneer. But not for long.

Following the horde of outsiders from a safe distance, it was easy for Jones to blend into the crowd of 'faithful' that had assembled as he had commanded.

As the ambulance sped off into the night and Detective Matt Browning, the Boston PD cop who'd found Riley and Anna huddled in a storeroom after barely surviving the purge of male members of the Sokoloff crime family, took Riley in the opposite direction, Jones felt a surge of dark satisfaction wash over him. This was it—the chance he'd been waiting for. Years of resentment, humiliation, and wounded pride had festered within him, a bitterness rooted in Ashley's rejection and Bryan Jensen's very existence.

That Outsider, that unworthy insect, had ruined everything. Not only had he stolen Ashley's loyalty and love—he'd taken what should have been Jones's rightful place at her side, helping to control the Coven, dominating the others who'd once dared to challenge him. With Ashley's power, he could have risen to a position of absolute influence, reshaping the Coven in his image. Instead, she dared to deny him and choose a life beyond the Coven, beyond him.

Jones let the venomous memories flow through him. Ashley had been his for the taking; her beauty, her power— all of her should have belonged to him. He'd pictured it countless times: the two of them as a force of supernatural mastery, untouchable. Dominating her in every aspect of life, not only in life but in bed. She would bear his offspring. Their child, born from that union, would have been the culmination of his line, carrying the legacy of the Coven forward with a strength unmatched by any. And yet, her loyalty had wavered the moment she met that Outsider. Jensen, he thought, barely able to stomach the name. That unworthy, cowardly, ordinary man had somehow captured her heart, turning her against her own kind, against him.

But now, fortune had aligned in his favor. The Outsider lay on the brink of death, his frail body torn to shreds. Jones felt a twisted satisfaction at the thought. Perhaps Bryan was suffering, feeling every wound, every fracture, knowing he was on the verge of slipping into oblivion—a fitting punishment for daring to touch what wasn't his.

***

As the SWAT team finally departed, Jones stepped out from his hiding spot, slipping through the darkened edge of the forest and skirting around the house until he stood before Ashley's ancestral home. Its defenses, the ancient wards, and the protective spells she'd woven had been weakened, likely shattered during the violent battle that had just taken place. He could feel it—an almost palpable stillness, as though the building itself had gone dormant, its power drained in the wake of Ashley's spectral rage.

With a quick, efficient motion, Jones withdrew a small knife from his coat pocket and pressed it against one of the wooden beams, extracting a small splinter from the structure. He held it up, studying the fragment as though it were a precious gem. This tiny piece will be enough to bring my shadows with me, he thought, tucking it into his palm with a satisfied smirk. This sliver of Ashley's home would tether the Shadows to him, allowing them to roam far beyond their usual confines, freeing him to unleash them wherever he wished.

He murmured a quiet incantation, binding the splinter's power to his own, sealing the link between himself and the

Shadows that were bound to the land. He felt a chilling rush of dark energy flow through him, like a shiver down his spine, as the spectral beings stirred at his call. They had been waiting, lingering for centuries, trapped by ancient magic, but now—now they were his to command, to wield against the enemies that dared to stand in his way.

*** 

Jones's eyes glinted as he turned back toward town, every step bringing him closer to the final phase of his plan. He had maneuvered for this moment for years, weaving layers of deception, ensuring no one suspected his true ambitions. The town knew him as a respected lawyer, a figure of authority, someone to be trusted. But beneath that polished exterior lay a mind as calculating as it was ruthless.

Let them think I'm there to help, he thought, a cold smile creeping across his face. He would pose as Jensen's lawyer, a perfectly legal excuse to visit the hospital and hover close to his enemies. The foolish townspeople would grant him access without question—no one would dare keep him from his 'client.' And once inside, he would set the Shadows upon them, let them descend upon Anna, on Riley, on anyone foolish enough to be nearby. There would be no witnesses, no survivors—only the silent, terrifying marks of spectral vengeance.

As he walked, Jones's thoughts drifted back to Ashley's rejection, to the slight she had dealt him in front of the Coven. She had humiliated him, dismissed him as if he were nothing. The arrogance, he fumed. She thought herself above us, above me. And now, her memory is nothing but an echo, a ghost clinging to the fringes. He dismissed the rumors about her spirit as mere superstition, a story whispered by the weak-minded to comfort themselves against the unknown. Ashley was gone. The only threat left was her daughter. That cursed offspring she'd left behind with Jensen; now, little more than a memory would be dealt with; he would claim the ancestral home and use it to fuel his rise to power.

Jones's resolve hardened as he neared his car, glancing back one last time at the darkened trees surrounding Ashley's home. This is my destiny, he thought. With Jensen and his pathetic 'family' out of the way, nothing would stand in his path. He would show the Coven what true power looked like, bending them to his will, and in time, even the outsiders would cower before him. And the outside world, the world of Outsiders, would pay for what they'd done. They would pay. Finally, after so many centuries of hiding his true identity, they would grow to fear the name 'Gregor Vasilević.'

***

Sliding into the driver's seat, Jones cast a glance at the sliver of wood he'd extracted, feeling a surge of twisted satisfaction at the thought of what was to come. Let them cling to their wards, their prayers, he thought with a smirk, his fingers brushing over the splinter. They have no idea what's waiting for them. He could already picture the scene—the panic, the helpless terror as the Shadows descended upon the hospital, sweeping through the halls like a plague, sparing no one who dared stand in his way.

As he drove toward the hospital, he couldn't help but savor the thought of his enemies' fear, the exquisite agony they would feel as they realized they were powerless against him. The Shadows, carrying centuries of vengeance, would tear through the hospital, and he, Ed Jones, would stand at the center of it all, untouched, orchestrating their end with a cool, unfeeling precision.

Unbeknownst to Jones, his hubris would be his undoing. The Ward of Protection Riley held, the very piece of magic he dismissed as insignificant, would stand as a barrier to the Shadows he believed so unstoppable. Jones, blinded by his ego and his lust for revenge, had overlooked the strength of the bonds that tied Bryan, Anna, and Riley together—the very thing he lacked, the same thing that would bring him down.

As Jones continued his journey, the Shadows began to stir at his command, hovering just outside the range of the sliver's influence, ready to strike. The final confrontation was close, and Jones could almost taste the power he believed was rightfully his. But for all his careful planning, for all his ruthless ambition, he remained ignorant of the forces he could not see—the Ward, the fierce loyalty of Bryan's new family, and Ashley's lingering presence poised to protect her loved ones one last time.

His confidence would be his greatest weakness, and by the time he realized it, it would be far too late.

***

The ambulance tore through the dark, winding roads, its sirens screaming into the night. Inside, Anna clutched Bryan's hand, her fingers sliding over the thick, blood-soaked bandage that covered his missing fingers. The raw horror of it churned in her mind, her heart seizing at each erratic beep of the heart monitor. He lay pale and motionless on the stretcher, the barest whisper of life left in him, and every stuttering blip on the monitor was a countdown to the moment he might slip away.

"Pressure's dropping!" Robert, the lead paramedic, shouted, his voice rising above the wail of the sirens. He pressed down hard on Bryan's bandages, his brow knit with grim concentration. "We're losing him here!"

Jace, his partner, wrestled with the IV line, glancing anxiously at the monitor. "How's he even hanging on? Look at his BP—he's practically a corpse." He grimaced at the sight of Bryan's hand, noting the steady seep of blood through the ragged cloth. "We've got to do something about that hand— he's bleeding out faster than we can stabilize him."

Anna's breath hitched. "Please... please help him! Do something!" Her voice cracked, desperation clawing at her throat.

"We're doing everything we can, ma'am," Robert said, but even his words carried an edge of doubt. He leaned closer to Bryan, willing him to hold on. "Hang in there, buddy. Don't you check out on us."

The ambulance lurched as it sped through the downtown streets of Havenwood. Residents peeked out from their windows, their expressions shifting from confusion to alarm as the flashing lights and two police cruisers blazed past, their sirens joining the cacophony as they raced through the sleeping town.

With a screech, the ambulance halted near the open field by the high school, where the whirling rotor blades of an air ambulance cut through the air. The medical team inside was ready, waiting, as the paramedics wheeled Bryan toward them.

"Move! Move!" Robert barked as they maneuvered the stretcher across the field. Anna followed, barely able to keep up, her gaze locked on Bryan, willing him to stay and fight despite the gruesome sight of his wrecked hand.

The medivac helicopter doors slid open, and the trauma team inside sprang into action, quickly securing Bryan onto the stretcher. Anna clambered in behind them, her hands still clutching Bryan's, refusing to let go.

"Get him on the monitor, stat!" a nurse ordered over the roar of the rotors, her tone sharp and commanding. The heart monitor beeped erratically as they adjusted Bryan's IVs, the rhythm fluctuating wildly.

The flight surgeon, his face set in concentration, examined Bryan's vitals on the monitor and shook his head. "Massive blood loss. Looks like severe internal injuries. This guy should be dead already." His gaze flicked to Bryan's hand, wincing at the missing fingers. "We're losing him through that hand alone. We need immediate cauterization if we're going to slow the bleed."

The nurse pried open one of Bryan's swollen eyes, studying his pupil reaction. "Jesus... no response. And his pupils are blown. It's like he's gone, but his heart's still beating."

Anna's throat tightened. "He's not gone... please, he's still here. Just... just keep him here." Her hand clutched his all the more fiercely, feeling the rough cloth where his fingers had once been, her heart shattering at what he had endured.

One of the paramedics, struggling with the IV line, muttered to the nurse beside him, "How's he even holding on? He's bleeding out faster than we can stabilize him."

"Miracle, if you ask me," the nurse replied, glancing at Anna with something like pity. "Ma'am, whatever he's holding on for… you're the reason. Keep talking to him."

Anna leaned close, her hand trembling as she brushed it across Bryan's forehead. "I'm here, Bryan. You saved us—me and Riley. Don't leave us now. Don't give up. We need you."

As she spoke, images began to flash through her mind—moments that felt like fragments of a life she had dared to imagine.

She saw Bryan that first time at her doorstep, awkwardly asking if Riley could come out to play catch. His eyes had held that shy earnestness, that vulnerability he tried so hard to hide, and the way he had looked at her as if he needed her approval more than he'd ever admit.

Then Riley's accusing words echoed in her mind, laced with bitterness: "You know what they're doing to him!" Anna's breath hitched, shame flooding through her. She remembered how Riley had looked at her that night—face pale, voice trembling, his words a fierce indictment of the mistake that had unleashed a chain of horrors. And here, in the blood-soaked reality before her, she couldn't ignore the evidence of that horror. Alexi's sadistic acts were carved into every bruise and wound only inches from her—a nightmare made real by her stolen kiss. All because of a kiss.

The kiss. The one plastered across the front of a nationally syndicated magazine, the kiss that had cost the man in front of her so dearly. Her mind flickered to that moment—the warmth that had spread through her from that stolen kiss on the lawn, her lips on his, hope surging through her at the world of possibilities that might follow it. She could still feel the warmth of her hand on his cheek, could still remember the brief light in his eyes that a flash of fear had quickly overshadowed—fear that now felt like a cruel omen of what would come. That kiss had drawn Ashley's wrath, drawn her back from wherever she'd been watching, lurking, abandoning Bryan to a fate he didn't deserve.

Another memory forced its way into her mind: Bryan and Riley, laughing in the yard, throwing the ball back and forth in the late afternoon sun. She could almost hear the crunch of grass and leaves underfoot and see the smile that softened his face as he gently corrected Riley's stance, showing him how to keep his eye on the ball. The way Bryan's eyes had flicked to her—half a smile that warmed her from the inside out, before all of this, before her heart had set in motion the events that would shatter him and his precarious world.

And that last kiss, in her kitchen, just before she and Riley fled for safety. The way her heart ached when she witnessed this man, once a stranger and now the center of her universe, consoling her son, giving the small boy hope where none existed. The kiss that had changed everything—their lips had barely brushed, but in that instant, she'd felt something ignite, something so powerful she knew she couldn't deny it anymore. She had fallen in love with this man, this imperfect, wounded, wonderful man.

Her voice broke as she spoke, her whispers fierce. "You can't leave, Bryan. I love you. Riley loves you. Don't you dare leave us after everything... Don't you dare."

Through the headset, the pilot's voice crackled as he relayed information to the hospital. "Trauma One, this is Medevac Bravo. We have a critical inbound. Male, approximately thirty-five. Massive blood loss, potential internal hemorrhaging, multiple fractures. Vitals are unstable; ETA six minutes."

The helicopter shook as the wind picked up, jostling them all, the rain pounding against the windows with increasing force. Anna tightened her grip on Bryan's hand, her heart aching with every turbulent shift. Beside her, the nurse adjusted the IV; her brow furrowed as she checked Bryan's vitals again.

"His pressure's tanking again," she said urgently. "We're losing him, and I have no idea how he's even hanging on. Nothing about this is making sense."

The flight surgeon leaned in, shouting over the noise, "If he's still got a pulse, we're going to fight like hell. Prep the O-neg and crank that transfusion rate!"

The helicopter rocked again, rain slamming against the windows, and Anna felt a chill run through her. It was as if nature itself were conspiring against them, determined to pull Bryan away. She pressed her forehead against his, her voice barely audible over the noise. "Please, Bryan. Hold on. You're not leaving me. Not like this."

The nurse adjusted her headset, turning back to the monitor with a frown. "His pulse is erratic. Barely holding. And with his injuries… there's no medical reason he should still be here."

One of the medics muttered under his breath, "I don't know if it's luck or something else, but he's hanging on by a thread. We've got to keep him tethered."

Anna's mind drifted again, the memories flashing brighter and more vivid as she clung to him. She could see their life stretched out before her—the quiet mornings, the laughter, the way he could calm her fears with a single look. This was the man who had risked everything for her, who had promised in his own quiet way that he'd be there for her and Riley.

The co-pilot's voice crackled again, relaying the details to the waiting trauma team. "Inbound with severe trauma. Blood pressure unstable, extensive bleeding. Prep OR and notify the surgical team. Repeat and notify the surgical team. We'll be down in thirty."

The helicopter lurched again as they began their descent, the city lights of Boston stretching out below like a beacon. Anna caught sight of the hospital, its floodlights blazing against the darkness, and felt a surge of desperate hope.

The pilot's voice was tense as they approached. "This weather's cutting it close. Hold tight for landing."

With a hard jolt, the helicopter finally touched down. Paramedics and trauma staff rushed to the doors, bracing against the storm as they slid open and pulled the stretcher out, each one shouting instructions as they fought against the gusts of wind and rain.

"Keep his head stabilized!" a trauma nurse shouted, her voice barely audible over the storm.

"Vitals are crashing—get him inside now!" another shouted as they wheeled Bryan toward the emergency entrance, lights from the ER casting harsh shadows over his pale face.

Anna stumbled after them, drenched and trembling as they rushed him through the double doors into the bright, sterile chaos of the trauma unit. She stood frozen for a moment, the chaos behind her a blur of voices and flashing lights.

***

The hospital doors burst open, and the trauma team surged forward, wheeling Bryan's stretcher down the brightly lit corridor. Anna trailed closely behind, her heart pounding, her gaze locked on his pale face as he was swallowed into the chaos ahead. She could barely keep up, stumbling as she watched the flurry of activity around him, each movement sending a fresh wave of fear crashing through her.

The nurses worked swiftly, adjusting IVs and tightening restraints, their hands steady but their faces tense. One nurse leaned close to Bryan, checking his vitals, her lips pressing into a thin line as she glanced at a nearby colleague.

"BP's still dropping—prep the crash cart," she murmured, her voice low but urgent. As she looked down the hallway, her words dropped to an even softer whisper, "And... we're going to need a priest."

The words struck Anna like a physical blow, reverberating through her with the cold, crushing weight of despair. A priest! Her steps faltered, her fingers instinctively reaching out to brace herself against the wall. It was as if the very air had thickened around her, pressing down until she could barely breathe. Her mind struggled to process what she'd just heard, the quiet, matter-of-fact tone in the nurse's voice seeming to drain the room of any remaining hope.

"No... please, God, no," she whispered, her voice cracking as she staggered forward, unable to tear her eyes from

31

Bryan's still, pale face. She felt her pulse quicken, a desperate urge rising within her to rush forward, to grab them all, to make them see that they had to keep trying, to fight harder. Her eyes, wide with fear, followed the nurse as she moved away, leaving Anna rooted in the hallway, her heart splintering under the weight of that single word.

She glanced down the hall, catching a last glimpse of Bryan as the team maneuvered his stretcher around a corner. His hand lay limp against the sheet, his body so still it seemed lifeless. A voice echoed faintly in her mind, a haunting reminder of the fragility of hope within these sterile, unforgiving walls.

Swallowing hard, she forced herself to move, trailing after them on unsteady legs, her heart caught between love and terror. She knew what life with him could be—she saw it clearly now, a life filled with laughter, love, and quiet moments that could become their own. Her voice was barely a whisper, and she begged him to stay, to keep fighting, and to come back to her.

Up ahead, the trauma team circled Bryan, voices overlapping in a discordant symphony.

"BP's at 60 over 30—he's crashing!"

"Prep for immediate transfusion! How is he still alive with this much blood loss?"

"Get him on oxygen—stat!"

Each command was a lifeline, every second a desperate effort to keep him tethered to life. Anna felt herself trembling as she watched, helplessly rooted at the edge of the chaos. The cold fluorescent lights seemed harsher, the sterile smells of the hospital overwhelming her senses. Yet even in the midst of it, she could see it—an image of what their life together could be, of Bryan by her side, of Riley someday calling him "Dad."

Her heart ached with that fragile vision, the knowledge that she'd give anything to make it real, to see him open his eyes and come back to them. She held her breath, fighting back tears as she clung to that hope, whispering to him as if somehow her words could reach him through the blur of pain and darkness.

"Please, Bryan... stay with us. Don't give up. We need you. I need you."

With every whispered plea, she felt herself slipping further into the depths of her fear—the quiet terror that he might not come back and the cold finality that a single kiss might have snatched away a future together.

*** 

As the surgical doors swung closed, Anna felt an overwhelming emptiness press down on her, as if that door had sealed her off from everything she had left to hold onto. Bryan was in there, on the table, his life at the mercy of surgeons who couldn't possibly understand what he had endured, what he had fought through just to make it this far. She sat down slowly, eyes unfocused, lost in the sterile white of the waiting room, her mind already spiraling into the dark.

Every thought drove her further inward, dragging her down under the weight of things left unsaid, of betrayals hidden behind false smiles. Marshal Taylor's face flashed in her memory, unbidden—the woman she'd trusted, talked to, leaned on, her supposed friend. Every conversation, every

33

warm moment of 'girl talk,' now felt hollow, twisted with the knowledge that Taylor had been hiding a knife behind her back. How many details had she casually let slip in those private moments? Had Taylor watched her, listened to her, all the while planning exactly when to strike? How much had she shared with Alexi? It was like filth clinging to her skin, each thought darker and more damning, making her feel raw and tainted, like she'd been played for a fool.

And then there was Bryan. Anna's mind reeled back to him, her heart pounding as she thought of the quiet, reclusive man she had so wrongly judged. When they'd first met, she'd seen him as someone who'd checked out of life, someone too broken and distant to care. And yet, he had stepped up when she needed him most. The weight of that realization was crushing. He had died for her once, right there in her arms, a sacrifice she'd never forget. Now he was lying in surgery, fighting for his life all over again, and the worst part—the thing that tore at her most—was that he wouldn't be there at all if it weren't for her. A kiss. That's all it had been. A single kiss that she'd thought would spark something meaningful, something real. It was innocent, even hopeful, but how could she have been so naive?

Riley's words echoed through her mind, cold and accusing. "You know what they're doing to him." And, God help her, she did know. Deep down, she'd known what Alexi was capable of, what the price of defiance could be. She'd brushed off the danger, blinded by the promise of a fresh start, by her desperate hope for something good in a world filled with shadows. And now Bryan, the man who had fought so hard, who had endured so much, lay in surgery because of her. Because she hadn't seen the danger, hadn't protected her

34

family, hadn't been strong enough to resist that fleeting temptation.

Her hands were trembling, and she clenched them into fists, nails biting into her palms as she held back tears. If Bryan didn't survive, she knew that this guilt—this crushing, relentless guilt—would be with her forever. Every choice, every misjudgment, every blind spot had led them here. And if she lost him, she would never forgive herself. Not for the kiss, not for believing in Taylor, and certainly not for letting her guard down when she'd had so much more to lose.

And still, she sat. Helpless, with nothing left to cling to but the fading hope that Bryan, in his quiet, unbreakable way, would find a way to pull through—one last time.

***

On the dark, winding drive to Boston, the car is silent except for the low hum of the engine. Browning glances over at Riley, who sits with his head leaning against the window, clutching the Ward of Protection Bryan gave him. His small hands grip it tightly, almost desperately, as he stares out into the night. Riley's eyes, wide with shock and sorrow, seem lost, replaying the horrors of the night: Marshal Taylor's betrayal, her threats against his mom, and the way she looked at him with pure disdain.

For Riley, it's a nightmarish blur. He remembers Bryan, his rock and his hero, telling him to get his mom to safety. He remembers Bryan's words: I'll buy you as much time as I can and the horrifying realization that Bryan fully expected not to make it out alive. Riley knows Bryan kept his promise, sacrificing everything to save him and Anna. And now Bryan is fighting for his life in a hospital somewhere up ahead, and

Riley can do nothing to help. He clutches the Ward as tightly as he can, hoping it will be enough.

Browning, watching the boy out of the corner of his eye, feels the weight of Riley's pain pressing into the car's silence. He wonders what he could possibly say. He's not used to talking to kids, especially not one who's endured such horrific trials. Browning's guilt gnaws at him, knowing he's the one who handed Riley and Anna over to WITSEC, believing they'd be safe. But the betrayal of the trust placed in Marshal Taylor shattered more than just their safety—it left this young boy haunted, sitting beside him in shell-shocked silence.

As they travel deeper into the night, Browning notices Riley casting glances down at the Ward of Protection. It's just a trinket to him, a keepsake. But Riley holds it as if his life depends on it, as if it carries the last bit of hope he has left. Browning watches, feeling something he doesn't fully understand—a strange mix of pity and respect. What could this kid have gone through to cling to a token like that with such fervor? Kid's hoping for a miracle, he thinks to himself, but he knows all too well that prayers don't often reach where they're most needed.

The deeper they drive into the dark, the more Browning's helplessness gnaws at him. Here's this young boy, who's witnessed horrors that even seasoned cops would struggle to stomach, clinging to what looks like a child's good-luck charm. He wants to reassure Riley, but he knows words aren't enough.

At one point, Riley's grip on the Ward tightens, his knuckles white, and he starts rocking slightly, whispering to himself, perhaps prayers for his mother or Bryan. Browning feels his chest tighten. Jensen, the kid, had corrected him earlier when Browning addressed him as Sokoloff. 'Jensen, sir. Riley Jensen.' It's a name Riley chose with a fierce resolve, almost a vow to stand by the man who had risked everything for him.

Suddenly, Riley seems to crumble, overwhelmed by the weight of it all. Browning pulls over, unsure of what to do but feeling a need to offer some kind of comfort. In an awkward attempt to help, he reaches out, and though Riley resists at first, he finally leans into Browning, letting the silent tears fall as he clutches the Ward and cries like a child who's just lost his dad.

Browning can do nothing but hold him, feeling Riley's grief as though it's his own, understanding now that the weight Riley bears is far beyond what any ten-year-old should have to carry. And though he doesn't understand the Ward's power, or the supernatural bonds Riley seems to trust, he knows that to Riley, it's not just a relic. It's a lifeline, an anchor to Bryan's promise of protection, something tangible in a world that has offered him nothing but pain.

*** 

Rain drizzled in fine, misty sheets, pooling in the cracks of the alleyway. The city breathed in gasps of red and blue, emergency lights flashing through the damp darkness. Jones stood in stillness, hands in the pockets of his sleek, tailored coat, watching the entrance of Boston General like a predator studying wounded prey.

Behind him, cloaked in heavy, dark fabric, stood a man draped in heavy, dark robes that seemed to swallow the light around him. The man, a Custodian, hovered a step back. His pale fingers fidgeted with the hem of his sleeve.

"We shouldn't be this close," he murmured, his voice low, careful. His gaze flicked uneasily between the flood of officers and paramedics. "The police are everywhere. If they start asking questions—"

Jones didn't turn.

"—If they start asking questions," he said smoothly, "then we'll give them answers."

The corner of his mouth curled, the smirk almost polite.

"The right answers," Jones added. "The ones that lead them anywhere but to us."

The Custodian exhaled, still tense. "Still," he pressed. "The Huntress... she shouldn't be here."

Jones finally glanced at him, amused. "Oh?" he mused. "And why's that?"

The Custodian hesitated before forcing himself to answer. "Because she's dead."

Jones chuckled, low and dangerous.

"That's the problem with fools like you," he murmured. "You think death is an ending."

Jones' gaze flickered back to the hospital. "It's not."

The Custodian shifted uncomfortably, his boots scraping against the damp pavement.

Jones continued, voice light, almost indulgent.

"The dead don't haunt us for no reason. They haunt us because we refuse to let go."

A siren wailed in the distance. The Custodian hesitated, then gestured toward the hospital.

"Then why is she still here?"

For the first time, something flickered in Jones' expression. A shadow of irritation. It was gone just as quickly, replaced by a knowing smirk.

"Because some fools think love is stronger than vengeance." His exhale was almost pitying. "They never learn."

The Custodian fidgeted, clearly disturbed. There was something in Jones' voice—something too calculated, too sure.

"And Jensen?" he asked cautiously. "The child?"

Jones didn't respond immediately. Instead, his gaze flickered to the side of the building, where a rat scurried along the soaked concrete, its tiny claws scraping for purchase.

Absentmindedly, still speaking, he lifted a hand.

"The boy is a nuisance," he said. "But nuisances have their uses."

His fingers curled ever so slightly.

The rat stopped mid-scurry, its tiny frame jerking suddenly upright, paws flailing as if lifted by an invisible hand.

The Custodian stiffened, his breath catching. His eyes darted between Jones and the rat, watching as the small creature twisted in the air, spine arcing unnaturally, its squeaks high and desperate.

Jones' head tilted slightly. "Jensen, though..." His voice was soft, contemplative. Too quiet. Too calm.

The rat convulsed. Its tiny chest caved inward with a wet, muffled pop.

It stopped struggling. A moment later, it dropped lifelessly to the pavement, landing with a damp, final thud.

Jones didn't even glance down. "He should have died in that house."

A breath of silence. The rain hissed against the ground.

Then, Jones took a slow step forward, his gaze locked onto the hospital doors.

"Perhaps I was wrong," he murmured. "Maybe he's exactly where I want him to be."

The Custodian swallowed hard, eyes flicking back to the crumpled corpse of the rat. His fingers twitched under his cloak, a nervous habit. The flickering emergency lights caught the edges of his hood, making his pale face seem almost spectral.

Jones' smirk returned—predatory, knowing. "Gather your minions." His voice was quiet, but it left no room for disobedience.

The Custodian hesitated only a fraction of a second before bowing his head. His fingers curled inwards, his posture shifting. There was no physical gesture, no whispered incantation—but the air around them thickened, pressing inward like a gathering storm.

A moment later, the presence was gone.

Jones never looked away from the hospital.

Inside, Bryan Jensen was dying.

And Jones had come not to stop it, not to fight it—but to watch.

To make sure it happened.

To enjoy the show.

A flicker of movement caught his eye.

Jones turned, watching as a dark-colored sedan whipped around the corner, tires splashing through the slick pavement. The car lurched to a stop directly in front of the hospital entrance, coming to rest beneath a bright red NO PARKING sign.

Jones smirked.

Detective Browning didn't give a damn.

Even before the car had fully stopped, the passenger-side door swung open with force. A small figure shot out—fast, reckless, driven.

Riley.

Jones' smirk thinned slightly as he observed the boy dart across the wet pavement, barely waiting for the sedan to settle before slamming the door shut and racing toward the entrance.

Browning was slower. The detective threw the car into park, his movements hurried but controlled, then shoved open his door and rounded the vehicle in quick strides.

Jones noted the contrast. Browning was deliberate, professional. Riley was pure instinct. The child moved like a storm, driven forward by something deeper than fear—a force that cared nothing for logic or hesitation.

Interesting.

Jones clasped his hands behind his back, tilting his head slightly.

A child like that could be dangerous.

If pointed in the right direction.

If shaped properly.

The automatic doors slid open, welcoming the boy and his detective into the fluorescent-lit chaos of the Emergency Room lobby.

Jones let out a slow, measured breath.

The pieces were moving.

And, as always...

They were exactly where he wanted them.

"If only the boy knew what he could become," says Jones.

***

The automatic doors slid shut behind them, sealing Riley and Detective Browning inside.

Fluorescent lights buzzed overhead, too bright, too cold. The sterile hospital air smelled of antiseptic and the faintest trace of copper—blood, old and new.

The place was busy, but something about the energy felt... wrong.

Nurses and doctors moved quickly but spoke in hushed voices. Conversations were clipped, their glances shifting toward Riley and Browning, watching just a second too long.

Browning straightened, immediately aware of the attention. His cop instincts kicked in, eyes sweeping the room.

"Where's the doctor?" he muttered.

Riley didn't answer. He was already moving.

***

They reached the waiting area outside Bryan's room, where Anna sat hunched forward, her hands clasped tightly in her lap.

At the sound of approaching footsteps, Anna looked up. Her face was pale, her eyes red-rimmed.

The moment she saw Riley, she rushed toward him, pulling him into a fierce embrace.

Riley buried his face against her shoulder, gripping her tightly. After a night filled with terror, for just a moment, it was mother and son—holding onto each other, refusing to let go.

Browning stood nearby, ever watchful, ever-present.

Behind them, Dr. Harrison approached, his expression a mixture of exhaustion and disbelief.

"We've stabilized him," the doctor said. "But only time will tell."

Anna's grip on Riley tightened.

Dr. Harrison shook his head, rubbing his temple. "His injuries..." He hesitated. "Frankly, I don't understand how he's still alive."

Browning exhaled, shifting his stance. "I need to speak with him the second he wakes up."

But before the conversation could continue, the energy in the room shifted.

A new presence filled the space, effortless and commanding.

Ed Jones stepped into the waiting area, his silver hair perfectly combed, his polished suit pristine despite the storm raging outside.

Behind him, a young woman followed, clutching a briefcase against her hip, her expression cold, calculating.

Browning immediately stiffened, his jaw clenching.

Jones, however, smiled.

"I'm afraid your interview will have to wait, Detective." His voice was calm, almost amused.

He produced a business card, flicking it toward Browning without actually handing it to him. "Edward Jones," he introduced himself. "Bryan's attorney."

His gaze flickered toward Riley.

"And given tonight's events, I've been authorized to represent Ms. Sokoloff and her son as well."

Anna stared at him, caught off guard, overwhelmed.

Jones held her gaze, his smile just a fraction too sharp.

Browning glared but said nothing. The air between them simmered, heavy with unspoken threats.

Then—something changed.

The waiting area felt colder.

Browning noticed it first—the fine hairs on his arms standing on end.

Then—

A loud, metallic crash.

A nurse had dropped a tray. The instruments scattered across the tile, the clatter too sharp, too jarring. The nurse didn't pick them up right away. She just stood there, staring, her hands shaking.

Riley turned sharply toward the noise.

The fluorescent light above them flickered.

Dr. Harrison hesitated, his mouth opening—then closing again.

Then—a scream. Distant. Muffled. Cut short.

Browning's hand instinctively moved toward his gun.

Riley's fingers tightened around the Ward of Protection.

Jones remained perfectly still.

A doctor rounded the corner, moving too fast, too sudden. His white coat billowed unnaturally like it was caught in a breeze that didn't exist.

He spotted Riley—and lunged.

A hand clamped onto Riley's shoulder, too strong, too cold. "Where do you think you're going?"

Riley froze, his breath caught in his throat.

The man's fingers dug in, his grip unnatural. His eyes were wrong. Too dark. Too empty.

Browning reacted instantly. He shoved the doctor back hard. "Back off."

The doctor stumbled, blinking.

Then—without a word—he turned and walked away. Just... walked away.

Riley watched him go, his pulse hammering. Then, at the end of the hall—he saw it.

A shadow.

Watching.

Then, it moved.

The lights went out. Darkness swallowed the hospital in an instant.

For a heartbeat, silence.

Then—the emergency backup kicked in, flooding the halls in pulsing, blood-red light.

That's when Riley saw them.

The hallway was stretching. The shadows at the far end were moving—not passively, but with intention. Watching. Then, one lurched forward. Fast. Too fast.

Browning drew his gun in an instant.

"Riley, get back—"

The hallway exploded into motion.

A security guard screamed as something yanked him into a vent. A nurse stumbled backward, her eyes rolling white as her body convulsed.

The air turned freezing.

And the Shadows attacked.

## CHAPTER 2 - BOSTON GENERAL

Outside Boston General Hospital, winds howled, and sheets of rain hammered against the building with relentless fury. Lightning flashed across the night, casting jagged shadows that clawed up the hospital walls, illuminating the dark figures advancing in silence. These were The Shadows—malevolent shapes that slithered along walls, slipping into cracks and crevices and moving unnoticed within the chaos of the storm.

Inside the hospital, the basement hummed with the rhythmic thump of machinery. A fifty-something engineer, wearing earmuffs that isolated him in a bubble of mechanical white-noise, moved among the machines with a worn clipboard. The basement's warmth felt oddly chilly, but he dismissed it as a draft. He didn't notice the shadow moving soundlessly toward him until an icy grip wrapped around his body. His scream died in his throat as his strength ebbed, leaving him pale and lifeless on the cold concrete floor.

The Shadows dispersed with purpose, infiltrating the hospital through ventilation grates, elevator shafts, and electrical ducts. A hospital aide working a late shift in the elevator felt a creeping chill before his life was drained in an instant. In the electrical room, a dark figure hovered over the main power switch, pulling it in a whispering flick. The hospital plunged into sudden darkness, and for a single heartbeat, there was silence—before the emergency lights flickered on, casting an ominous red glow through the halls.

***

Inside the Intensive Care Unit, Detective Browning instinctively stepped in front of Anna and Riley, his pistol draw, his eyes scanned the shadowy corridor. Ed Jones, the lawyer, stiffened, his smug expression slipping as he caught his pale reflection in the window, a rare flash of vulnerability in his gaze. Nurses and staff scrambled in the dim light, footsteps echoing as shadows flickered and slithered along the walls.

"Bryan!" Anna gasped, her voice taut with desperation. She bolted toward Bryan's intensive care room, Riley close at her side, clutching the Ward of Protection Bryan had given him. Browning moved swiftly after them, his posture tense and protective. Jones hesitated, fear in his eyes, before following with a steeled expression.

In a hallway corner, a security officer looked up just as the vent cover crashed to the ground. A shadow lunged, pulling the officer up with a sickening crunch as his body twisted into the vent. His scream echoed through the walls, then faded to silence, leaving only blood smeared on the floor.

***

Anna, Riley, and Browning burst into Bryan's intensive care room, where the emergency power kept the life-support monitors beeping steadily. Anna gripped Bryan's hand, her gaze fixed on his unconscious face as she fought back the growing dread.

Dark, amorphous shapes seeped under the door, pooling at the threshold and creeping forward. Riley clutched the Ward, stepping back as it began to glow faintly, casting a soft protective light around him. The Shadows recoiled, letting out an unearthly shriek that chilled everyone to the bone.

Jones, standing by the door, paled, his mask of confidence cracking. His eyes darted between Riley and the Shadow, realizing the artifact's power with a look of fear and greed. Outside the room, the other Shadows froze, heads snapping toward the light. Sensing the Ward's power, they retreated, slithering back through vents and grates, dissipating into nothingness as though driven off by an unseen force.

***

The door clicked shut, and the lights flickered, casting the room in an uneasy stillness. Browning stood protectively in front of Anna and Riley, weapon raised, keeping his focus on the now-empty doorway. The others remained tense, unaware of the figure that had appeared silently behind them.

Ashley materialized on the other side of Bryan's bed, her spectral form flickering between solid and transparent. Her gaze swept over the room, lingering on each person, her eyes cold and calculating. She took a silent step forward, her form shifting into something monstrous, eyes glowing with terrifying, otherworldly power. She was a wraith of vengeance, her gaze dark and full of purpose.

The Shadows, sensing her presence, froze in their retreat. Ashley raised her hand, and a wave of dark energy swept forward, cutting through Browning, Anna, Riley, and Jones without touching them, sending an icy shock through their bodies. The Shadows shrieked and twisted as Ashley's power surged, her presence tearing them apart one by one. Tendrils of darkness snapped and dissipated, leaving nothing but silence in her wake.

As the Shadows vanished, the room stilled, the unnatural chill lingering. Anna glanced at Riley, thinking the Ward had held the Shadows back, while Browning lowered his pistol, believing they were safe.

But Jones, rooted to the spot, trembled. He alone saw Ashley standing across the bed, her terrifying gaze locked on him. She stepped forward, her figure towering, her eyes glinting with a cruel knowledge. At that moment, he knew she recognized him—the man responsible for her death, the one who had orchestrated the plan that had led to this moment.

Her gaze held him captive, a silent, menacing promise that she hadn't forgotten or forgiven him. Jones's hands shook, his breath catching in his throat as he backed away. His gaze locked with hers, knowing his time would come.

Then, with a flicker of her eyes, Ashley turned away. Her form dissipated into the air, leaving him rattled, a thin sheen of sweat on his brow.

The hospital's power flickered back on, the regular lights flooding the room in a harsh, sterile light. Browning scanned the scene, taking in the aftermath. The hallways outside were littered with bodies—nurses, officers, aides—some pale and drained, others torn apart in brutal violence. The silence held, thick and heavy, as though the hospital itself were catching its breath.

Outside the room, a nurse, bloodstained and trembling, leaned against the counter, her face ashen as she struggled to breathe. Another nurse backed away from a fallen officer, barely containing a scream as she pressed her hand to her mouth.

A surviving security guard stumbled to the wall, slapping the emergency button, setting off alarms that blared through the building, the shrill sounds echoing through blood-streaked halls. Phones rang in a cacophony as doctors and staff raced to call for emergency assistance. A nurse pulled the fire alarm, and red lights flashed as a robotic voice announced, "Code Black—Emergency Protocol Initiated. Evacuate Non-Essential Personnel."

In the midst of the chaos, Browning held his ground, eyes steady, weapon ready. He stood as a shield for Anna, Riley, and Bryan, his expression resolute and defiant, challenging any threat that might return.

Riley clutched the Ward tightly, its faint pulse a reminder of its power. He looked up at Anna with wide, steady eyes, a newfound courage in his gaze, while Browning regarded him with a nod of respect. "You did good, kid," he said, his voice rough but genuine.

Jones took a shaky step back, his eyes darting between Riley and Browning. He cast a furtive glance to where Ashley had been, a haunted look in his eyes. He backed away, calculating his next move, feeling her silent promise hang over him, a looming judgment he couldn't escape.

As the alarms wailed, more officers and medical staff arrived, organizing the survivors. A doctor called out, "We need to triage—move the injured to the trauma bay!" Nurses moved swiftly, pulling those with a pulse onto gurneys, away from the bloodshed.

An EMT, visibly shaken, called his supervisor, his voice cracking. "We need a full response team. It's—" he swallowed, "—a massacre up here."

The hospital PA crackled as a police officer announced, "This is Boston PD. All non-essential personnel evacuate immediately. Secure intensive care and await further instructions." Orderlies wheeled patients in stable condition out of the intensive care unit, locking doors in case of further threats.

As the lights steadied, Browning glanced over his shoulder at Anna and Riley, offering a grim nod. Then, his face set, he turned back, unwavering in his promise to protect them. In the wake of Ashley's wrath, the hospital had found a fragile calm, but a sense of unfinished business lingered like a shadow ready to strike again.

*****

Rain drizzled steadily, pooling in the parking lot's uneven cracks, mingling with blood and debris tracked out of the hospital. Emergency lights strobed against the wet pavement, their reflections fragmenting like fleeting phantoms moving in the mist.

Detective Browning stood beneath a hastily erected canopy of the Emergency Command Post of the Boston PD, his trench coat soaked and his expression grim. His eyes lingered on the shattered windows of the hospital, now boarded with splintered plywood, jagged edges still visible like scars against the storm-lit structure. He lit a cigarette, the faint glow briefly illuminating the dark circles under his eyes.

"Detective Browning!" Captain Morales's sharp tone cut through the rain as she approached, clipboard in hand. Her usual no-nonsense demeanor was replaced with an edge of incredulity. "What the hell am I looking at here? Fifteen dead, bodies drained like someone pulled the damn plug, and I've got reports of... shadows." She spat the word like it burned her mouth.

Browning took a drag from his cigarette, exhaling slowly before turning to her. "It's a mess," he admitted, his voice low and rough. "And it's not random. Whatever this is, they were targeting someone specific."

Morales's brow furrowed, her lips pressing into a thin line. "Targeting who?"

"Bryan Jensen," Browning replied, his gaze shifting toward the ICU's darkened windows. "The guy in critical care. Him and his family."

"Why?" Morales demanded, stepping closer. "What makes him so special?"

"Still working that out," Browning muttered. He flicked his cigarette to the ground, grinding it out under his boot. "But I can tell you this much—it wasn't just bad luck."

Morales's frown deepened as she glanced over the hastily arranged command post. Her officers moved like ghosts, faces pale and voices hushed. The crime scene photos laid out on a table between them painted a picture of carnage: bodies drained, walls gouged with claw-like marks, and blood splattered in grotesque patterns.

"Jesus," she muttered, shaking her head. "And this... Ward? You believe that?"

Browning gave a tight nod. "I saw it with my own eyes, Captain. Whatever those things were, they didn't want anything to do with it."

Morales barked a bitter laugh. "Wards. Shadows. This is a goddamn horror movie, Browning. You expect me to put that in my report?"

"You can write whatever you want," Browning said, his tone sharp. "But whatever came through here isn't done. And if we don't get ahead of it, it won't stop with this hospital."

Morales stared at him, her disbelief warring with the gravity of his tone. After a long moment, she nodded curtly. "Fine. But you're on point for this, Browning. I want answers, and I want them fast."

He gave a faint smirk, though there was no humor in it. "You and me both, Captain."

***

The faint beeping of life-support machines punctuated the oppressive silence in Bryan's hospital room. The sterile scent of antiseptic hung in the air, mingling with the faint metallic tang of blood carried in from the chaos outside.

Anna sat at Bryan's bedside, her hands clasping his as though sheer willpower could pull him back from the brink. Her back was rigid, her body tense despite the dark circles under her eyes and the slump of exhaustion weighing her down. Riley stood nearby, the glowing Ward of Protection resting against his chest like a faint heartbeat.

The door opened quietly, and Browning stepped in, his gaze sweeping the room. His eyes lingered on Anna, then

Riley, and finally Bryan's pale, battered form. The tension between them was palpable, an unspoken understanding of the night's gravity.

"What's that?" Browning asked, nodding toward the Ward, his tone edged with skepticism.

Anna's head snapped up, and her posture immediately became defensive. "It's... just something to keep him safe."

Browning arched an eyebrow, his sharp gaze locking onto hers. "Uh-huh. And him?" He gestured toward Bryan. "Who is he to you?"

Anna hesitated, her lips parting as if to speak before faltering. She glanced at Bryan, then back at Browning. "He's my... my neighbor."

Browning smirked faintly, folding his arms. "Neighbor. Sure. Neighbors always stick around through the worst night of your life, right?"

Anna bristled, straightening in her chair. "He's a good man. You wouldn't understand."

"Try me," Browning said, his tone softening slightly as his gaze shifted to Riley. The boy was watching him intently, his small hands gripping the edges of the Ward.

"You don't need to understand," Riley said, his voice calm but firm. "We're staying. We're keeping him safe."

Browning studied him for a long moment, then nodded slowly. "Alright, kid. I get it. But staying here? You'd better be ready. Whatever came for him isn't done."

Riley's expression hardened. "We don't run, Detective. We fight."

Browning looked at Riley, his expression shifting as he took in the boy's resolute tone. After a moment, he sighed and ran a hand through his damp hair. "Alright, kid. Fine. You win. But if you're all staying, you'd better be ready. Whatever hit this place isn't gone. Not by a long shot."

Anna's eyes softened for a moment as she glanced at Riley, then back at Bryan. "We're ready."

Browning's lips quirked into a faint smile, more of a grim acknowledgment than amusement. "Neighbor... yeah, okay, neighbor it is."

***

The hospital settled into a tense silence as dawn approached. Anna refused to leave Bryan's side, Riley stationed resolutely at her shoulder. Browning stood just inside the doorway, his gaze flicking between them.

The ICU had devolved into a chaotic mess. Nurses rushed between rooms, their uniforms streaked with blood, as doctors barked orders that were barely audible over the shrill alarms echoing through the hallways. The fluorescent lights flickered intermittently, adding to the sense of unease.

Ed Jones sat in a plastic chair near the triage area, his posture slumped but his mind racing. The makeshift waiting room was filled with nurses, orderlies, and security officers—survivors of the chaos who clutched Styrofoam cups of coffee like lifelines. Their murmured conversations blurred into an indistinct hum, but Jones barely registered it. His thoughts were consumed by one thing: Ashley.

She had burned to death. He was certain of it. He had made sure of it. Yet she had stood in that room, her spectral presence shattering every rule he had spent his life mastering.

"Coffee?" A nurse offered him a cup, her hand trembling.

Jones blinked, feigning shock as he reached for it. "Uh... no thanks," he muttered, his voice thin and shaky.

The nurse gave him a sympathetic smile before moving on. His gaze flicked toward the ICU, where Anna, Riley, and Browning still lingered. Witnesses. Survivors.

He couldn't leave. Not yet. Not until he was sure she was gone.

Ed Jones sat slumped on a waiting room bench just outside the triage area, his suit rumpled and damp from sweat. Around him, survivors—nurses, security guards, and hospital aides—huddled in various states of shock, their faces pale and their hands trembling as they clutched Styrofoam cups of coffee or bottles of water handed out by staff.

Jones shifted uncomfortably, his eyes darting around the room. He had to appear shaken, like everyone else, but his mind raced. His clammy hands gripped the armrest of the chair, his fingernails digging into the worn vinyl. Was she still here? Could she return? Ashley's spectral presence had shattered everything he thought he knew. She was supposed to be gone—burned to death, erased. Yet she had stood in that room, staring right through him as though she could see into his soul.

The thought made his stomach churn.

"Coffee?" a second nurse offered, leaning down with a sympathetic smile. She held a tray of steaming cups, her own hands trembling slightly.

Jones blinked, forcing his face into what he hoped passed for shell-shocked gratitude. "Uh… yeah. Thanks," he muttered, reaching for the cup with an unsteady hand.

The nurse gave him a pitying nod before moving on to the next cluster of survivors. Jones watched her go, using the distraction to scan the room for any sign of Ashley. The faint scent of burned hair and scorched fabric seemed to linger in his nostrils, though no one else reacted. Was it real? Or just his mind playing tricks on him?

He sipped the coffee, grimacing at the bitterness. He needed to stay calm, to blend in. He couldn't afford to draw attention—not when there were so many witnesses. His gaze flicked toward the triage room, where Anna, Riley, and that stubborn detective were still gathered around Bryan's bed. He couldn't risk staying too close to them; their proximity to Ashley made them dangerous. But leaving now would look suspicious.

A pair of uniformed officers passed by, talking in low voices. Jones tensed, forcing himself to focus on his coffee. His mind reeled as he tried to process what he'd seen.

She burned to death. I know she did. I made sure of it.

The memory of Ashley's lifeless eyes as the fire consumed her was vivid, but the Ashley in that hospital room had been anything but lifeless. She'd looked through him, her gaze sharp and unrelenting, as if she knew everything. And those… powers. The way she'd torn the Shadows apart—it was unnatural.

Jones's breath hitched. What if she came back? What if she decided to reveal the truth?

His eyes darted toward the far corner of the room, where a group of nurses whispered among themselves, their glances shifting nervously toward the ICU hallway. Survivors. Witnesses. They'd seen it too, hadn't they? The spectral form. The unnatural energy. Jones clenched his jaw. These people didn't understand what they'd seen. Not like he did.

They don't know her. They don't know what she's capable of.

And neither did he, he realized with a chill. For the first time in his carefully controlled life, Ed Jones felt powerless. Ashley Jensen was no longer a distant memory or a regrettable casualty. She was a living force, untethered by the rules he'd built his life around.

His hand shook as he lifted the coffee to his lips. The hot liquid scalded his tongue, but he barely noticed. All he could think about was whether she was still here, lingering unseen in the shadows. Watching him. Waiting.

A sharp laugh from one of the nurses startled him, and his head snapped toward the sound. He scowled, forcing himself to relax. Just a laugh. Just a human sound.

But the fear remained. For all his calculated moves, for all his manipulations, Jones was in uncharted territory. He had no contingency for a ghost bent on vengeance.

## CHAPTER 3 - HEALERS

The pale light of dawn filtered weakly through the blinds in Bryan's hospital room, doing little to dispel the oppressive atmosphere. The faint hum of monitors and the occasional murmur of hospital staff punctuated the silence.

Anna sat in a chair that had been brought into the room overnight, her back against the hard cushions as Riley lay curled up in her lap. His head rested heavily against her arm, his breathing slow and even. Dark circles rimmed Anna's eyes, and she blinked rapidly, fighting the pull of exhaustion. Her free hand rested on Bryan's, her thumb absently tracing over the bandages that wrapped his fingers.

The door creaked open, and Browning slipped inside. His face was drawn, his shoulders hunched slightly as though the weight of the night had settled permanently on him. He glanced at the scene before him—Anna barely upright, Riley sound asleep, and Bryan, still unmoving but alive.

"You need to rest," Browning said softly, keeping his voice low to avoid waking Riley.

Anna shook her head, her gaze fixed on Bryan. "I can't," she whispered. "I won't leave him."

Browning hesitated, his jaw tightening. He had spent half the night fending off hospital staff who were less than pleased about Anna and Riley refusing to vacate the ICU. He'd burned through his patience and his authority, but the sight of them now—clinging to each other in quiet defiance of the chaos—kept him from pushing the issue.

He stepped closer, lowering his voice further. "Listen, I have to go. There's a lot I need to sort out back in Havenwood. But I'll try to bring you fresh clothes and... whatever else you need."

Anna looked up at him then, her eyes glassy with exhaustion. "Thank you," she said, her voice cracking slightly. "For everything."

Browning nodded, looking uncomfortable. "Just... try to rest," he muttered. He turned to leave, pausing at the door to glance back at them. His eyes lingered on Riley for a moment before he stepped out, the soft click of the door closing behind him, leaving the room in silence once more.

The stillness didn't last long. About an hour later, the door opened again, and Anna straightened, her body tense despite her exhaustion. A tall man in an immaculate suit stepped inside, his movements fluid and deliberate. Ed Jones.

Behind him, a woman in a crisp white coat followed, carrying a small black bag. Her presence radiated an almost unnatural calm, her piercing eyes flicking over Bryan's prone form with clinical precision.

Anna frowned, her arms instinctively tightening around Riley. "What do you want?" she demanded, her voice low but sharp.

Jones raised his hands in a placating gesture, his smile thin and practiced. "Relax, Ms. Sokoloff I'm here to help. This is Dr. Vance, a specialist who's been brought in to assist your neighbor. She's here to make sure Mr. Jensen gets the best care possible."

Anna hesitated, her gaze shifting to the woman. The doctor's expression was unreadable, but there was something about her presence—something steady and confident—that made Anna pause.

"We've contacted the hospital's administration," Jones continued smoothly, "and they've authorized her to take over his treatment. I understand you've had a long night, and we all want the same thing—for Mr. Jensen to recover."

Anna glanced down at Riley, still asleep in her lap, and then at Bryan. The weight of exhaustion bore down on her, clouding her judgment. "You're sure she can help him?" she asked, her voice wavering.

The healer, Dr. Vance, stepped forward, her voice calm and reassuring. "I specialize in cases like his. I've seen patients come back from worse. You have my word—I'm here to help."

After a long moment, Anna relented, nodding as she shifted slightly to allow them access to Bryan. She watched warily as Dr. Vance set her bag on the bedside table, her movements precise and deliberate.

Jones stepped back, a satisfied glint in his eyes as he observed the scene. For now, his role was to remain in the background, letting the healer do her work. But his mind raced with calculations, his focus lingering on Anna and Riley as much as Bryan.

The healer placed her hands lightly over Bryan's chest, her fingers brushing against the bandages. For a moment, the air in the room seemed to still, and Anna shivered, though she couldn't explain why. Riley stirred faintly but didn't wake.

"This will take some time," Dr. Vance said, her voice distant, almost distracted. "You may want to step out for a while."

Anna's eyes narrowed. "I'm not leaving him."

Dr. Vance glanced at her, and for the briefest moment, something flickered in her expression—something almost like respect. "As you wish."

"Well, if you'll excuse me, Mrs. Sokoloff, I have legal matters to attend to." Jones nods and departs. "If you need anything... anything, just let me know." Jones smiles before leaving.

*** 

The alleyway was a forgotten scar on Boston's underbelly, nestled between crumbling brick buildings and bathed in the dim, flickering light of a single malfunctioning streetlamp. The snow on the ground had turned to slush, blackened with soot and filth, and the air reeked of oil and decay. It was the kind of place where even rats hesitated to linger.

Jones stepped into the darkness, his polished shoes making an incongruous clicking sound on the frozen pavement. Though calm, his face carried an edge of irritation that simmered just beneath the surface. He paused beneath the shadow of a rusted fire escape, his sharp eyes scanning the empty alley for any sign of life.

Satisfied that he was alone, he turned toward the farthest corner, where a faint shimmer of light danced against the bricks. A figure stepped forward, emerging from the shadows as if drawn by Jones' presence.

The Custodian was draped in heavy, dark robes that seemed to swallow the light around him. His hood obscured most of his face, but Jones could see the faint glimmer of fear in his eyes as he approached. The air between them crackled faintly with energy, a subtle reminder of the magic that bound them both.

"You kept me waiting," Jones said, his voice cold and clipped.

"My apologies," The Custodian replied, his tone deferential but uneasy. "The Soulless made me aware of your summons only moments ago."

Jones sneered, his lip curling. "Excuses. Do you think I care about your shadows? They failed me, as did you."

The Custodian flinched but said nothing. Jones took a step closer, his presence radiating authority.

"Twenty-five," Jones hissed, his voice barely above a whisper. "Twenty-five shadows, gone. Destroyed. And for what? A single man and a woman who shouldn't even exist."

"She was... relentless," The Custodian offered hesitantly. "Even in death, she hunts them as she did in life. Her power—"

"—Her power is not the problem," Jones snapped, his voice cutting through the cold air like a blade. "The problem is your incompetence."

The Custodian stiffened but held his ground. Jones continued, his voice low and venomous.

"She shouldn't have been able to reach Boston. It's beyond her range. She's dead, after all. So, tell me—how did she get here?"

The Custodian hesitated, his hood dipping slightly as if to avoid Jones' gaze. "There is... a boy," he said at last. "One who carries a Ward of Protection. It's possible he could have—"

"—Possible isn't good enough," Jones interrupted, his tone icy. "I need answers, not theories. The Ward could explain it, or it could be something else entirely. I will not be blindsided again."

The Custodian shifted uncomfortably, his hands disappearing into his sleeves. "I will investigate further."

"You'll do more than investigate," Jones said, his voice dropping to a deadly calm. "You will keep constant contact with the one at the hospital. Nothing—nothing—must go unreported. Do you understand me?"

"Yes," The Custodian murmured, his voice barely audible.

Jones took a step closer, his eyes narrowing. He caught movement at the mouth of the alley—just a flicker, a figure passing by. A man, bundled against the cold, glanced briefly into the shadows. His gaze lingered for a moment too long, curiosity drawing his eyes toward the two figures.

Jones's lips curved into a faint, dangerous smile. He glanced at the Custodian, his expression hardening, and then back at the passerby. No words were exchanged, but the meaning was clear. The Custodian inclined his head in understanding.

Jones reached into his pocket and withdrew a single match. He struck it against the brick wall, the flame flaring to life. He brought it to the unlit cigarette between his lips, inhaling deeply as the orange glow illuminated his sharp features.

"And if you fail me again..." Jones let the words hang in the air, exhaling a stream of smoke that swirled in the icy breeze. The Custodian flinched at the unspoken threat.

***

The man walking home from his late shift pulled his coat tighter against the chill, his boots crunching against the frozen sidewalk. He couldn't shake the unease that prickled at the back of his neck. Something about those two figures in the alley... something wasn't right.

He quickened his pace, his breath puffing in the cold air. The distant sound of a car horn echoed through the empty streets, but it did little to drown out the growing sound behind him—the faint whisper of movement, too soft to be the wind.

He glanced over his shoulder, his heart hammering in his chest. The alley behind him was empty. Or so it seemed.

Then he saw it: a shifting shadow, darker than the night, detached from any source of light. It moved with a predatory grace, its form amorphous and menacing.

He broke into a run, his boots slipping on the icy pavement. The shadow followed, closing the distance effortlessly. He didn't have time to scream before it engulfed him.

The struggle was brief, the man's desperate gasps swallowed by the silence of the city. When the shadow retreated, all that remained was his lifeless body sprawled across the frozen ground. A faint, dark mist lingered for a moment before dispersing, leaving the street as quiet and empty as before.

***

The morning sun is a pale suggestion behind a thick mist that clings to the cul-de-sac, failing to bring warmth or clarity to the scene. Detective Browning's car slows as he approaches, his eyes sweeping the eerie tableau before him. A cluster of vehicles—two black SUVs, Anna's SUV, the Marshal's sedan, and Bryan's weathered truck—are scattered in a rough semi-circle, abandoned and silent, their presence a grim reminder of last night's violence.

He kills the engine and steps out, his breath fogging in the chill air, a subtle bite that seems to seep right to his bones. Whether it's the brisk morning or the dreadful weight of what he's about to witness, he can't be sure. But the silence feels wrong, heavy as if the air itself remembers.

The forensic van idles nearby, a beacon of order in this unnatural place. Techs move around the scene in pale coveralls, their faces obscured by masks as they meticulously catalog each shattered piece of glass and every ominous bloodstain. Browning's gaze lingers on the open trunk of one SUV, a dark stain smeared across the tailgate—a vivid reminder that Sokoloff and his men left no intention of surrendering.

He approaches the scene slowly, feeling the full impact of the quiet devastation that surrounds him. There's a low hum of voices, officers huddled in tense whispers, shifting glances over the carnage. As he passes, some offer nods of acknowledgment, though their eyes betray the unease that hangs over them like a pall.

Officer Harmon stands near the forensics van, his SWAT gear looking out of place in the muted daylight. His face is pale and drawn, but his eyes flicker with something just short of terror.

"Detective," Harmon greets him, his voice barely above a whisper, glancing toward the clearing where Bryan's house once stood. "There's... no house, sir. Nothing left but grass and trees. We searched every square inch. Whatever was here is gone."

Browning's brow furrows as he stares into the empty lot. "What do you mean, gone? Your report said two bodies, both left on scene."

Harmon nods, almost dazed. "That's the thing, sir. I saw them—so did you. Sokoloff was down. His guard was down. But now? There's nothing. Not even rubble. No evidence a structure was ever here."

Browning shifts uncomfortably, glancing back toward the spot where Bryan's home had once loomed. "And the bodies?"

Harmon swallows, his face growing ashen. "We're still looking, but..." He gestures toward the forensic team, who are working with tense, nervous movements, as though afraid to look too closely at the ground beneath their feet.

"Something about this isn't right," Harmon murmurs, stepping closer to Browning. "I mean, I've seen some messed-up stuff in my time, but this? What we found last night—what was in that basement..."

Browning crosses his arms, nodding for Harmon to continue, bracing himself.

"Jensen's basement," Harmon continues, his voice rough. "Whatever... killed that guy tore through him like he was paper. His heart ripped clean out, limbs scattered around like it was nothing. The house was shredded, Detective. Windows are broken from the inside out, and furniture is tossed around like toys. It was like something went through there, pure rage. And it wasn't Bryan or the kid. No way. Whatever happened in that basement was... inhuman."

Browning feels the chill deepen, his jaw clenching as he tries to process Harmon's words. He'd seen the basement himself, glimpsed the twisted remains. But hearing it spelled out now, in the cold light of day, it settles heavily in his mind.

"What about Jensen?" Browning asks, his tone edged with skepticism he's struggling to hold onto. "How do you explain him standing at that door, holding off Sokoloff?"

Harmon's gaze drops, his hands flexing at his sides. "I can't. That man was barely breathing when we evac'd him. I saw the blood, the cuts... there's no way he should've been on his feet. And the kid—Riley—he's got some kind of mark on him, doesn't he?"

Browning's silence is an answer in itself.

"Look, I know it sounds crazy," Harmon continues, his voice thick with desperation. "But it's like something was... protecting them. It was as if the house came alive, and whatever it was, it didn't want Sokoloff in there. And now it's

71

gone, every trace of it. Detective, you've got to see this for what it is."

Browning's expression hardens, but the seeds of doubt are planted deep. His mind drifts back to the basement, the horror of the torn body, the strange, oppressive feeling that had lingered in the air, pressing down like a weight that didn't belong. The basement scene, grotesque and unyielding, flashes through his mind: walls gouged deep with claw-like marks, broken fragments of furniture, and splatters of blood that seemed to defy logic.

"There's no such thing as ghosts, Craig," Browning says finally, his voice lacking conviction.

Craig holds his gaze, his face a study in grim resolve. "Then tell me, Detective... what the hell are you putting in your report?"

For a long moment, Browning says nothing, his gaze focused on the empty lot, the trees seeming to sway in anticipation. He feels the creeping sense of dread in his bones, a sense that whatever haunted this place is far from done with them.

Finally, he turns, the weight of the morning's revelations settling heavily on his shoulders. "Keep me posted," he mutters, heading back to his car, feeling the stares of his team behind him.

As he drives away, the mist clings to the cul-de-sac, swallowing the scene behind him in unyielding silence, leaving the unanswered questions hanging in the air like a specter.

***

The harsh fluorescent lighting inside Boston General buzzes faintly, casting a sterile glow over the small ICU room. The air carries the sharp scent of antiseptics and the faint hum of medical machinery. Bryan's bed dominates the center, surrounded by equipment monitoring his every breath and heartbeat. Tubes and wires snake their way from his body to beeping monitors, the only signs of life from the man who lies motionless.

Yet, the room feels anything but clinical.

A chair pulled close to Bryan's bedside holds Anna, her fingers entwined with his, her head resting against the edge of the mattress. Her face is a map of exhaustion, dark circles framing her bloodshot eyes. A small portable bed, awkwardly jammed into the corner, holds Riley, curled up with a drawing pad clutched to his chest. His shoes are kicked off, lying haphazardly beneath the bed.

Personal touches fill the space—Anna's coat draped over the back of a chair, Riley's scribbled drawings taped to the wall, depicting stick-figure renditions of the three of them standing together. Amidst the cold, clinical environment, the room feels occupied, claimed, as if Anna and Riley have refused to let it belong to the hospital.

It starts with a twitch. Just the slightest movement of Bryan's fingers, unnoticed at first. Then, his chest rises a fraction more deeply, his eyelids fluttering. The heart monitor beeps slightly faster.

Anna stirs, her brow furrowing. She lifts her head, her tired eyes locking on Bryan's hand. "Bryan...?" she whispers, her voice raw with disbelief.

The fluttering of his eyelids turns into a slow, labored opening. His brown eyes are unfocused, blinking against the harsh light. His lips part slightly, and a hoarse, barely audible sound escapes.

Anna's breath catches, her hand tightening around his. "Bryan! Oh my God—Bryan, you're awake!"

Riley bolts upright, the drawing pad tumbling to the floor. "Dad? Dad!" He scrambles to the bedside, grabbing Bryan's arm with both hands. "You're back! You're alive!"

Anna's tears fall freely as she brushes Bryan's hair back from his forehead, her voice trembling. "We thought we lost you. We thought—" She can't finish, her sobs cutting her off.

Bryan's voice is gravelly and faint. "Anna..." His eyes dart between them, unfocused but recognizing the faces that anchor him.

Anna leans closer, her tears falling onto Bryan's hand. She laughs softly, a sound somewhere between joy and disbelief. "Hello, handsome... You look like hell."

Bryan's lips twitch into the barest hint of a smile. His voice is still hoarse, but there's a glimmer of his dry humor. "Well, you could use a brush through your hair. Just saying."

A moment of soft laughter fills the room, a collective exhalation of breath no one realized they were holding.

Bryan's gaze shifts to Riley, who stands motionless, waiting, his wide eyes glued to the man in the bed. Bryan lifts his hand weakly, placing it on Riley's shoulder. "You did it."

Riley's face transforms, his eyes filling with tears as a grin splits his face. "I—I did?"

"You did," Bryan repeats, his voice stronger. "I'm proud of you."

No one had ever said those words to Riley before. The boy beams, his chest swelling with pride as he clings to Bryan's hand.

The quiet moment shatters as raised voices echo through the corridor. Bryan winces at the noise, his expression tightening.

"I'm not going anywhere!" Browning's voice booms. "You can shove your orders—"

"—You're suspended!" another voice, sharp and authoritative, interrupts. "You're lucky the FBI hasn't dragged you in yet!"

Anna stiffens, her relief turning to anger. She stands abruptly, her chair scraping loudly against the floor. "Stay with him, Riley," Anna says, her tone sharp. She storms to the door, flinging it open.

The argument in the hallway halts abruptly as Anna appears, her presence commanding. "What the hell is going on out here?" she snaps, her voice carrying the full weight of her frustration and exhaustion.

Both Browning and Captain Morales freeze, momentarily stunned by the fiery woman in front of them.

"This is a hospital. My neighbor—no, my family—is trying to recover after saving all of us, and you're yelling like children. If you have a problem with Detective Browning, take it elsewhere." She steps forward, crossing her arms.

"And for the record, he's Bryan's legal representative. You'll deal with him if you want to deal with us."

Morales opens her mouth to object, but Anna cuts her off with a glare that could pierce steel. "And if you wake him up again with this nonsense, I swear to God—" She doesn't finish, but the threat lingers in the air.

Inside the room, Bryan hears the exchange, his lips curling faintly into a smile. He leans back, his strength waning but his determination steady. "She's good," he rasps to Riley. "She's really good."

Riley grins. "Yeah, she is."

Anna returns, closing the door behind her and muttering under her breath. She pauses, her resolve crumbling as she sees Bryan awake and smiling faintly. "Sorry about that," she murmurs, sitting back at his bedside.

Bryan reaches for her hand, his grip weak but steady. "Don't apologize," he says. "You... you did good."

For the first time since the incident, Anna allows herself to hope. Bryan is alive, and no matter the chaos outside, they are together.

The medical team arrives swiftly after Bryan's awakening, their professionalism cutting through the emotional haze of the room. The lead nurse, clipboard in hand, speaks firmly but gently. "We need to examine him now. You'll need to step out, at least for a few minutes."

Riley bristles immediately, his hand tightening on Bryan's. "No! I'm not leaving."

Anna opens her mouth to object, but Browning steps into the doorway, his presence commanding. "I've got him," he says. His voice is calm, but his tone leaves no room for argument.

Riley looks up at Browning, his expression wavering between defiance and uncertainty. He glances back at Anna and Bryan, searching for reassurance.

Bryan, weak but steady, gives him a faint nod. "Go on, Riley. Get some air. I'm not going anywhere."

Anna adds softly, "It's okay, baby. We'll be right here."

Reluctantly, Riley lets go of Bryan's hand. Browning rests a reassuring hand on the boy's shoulder. "Come on, kid. Let's find something to eat."

***

The hospital cafeteria has utilitarian and unremarkable rows of tables under harsh fluorescent lights, an assortment of pre-packaged snacks, and questionable hot food options lining the counters.

Browning's cop instincts kick in, and he immediately scans the room. Only a few of the tables are occupied. The conversation is muffled, and no one seems to notice or pay attention to the newcomers.

Riley stares at the trays of food with undisguised skepticism.

"Do they even try to make this stuff taste good?" Riley mutters, eyeing a tray of meatloaf.

Browning chuckles, grabbing a tray. "Probably not. But don't worry, I've got this figured out."

He picks out a sandwich, an apple, and a carton of milk for appearances' sake. Then he loads the tray with cookies, a large slice of pie, and a mountain of ice cream. "There. A balanced meal."

Riley's eyes light up as Browning hands him the tray. "For real? Mom would never let me have this."

Browning smirks. "Good thing I'm not your mom."

Riley grabs a juice box and follows Browning to a table by the window. They sit in silence at first, Riley eagerly digging into his ice cream while Browning sips his coffee.

Riley breaks the silence, his voice quiet but sincere. "Thanks."

Browning looks over, raising an eyebrow. "For what?"

Riley pauses, poking at his ice cream with his spoon. "For being here. For helping my mom and... and..." He hesitates, his voice faltering.

Browning leans back in his chair, watching the boy carefully. "Go ahead, kid. If anyone deserves it, it's that man in that room upstairs."

Riley looks up, meeting Browning's gaze. He seems to measure the older man's words, the thought behind them, before nodding. "Yeah. He does."

They sit in silence again, the weight of Riley's words hanging in the air. Finally, Riley speaks again, his voice quieter this time. "It's not your fault."

Browning's brow furrows. "What?"

Riley takes another bite of ice cream before continuing, his tone matter-of-fact. "We didn't know who they were either. Simmons or Taylor. None of us knew."

The words hit Browning like a hammer. He stares at Riley, his gruff exterior faltering for a moment. For a career cop who'd built his identity on his ability to read people, failing to see the truth about Simmons and Taylor had been a blow to his pride and his conscience.

But hearing it from Riley—a boy who had faced more than most grown men—shifted something inside him. This wasn't pity. This was understanding. Forgiveness.

Browning clears his throat, his voice softer than usual. "You're a smart kid, you know that?"

Riley shrugs, shoving a cookie into his mouth. "Yeah, I know."

Browning chuckles, shaking his head. "All right, smart guy. Finish up. Your mom will have my head if I bring you back late."

As Browning and Riley leave the cafeteria, Riley sips on his juice box, clutching it with both hands like it's a prize. The tray they used sits abandoned on the table—neither of them gives it a second thought. Browning leads the way, his long stride slower than usual to match the boy's pace.

The hallway stretches ahead, quiet except for the faint hum of hospital activity. They walk side by side; Riley focuses on his juice, Browning on the path ahead. After a few yards, Riley suddenly shifts the juice box to one hand and reaches up with the other, slipping his tiny fingers into Browning's larger hand.

Browning falters mid-step, glancing down in surprise. His first instinct is confusion, his brow furrowing as if trying to process what just happened. For a moment, he looks like he's ready to pull his hand away—but then he doesn't. Instead, he keeps walking, his grip adjusting slightly to hold the boy's hand more securely.

They walk a few more steps in silence before Browning's lips twitch into the faintest of smiles. It's not a grin—it's barely there—but it softens the hard lines of his face, marking a rare and quiet moment of vulnerability.

They pass a hospital employee coming the other way. The employee glances at them, curiosity flickering across their face. Without missing a beat, Browning shoots them a pointed look and growls in his unmistakable Boston accent, "Whatta you looking at?"

Riley freezes for a split second before a laugh bursts out of him. He looks up at Browning, his eyes wide with amusement. "You're so weird."

Browning smirks, his voice dry. "It takes one to know one," he glances at Riley. "Yeah, well, you're stuck with me."

Riley takes another sip of his juice, grinning. "Could be worse."

"Could be better," Browning quips, the smirk lingering.

The hallway stretches on ahead of them, and for the first time in days, Riley feels a sense of normalcy. The humor, the company—it's enough to make the hospital fade away, even if only for a moment. Browning, meanwhile, feels the small hand in his own and realizes, perhaps for the first time, that he doesn't mind being stuck with this kid.

***

As Browning and Riley make their way back to the ICU, the corridor becomes quieter, the sterile stillness of the ward pressing in around them. The boy still clutches his juice box, the cop's large hand swinging loosely at his side as they walk. The silence between them isn't awkward—it's companionable, a quiet acknowledgment of what they've shared.

As they near Bryan's room, Riley suddenly glances up, his expression shifting. He looks at Browning, then at their joined hands, and immediately pulls his own away, stuffing it awkwardly into his pocket. Browning, catching on, clears his throat and flexes his now-empty hand like he hadn't even noticed.

Neither of them says a word, but Riley glances at Browning out of the corner of his eye. "You're not gonna, like… tell them, are you?"

Browning snorts, rolling his eyes. "What, that you're a softie? Not a chance."

Riley huffs, sipping on his juice as if to reclaim some of his cool. "Good."

They reach the door, and Browning pauses, straightening his jacket. "You ready, tough guy?"

Riley nods, his usual smirk creeping back onto his face. "Ready. But, uh, you might wanna lose that smile before we go in. Don't wanna freak them out."

Browning's lips twitch like he's about to retort, but instead, he mutters, "Smartass," and pushes open the door.

When Browning and Riley return to the ICU, the boy walks a little taller, his steps lighter. Browning opens the door, glancing back at Riley with a subtle nod of reassurance.

Browning glances down at Riley, who is looking at two medical personnel standing at the nurses' station—his eyebrows tight as if deep in concentration. The boy drops his head and looks at the floor before looking up at Browning.

The two new 'best buds' step inside, their expressions carefully neutral as if nothing had happened. Bryan's gaze sharpens as the two enter. His brow raises slightly, taking in their neutral expressions, the faint ease in Riley's posture. Maybe this cop wasn't so bad after all, Bryan muses, his smirk soft and approving.

Anna's maternal instincts pick up on the subtle distance Riley and Browning put between themselves as if guarding a shared secret. Her eyes meet Riley's, hesitating briefly. She catches it—a tiny crack in the armor—and her lips twitch into a fleeting smile, too brief to embarrass him.

# CHAPTER 4 - THE HEALER

The hallway outside Bryan's room falls into a hushed quiet after Browning and Riley step through the door. The soft beeping of monitors and the occasional shuffle of nurses moving briskly to their next task create a soothing, almost rhythmic backdrop. Overhead, fluorescent lights buzz faintly, their sterile glow casting long shadows against the glossy floor.

No one notices the Orderly. They never do.

He's a man in his early 50s, slightly overweight, his uniform a bit too tight at the seams, with sleeves rolled up to reveal arms that carry the faint sheen of perpetual grease. His hair is thinning, combed in a way that suggests he stopped caring years ago. He shuffles with a purposeful yet unremarkable gait, clipboard tucked under one arm as if clinging to some semblance of authority in a world that barely acknowledges his existence.

In a facility dominated by higher-educated professionals—doctors, nurses, and specialists whose credentials hang framed in every office—the Orderly is a necessary cog in the machine. Not evil, not malicious, just... there. His job is indispensable yet invisible, a fact reinforced by the dismissive way people glance past him or, more often, don't look at him at all.

The doctors and nurses never include him in their conversations. To them, he's a background fixture, a shadow cast by the fluorescent lights. He empties bedpans, cleans up messes, and ferries supplies through the hospital's labyrinthine halls—tasks beneath the notice of the "important" people.

And that suits him just fine.

He pauses near the nurse's station, tilting his head slightly as he glances toward Bryan's room. For a brief moment, his expression shifts—neutrality giving way to a flicker of something else. Curiosity? Interest? Whatever it is, it vanishes almost instantly, replaced by the blank mask of a man accustomed to being overlooked.

Without a word, he veers off the main corridor and slips into a maintenance closet.

The Utility closet is dimly lit and cramped. Shelves sag under the weight of cleaning supplies, their labels faded and smudged from overuse. Brooms and mops lean together in one corner like weary sentinels, their bristles frayed and bowed. The faint scent of bleach mingles with the metallic tang of industrial disinfectant, clinging to the air like an unwelcome guest.

At the back of the room sits a small, nondescript table, scuffed and stained from years of neglect. The Orderly kneels, pulling a porcelain bowl from beneath the table—a surprising artifact in such a mundane setting. It is smooth, unblemished, and utterly out of place.

Setting the bowl on the table with careful precision, the Orderly retrieves a flask from his pocket. His fingers work deftly, despite their worn, greasy appearance. Water flows into the bowl, its surface rippling unnaturally, as if resisting the laws of physics.

He leans closer, his lips parting to release a low, melodic murmur. The words are indecipherable, ancient, carrying an almost hypnotic cadence that seems to pull the shadows closer. The air thickens, tinged with the faint metallic scent of ozone, as though a storm were building within the confined space.

The water begins to swirl, forming faint patterns of light and shadow. The Orderly watches, unblinking, as the ripples settle into a perfect stillness. Seconds stretch into an eerie silence, the kind that prickles at the edges of the mind.

Then, a voice echoes from the still surface of the water. Cold, commanding, and disembodied.

"Speak."

The Orderly leans closer, his expression unreadable. For a moment, the faint glow from the bowl reflects in his eyes, twisting his unassuming features into something vaguely sinister.

But only for a moment.

***

The ICU room was cloaked in a stillness that seemed almost alive. The soft beeping of the heart monitor and the faint hum of medical machinery provided a backdrop, yet the air felt heavy, expectant. Anna sat slumped in the chair by Bryan's bed, her fingers entwined with his motionless hand. Riley lay curled up in the corner on a makeshift cot, his small frame barely covered by a thin hospital blanket.

Anna's gaze lingered on Bryan. Her mind caught in an endless loop of what-ifs and prayers to a universe she wasn't sure was listening. How had he endured all this? How had she not seen the strength in him before? The dark circles under her eyes mirrored the exhaustion of her heart.

***

The hospital's security office was a fluorescent-lit cave of monotony. Greg, the night shift guard, leaned forward in his chair, one hand gripping his Styrofoam coffee cup while the other tapped at the console. The bank of monitors displayed the hospital's sprawling hallways, a network of sterile emptiness punctuated by flickering lights.

The ICU wing was quiet, its corridors empty save for the occasional nurse or the distant sound of wheels squeaking. Greg's eyes narrowed as he adjusted the focus on one of the cameras showing ICU Corridor 3. The feed was clear, but something about the stillness put him on edge.

He reached for his radio, hesitating as the back of his neck prickled. He glanced over his shoulder, finding only the shadowy corners of the room. "Get a grip," he muttered, returning his attention to the screens.

***

The corridor leading to Room 14 stretched out like a tunnel, dim and unnervingly quiet. The fluorescent lights buzzed faintly, but one bulb at the far end flickered sporadically. From the shadows, a figure emerged.

She walked with deliberate grace, her long black coat brushing the tiled floor as though untouched by gravity. Her sharp blue eyes glinted in the dim light, unyielding and cold. She didn't so much walk as glide, each step silent yet firm.

86

No cameras picked her up, and those who might have crossed her path failed to see her. The healer moved like an echo of something ancient, a presence that existed just beyond the veil of perception.

***

Greg leaned closer to the monitor, which showed ICU Corridor 3. His brow furrowed as he watched the flickering light. For the briefest moment, he thought he saw something—movement? A distortion? He rewound the footage but found nothing. The feed showed an empty hallway, the same sterile stretch of tile.

Greg rubbed his eyes and shook his head. "Need to cut back on the caffeine," he muttered, making a note to report the flickering light to maintenance.

***

The sharp click of heels against the tile broke the oppressive silence. Anna's head shot up, her grip on Bryan's hand tightening. A woman stepped into the room. She was old, impossibly old, with white hair coiled tightly at the nape of her neck and sharp blue eyes that seemed to pierce the air itself. Her long black coat hung off her thin frame, and she carried a worn leather bag that looked like it had seen centuries of use.

As she stepped fully inside, her fingers brushed the door handle. A soft, golden glow rippled outward, shimmering like water catching the first light of dawn. The air vibrated faintly with the hum of unseen energy.

Anna's breath caught as she watched the glass window on the door darken, its transparency fading into a dusky, impenetrable hue. The light in the room seemed to dim slightly, taking on a warmer, softer tone.

The woman turned to Anna, her sharp gaze locking onto her. "So we won't be disturbed," she said simply. Her voice was calm, deliberate, and carried the weight of someone unaccustomed to being questioned.

Anna exhaled shakily, realizing she'd been holding her breath. But the sensation of the room shifting, bending to the will of this stranger, left her uneasy.

***

A nurse pushed a linen cart past Room 14, her sneakers squeaking softly against the tiles. She glanced at the door's window, her gaze lingering for a moment.

Inside, she saw exactly what she expected to see: Anna slumped in her chair, her head resting against Bryan's forearm, her other hand clutching his. Bryan lay motionless on the bed, surrounded by softly beeping monitors. Everything looked normal, mundane.

The nurse moved on, her thoughts already shifting to her next task. If she had stayed longer, perhaps she might have noticed the faint shimmer that rippled across the window's surface, like heat haze distorting the air.

***

Anna stood, her body rigid. "Who are you?"

The woman didn't answer immediately. Her gaze swept the room, taking in every detail: the drawings Riley had taped to the wall, the jacket slung over the back of a chair.

88

Finally, her eyes settled on Bryan, and she nodded faintly as though confirming something only she could see.

"The Council sent me," she said at last. "Your Coven expressed concern."

"Concern?" Anna's voice wavered, and her grip on Bryan's hand tightened protectively.

The healer's eyes flicked toward Bryan. "This one has lived amongst us for a long time. He knows much about our ways... too much, perhaps. The longer he lingers in this state, the greater the risk of that knowledge being compromised."

Anna's heart raced, her protective instincts flaring. "If you think he's a threat—"

"—I am here to help, not harm," the Healer interrupted, her tone clipped. Her sharp blue eyes fixed on Anna with an unyielding intensity. "But there are limits even to what I can do. Magic bends, not breaks."

Anna swallowed hard, her unease growing. The healer's words were as much a warning as a reassurance.

The Healer moved to Bryan's bedside with the slow precision of someone who understood the weight of their actions. She set her worn leather bag on the small table beside him, her movements brisk and practiced. The faint scent of dried herbs and something metallic, almost coppery, wafted through the air as she opened the bag.

From within, she retrieved a series of items that looked out of place in the clinical environment: vials of dark liquid, bundles of dried herbs tied with red string, and a shard of crystal that gleamed faintly even in the dim light.

Anna stood a few feet away, her hands gripping the back of a chair as though it were the only thing keeping her upright. Riley had woken and climbed off his cot, padding silently to Anna's side. His small hand slipped into hers, and she squeezed it reflexively, her eyes never leaving the healer.

"What are you going to do?" Anna asked, her voice low, wary.

The Healer didn't look up. "What must be done," she replied.

She placed the jagged crystal on Bryan's chest, its sharp edge catching the faint light in the room. Her hands moved swiftly, arranging the herbs around his body in a circular pattern, each bundle tied at precise intervals. With a flick of her wrist, she uncorked one of the vials and poured its contents over the crystal. The liquid sizzled as it made contact, releasing a thin plume of smoke that smelled of burnt earth and metal.

Then the chanting began.

It started as a low hum, resonating deep in the healer's chest and vibrating through the air. The words were in a language Anna didn't recognize. Their cadence was ancient and rhythmic, each syllable heavy with purpose. The temperature in the room dropped sharply, the chill biting through the thin hospital blanket draped over Bryan.

Riley clung tighter to Anna's hand, his wide eyes fixed on the glowing crystal. "Mom," he whispered, his voice trembling, "what's happening?"

Anna knelt beside him, pulling him close. "It's... It's okay, Riley. Just stay quiet."

The crystal on Bryan's chest began to glow, a pale, otherworldly light that pulsed in time with the healer's chanting. Tendrils of the light spread outward, curling and twisting like smoke before seeping into Bryan's skin. His body jolted once, his chest heaving as though he'd been shocked. The beeping of the heart monitor spiked, the irregular rhythm settling into something steadier.

The Healer's voice rose, the chant reaching a crescendo. Her hands hovered over Bryan, palms down, fingers splayed. The light from the crystal intensified, bathing the room in an ethereal glow that seemed to bend the shadows, making the walls pulse and shimmer.

Anna's heart raced as she watched Bryan's face. His pale, sunken features began to change. Color returned to his cheeks, and the lines etched deep with pain softened. His breathing, shallow and ragged just moments ago, grew steady and even.

The glow from the crystal pulsed one final time before dimming, the tendrils of light withdrawing back into the shard. The healer's chanting ceased abruptly, the silence that followed so profound it felt like the room itself was holding its breath.

The air was heavy with the scent of herbs and burnt metal. The healer stood motionless for a moment, her eyes closed, her hands still outstretched over Bryan. Slowly, she lowered her arms, her breath coming in shallow gasps.

"It is done," she said, her voice calm but tinged with exhaustion.

Anna stepped closer to Bryan, her eyes scanning his face for any sign of consciousness. "He's... he's okay?" she asked, her voice trembling with hope and fear.

The healer turned to her, her sharp blue eyes meeting Anna's. "His body will heal," she said, her tone matter-of-fact. "But his mind... the scars... that is a matter beyond even my reach."

Anna frowned, her hand tightening on Bryan's. "What do you mean? What kind of scars?"

The Healer began packing her tools, her movements brisk and methodical. "The kind you will discover in time," she replied cryptically. "Scars that no magic can touch."

"Wait," Anna said, stepping forward. "You can't just leave. Who are you? What does this mean for him?"

The Healer paused at the door, her hand resting on the frame. She glanced back, her gaze softening just enough to reveal a sliver of emotion. "It means that he lives," she said simply. "For now."

And with that, she was gone, leaving behind the faint hum of energy and the lingering scent of ancient herbs.

***

The hallway outside Bryan's room was unnaturally quiet, its pale green walls washed in the dim light of flickering fluorescents. Anna leaned against the vending machine, the cold metal biting into her back as she tried to steady her racing thoughts. The healer's words replayed in her mind like a broken record.

The clink of the vending machine startled her as it spat out a candy bar. She bent to retrieve it when a voice broke the silence.

"Quite the night you've had."

She spun around, the candy bar clenched in her hand. A man in a janitor's uniform leaned casually against the wall, a clipboard under one arm. His face was unremarkable—grizzled and forgettable—but his eyes, pale and piercing, held her in place.

"Who are you?" she demanded, stepping between him and Bryan's door.

The man smirked faintly. "A Custodian," he said, his tone almost amused. "The kind who notices what others don't. Like how the air shifted when your friend in there came back."

Anna's chest tightened. "I don't know what you're talking about."

"Don't you?" He straightened, taking a step closer. "I saw her. The old one. She doesn't come out unless the stakes are high. And when she does…" He let the implication hang in the air.

Anna bristled. "If you know who she is, then you know you shouldn't be here."

He chuckled softly, the sound incongruously light. "I'm always here. People like me—we see things. And right now, I'm seeing a whole lot of trouble heading your way."

Anna's stomach twisted, but she forced her voice to stay steady. "Is that a threat?"

"A warning," he replied, his smile fading. "The Council saved him, but their involvement puts a target on all of you. And Havenwood? It's not as invisible as you think."

Her breath hitched. "You're lying. Havenwood's protected."

"For now," the man said. He stepped back, his gaze lingering on her. "But balances are fragile. And you've just tipped yours."

Before she could respond, footsteps echoed down the hall. The man glanced toward the sound, his posture stiffening briefly before he faded back into the shadows.

Anna stood frozen, her pulse pounding as his words echoed in her mind. "You've tipped the balance."

***

The hospital parking lot was a bleak expanse of asphalt under the faint orange glow of the overhead streetlights. The sharp chill of the night air was laced with the faint tang of exhaust fumes and the distant hum of a nearby highway. Potholes filled with murky rainwater dotted the uneven ground, reflecting the fractured light like shards of broken glass. Despite the stillness, there was an undercurrent of unease—a kind of quiet too perfect to trust.

Detective Browning stood by his car, his breath misting in the cold as he checked his phone for the time. His unmarked sedan was parked near the edge of the lot, away from the clusters of vehicles closer to the hospital's main entrance. He had insisted on taking Anna and Riley to a safe house—someplace discreet, far from prying eyes and Jones's reach. But first, he needed them out of the hospital, and that was proving to be harder than he'd anticipated.

Inside the hospital, Anna leaned against the window of Bryan's room, her gaze distant as Riley dozed lightly in the chair beside his bed. She stared at the vague shapes of cars in the parking lot below, the hospital lights casting strange halos across the glass. Something felt... wrong. A heaviness settled in her chest, the kind that didn't come from exhaustion or worry. It felt instinctive, primal—a deep, unsettling knowing.

Her eyes fixed on Browning, visible under the streetlights by his car. She saw the shadows move near him—unnatural, deliberate—and her breath caught. Grabbing the crowbar she'd insisted on keeping close since the attack at the house, she bolted out the door.

"Mom?" Riley stirred, half awake. Anna turned, her tone sharp but steady. "Stay here. Don't move."

The sharp click of her boots echoed through the hallways as she rushed toward the parking lot.

Browning scanned the area, his cop instincts humming. The lot was mostly empty, save for a few stragglers heading to their cars after visiting hours. A nurse in scrubs pushed a cart toward the entrance. A man in a leather jacket lit a cigarette near a dumpster. Browning's eyes lingered on each figure, cataloging their movements, their demeanor. Nothing out of the ordinary.

At least, not at first.

Out of the corner of his eye, Browning caught a flicker of movement—a shadow too quick and too deliberate to belong to the harmless mundanity of the parking lot. His hand instinctively moved to his hip, where his service weapon rested beneath his jacket.

The first figure emerged from the shadows near the far end of the lot. Tall and broad-shouldered, his face obscured by the hood of his sweatshirt. He moved with a deliberate slowness, his steps almost too casual, like a predator circling its prey.

A second figure appeared a moment later, smaller but no less imposing, his hands buried in the pockets of a heavy coat. Unlike the first, this one's gaze locked on Browning immediately, sharp and unwavering.

Browning squared his shoulders, planting his feet firmly as he turned to face them. "Evening," he called, his voice calm but carrying an edge. "Something I can help you with?"

The taller man stopped a few paces away, his face still hidden. "You're in the way."

Browning's lips curled into a faint smirk. "Funny. I was just about to say the same thing."

The smaller man stepped closer, his head tilting slightly as he studied Browning. There was something off about his movements, a fluidity that felt unnatural, almost too smooth. "You've got something that doesn't belong to you," he said, his voice low and gravelly. "Best hand it over."

Browning's grip on his weapon tightened, though he didn't draw it—yet. "You're gonna have to be more specific."

The taller man chuckled, a sound that echoed unnervingly in the empty lot. "We're not here to negotiate."

"Good," Browning said evenly. "Neither am I."

The smaller man moved first, his hand darting out of his pocket with alarming speed. Browning's gun was out in an instant, the weight of it steady in his hand as he fired a warning shot into the ground.

The crack of the gunshot split the air, the sound ricocheting off the surrounding buildings. The taller man flinched, his hood falling back to reveal a face that was strangely featureless—pale skin stretched too tight, eyes black and void-like. Browning's stomach churned at the sight, but he didn't let it show.

"You really wanna test me?" Browning growled, his voice steady despite the adrenaline surging through his veins. "Because I've got all night."

The smaller figure didn't flinch, didn't hesitate. Instead, he lunged his movement a blur as he closed the distance between them. Browning barely had time to react, sidestepping the attack and bringing the butt of his gun down hard on the man's shoulder. It connected with a sickening thud, but the figure barely staggered.

The taller man moved next, faster than someone his size had any right to be. Browning turned to fire again, but the figure was already on him, slamming into him with enough force to send him sprawling against his car. The gun slipped from his grip, clattering to the ground just out of reach.

"You should've walked away," the smaller man hissed, looming over him.

Browning gritted his teeth, his hand fumbling for the backup knife strapped to his ankle. His fingers found the hilt just as the taller man reached for him.

"Bad idea," Browning muttered, driving the blade upward into the man's side. The figure recoiled with a guttural hiss, black ichor spilling from the wound instead of blood.

The smaller man snarled, reaching for Browning again, but headlights suddenly flooded the lot, the sound of tires screeching breaking the tension. A car skidded to a halt a few yards away, its driver's door swinging open to reveal Anna, her face pale but determined as she brandished a crowbar.

"Get away from him!" she shouted, her voice trembling but fierce.

The two figures froze, their inhuman gazes snapping toward her. For a moment, it seemed as though they might press their attack—but the sound of distant sirens cut through the night, growing louder.

The taller man sneered, his expression twisting into something almost monstrous. "This isn't over."

With that, both figures melted back into the shadows, their movements unnaturally fluid as they disappeared into the darkness. The parking lot fell silent once more, save for the approaching wail of the sirens.

Anna ran to Browning, dropping the crowbar as she helped him to his feet. "Are you okay?"

Browning winced, brushing dirt from his jacket. "I've had worse." He retrieved his gun, checking the chamber before holstering it. "You shouldn't have come out here."

Anna glared at him. "And let them kill you? Not a chance."

Riley's voice called from the car. "Mom! Are you okay?"

Anna turned, waving to him. "I'm fine, baby. Stay in the car."

Browning sighed, his eyes scanning the shadows where the attackers had vanished. "They're not just after Bryan," he muttered. "They want all of you."

Anna's jaw tightened. "Then we'd better make sure they don't find us."

Browning nodded, his expression grim. "Let's move."

Together, they hurried back to the car, the distant sirens growing closer as they sped into the night.

## CHAPTER 5 - THE FBI

The FBI field office in Boston was a maze of glass-walled conference rooms and bustling cubicles, its air heavy with the constant hum of activity. Keyboards clattered in rhythm with the low murmur of overlapping conversations, and the occasional ring of a desk phone cut through the background noise. The faint scent of stale coffee lingered everywhere, mingling with the sharp tang of toner from overworked printers. Overhead, fluorescent lights buzzed softly, their harsh glare washing the office in an unrelenting, antiseptic brightness.

Agent Michaels sat at a long, rectangular table in one of the larger conference rooms. The centerpiece was an oversized map of the city spread beneath stacks of folders, photographs, and evidence bags. Red strings connected pushpins marking key locations—Havenwood, Anna's house, Bryan's residence, and now Boston General Hospital. On the wall behind him hung a collage of crime scene photos, mugshots, and surveillance captures, each meticulously annotated.

Michaels leaned back in his chair, his fingers rhythmically tapping a pen against the edge of the table as he scanned the map. He looked calm, but his sharp, calculating eyes betrayed his unease. Something wasn't adding up, and he hated it.

The door opened with a brisk hiss, and Agent Carter strode in, a coffee cup in one hand and a thin manila folder in the other. Her tailored suit was impeccable, her dark hair pulled into a sleek ponytail that bobbed slightly with each click of her heels against the linoleum floor. She carried herself with the no-nonsense precision of someone who had no time for games.

"Michaels," she said, setting the folder down in front of him "We've got something."

He glanced up, his brow furrowing. "Please tell me it's good news."

"That depends," Carter replied, flipping the folder open. Inside were grainy surveillance photos showing Anna, Bryan, and Riley entering Boston General, their figures partially obscured by shadows but unmistakable. Standing nearby was Detective Browning, his profile caught mid-turn as he surveyed their surroundings.

Michaels leaned forward, his expression hardening. "Browning's playing a dangerous game," he muttered. "BPD isn't going to let him protect them forever."

Carter took a seat across from him, setting her coffee aside. "That's the least of our worries," she said. "Jones is the name on everyone's lips upstairs. Organized crime, foreign ties, a connection to the Sokoloffs—and now this shadowy 'Havenwood' everyone keeps whispering about? Feels like we're trying to untangle a web we can't even see."

Michaels picked up one of the photos and studied it intently. "Sokoloff goes on a killing spree; he kills every male in his family, except his son, who he tracks down living next door to, for intents and purposes, a hermit. And this guy Jensen—of all people—squares off against these guys and walks out of that house alive. That doesn't happen by coincidence."

"Maybe not," Carter said, leaning back in her chair. "But Jensen's clean. No criminal record, no shady connections, nothing tying him to Sokoloff except Anna. Hell, he's just an author."

Michaels raised an eyebrow, setting the photo down. "An author?" he echoed. "You're underselling him. He's not just an author; he's 'Alan Hoyle,' New York Times best-selling author with a global audience. People from all walks of life read his work. High-level people."

Carter tilted her head, intrigued but skeptical. "High-level?"

"Politicians, CEOs, academics," Michaels clarified, gesturing at the open file. "Some of his fans sit in seats of power so high you'd get a nosebleed trying to see them. And the guy's rich. Not millionaire-rich. He's 'Richie Rich' rich. Do you know what that means if he gets the press involved?"

Carter's brow furrowed as the implications sank in. "The Bureau wouldn't just have a mess on its hands—it'd have a PR disaster. The kind that brings cameras and questions to the Director's front door."

"Exactly," Michaels said, his tone sharp. "We need to be careful with this guy. One word to the media, and we'll have journalists crawling all over this. It wouldn't just blow the case wide open; it'd blow us right out of the water."

Carter frowned, leaning forward. "Then we tread lightly. If he's clean, why is he in the middle of all this? How does he connect to Havenwood?"

Michaels tapped his pen against the table, his expression contemplative. "That's what we're going to figure out. Let's review what we've got on Havenwood."

Carter flipped open another file, her tone turning matter-of-fact as she read aloud. "Havenwood. Population: just over 3000. No fluctuations in decades. Surrounded by dense forest, the town owns all the land for miles. No real estate turnover. No available properties. Picture a typical, self-sufficient small town. People get born, people get buried, and in between? Not much else happens."

She paused, her lips curling into a faint smirk. "Hell, the place only has one stoplight."

Michaels allowed himself a slight chuckle. "Sounds like a dream for anyone trying to stay off the radar."

Carter continued, her voice tinged with curiosity. "They lean conservative, like most towns that size. No reported problems until recently. Not a single major crime in decades—at least, not one that made it out of their bubble. The Bureau's records on them are laughably thin. No scandals, no federal investigations. It's like they've been deliberately boring."

She set the file down and tapped her pen against the map. "The only vacant houses in the area? The ones housing our WITSEC team and the Sokoloff woman and her kid. No coincidence there."

Michaels frowned, leaning forward. "So, what? They're a tight-knit community? They don't like outsiders?"

Carter shrugged. "More like outsiders don't stick around. Gas up, grab a bite, and keep moving. That's their thing, except for Jensen. He's the exception. Why does a guy like Jensen decide to ditch civilization and move to 'Boring, USA?' And how does he end up in the middle of all this?"

Michaels's pen stilled as he stared at the map. "That's the million-dollar question. Why him, and why now?"

Carter opened another file, this one stamped with an official seal. She flipped to a black-and-white image of the interior of the house, taken during the forensic sweep after the accident. The place had been ripped apart. It didn't match Sokoloff's usual MO. If nothing else, Alexi Sokoloff was efficient, systematic, and didn't leave any traces behind.

She pointed to a photo of a framed picture hanging on the wall—a candid shot of Bryan, Ashley, and Brianne. They were smiling, caught in a moment of warmth and love.

Carter's voice softened as she studied the image. She dropped another file on the table. "And then there's this. Wife and daughter. Ashley and Brianne Jensen. Both were killed in a freak accident about seven years ago. Fuel tanker ran a light…"

"Damn," Michaels said, his voice heavy with skepticism. "Anything else?"

"Accident report's sketchy," Carter replied. "Two fatalities, no survivors, and no witnesses. And now the widower is lying in a hospital bed, tortured to within an inch of his life. Coincidence?"

Carter shook her head, her expression tight as she gestured to the photo. "Who'd think the guy in ICU is this guy?" she said, tapping the image of Bryan, Ashley, and Brianne. "The guy smiling like he had it all figured out?"

Both agents stared at the old photo of Bryan's family in silence, the weight of unanswered questions settling over the room like a heavy cloud.

***

The safe house waiting room was a forgotten relic of the 1970s, its faded wallpaper and sagging furniture a testament to years of neglect. Mismatched chairs surrounded a scratched coffee table stacked with curling magazines that promised outdated celebrity gossip and irrelevant tips for a bygone era. The air smelled faintly of mothballs and something metallic, a scent Anna couldn't place but found unsettling.

Anna sat in one of the chairs, her leg bouncing nervously, the muted creak of the old springs amplifying her restlessness. She clutched her phone, her grip so tight her knuckles were white. The soft glow of its screen offered no comfort—no messages, no calls, no updates—just silence.

Riley sprawled across a battered couch a few feet away, engrossed in his handheld game console. The beeps and chimes punctuating his progress grated on Anna's nerves like nails on a chalkboard.

"Do you have to play that right now?" she snapped, her voice harsher than she intended.

Riley flinched, his hands freezing mid-movement. He turned to her, his eyes wide with surprise and a hint of hurt. "What else am I supposed to do? We've been sitting here for hours."

Anna exhaled sharply, pressing her fingers to her temples. "I'm sorry," she murmured, her tone softening. "I didn't mean to snap."

Riley hesitated before returning to his game, though he turned the volume down. The room settled back into an uneasy silence, broken only by the occasional faint beep from the console and the sound of Anna's restless foot against the floor.

The door opened abruptly, startling them both. Detective Browning entered, his face set in a grim mask. He shut the door behind him with deliberate care, scanning the room before speaking.

"We've got a problem," he said, his voice low.

Anna was on her feet in an instant, her stomach twisting into knots. "What is it?"

Browning crossed the room in a few long strides, his hands resting on his hips as he lowered his voice. "The FBI. They've got surveillance on the hospital, and it's only a matter of time before they figure out where we've gone."

Anna's pulse quickened. "What do we do?"

Browning hesitated, glancing briefly at Riley, who had paused his game and was now watching intently. "They want to talk. Formally. Interrogations—for all of you."

"No," Anna said immediately, her arms crossing defensively. "Bryan can't handle that right now. He's still—"

"—They don't care, Anna," Browning interrupted, his tone firm but not unkind. "If we don't cooperate, they'll come to us. And if that happens, it'll be out of my hands."

Riley spoke up, his voice tinged with defiance. "They think Bryan's guilty of something, don't they? That's why they're doing this."

Browning turned to him, his expression softening. "They're just trying to connect the dots. But yeah, they're looking at him harder than anyone else."

Anna's protective instincts flared, and she squared her shoulders. "Then we need to be ready."

Browning gave a slow nod, his jaw tightening. "We don't have much time. If we're going to play ball, we do it on our terms. Not theirs."

***

The safe house living room was cloaked in the fading light of late afternoon, the heavy curtains allowing only narrow slivers of golden sunlight to pierce the gloom. The mismatched furniture seemed to huddle together in the dimness—a sagging couch, a battered coffee table, and an armchair with threadbare arms. The faint smell of mothballs and old wood lingered in the air, adding to the sense of disrepair.

Bryan sat on the couch, his pale face illuminated by the dim light. His bandaged hands rested on his knees, and his breathing was shallow but steady. Determination burned in his eyes, though his body clearly struggled to match his resolve. Across from him, Riley perched on the arm of the couch, his wide eyes fixed on Bryan like a lifeline.

Anna stood near the doorway, her arms crossed tightly over her chest. Her gaze flicked between Bryan and Riley, her worry palpable. "You don't have to do this now," she said, her tone a careful balance of concern and authority.

Bryan shook his head. "I do," he rasped. His voice was hoarse but firm. "If I don't start moving now, I'll just sit here. And that's not an option."

Riley hopped down from the couch, his small hands reaching out instinctively. "You sure, Bryan?"

Bryan's lips twitched into a faint smile at the boy's use of his name. "I'm sure, kid. But I'll need you to spot me."

Riley nodded, his face serious. "Okay, but if you fall, I'm calling Mom."

Bryan chuckled softly, though the motion made him wince. "Deal."

He planted his hands on the edge of the couch and pushed himself upright. The effort was visible in every strained muscle and bead of sweat that broke out on his brow. His legs trembled under the weight they hadn't borne in days, but he didn't falter.

Anna took an involuntary step forward, her hands twitching at her sides. "Bryan—"

"—I'm fine," he interrupted, his voice sharper than he intended. He softened slightly as he glanced at her. "I need to do this."

Riley stayed close, his small hands hovering near Bryan's arm like a safety net. "You're doing good," he said, his voice full of encouragement. "Better than me when I tried to ride a bike without training wheels."

Bryan snorted, the sound dry but genuine. "That bad, huh?"

"Worse," Riley said with a grin. "I went straight into a mailbox. Mom has pictures."

Anna rolled her eyes but couldn't suppress a faint smile. "That was years ago, Riley. And you were fine."

"Yeah," Riley said, stepping forward as Bryan took a shaky step. "But I didn't look this bad doing it."

Bryan barked a laugh, pausing to catch his breath. "Careful, kid. I might look bad, but I'm still strong enough to ground you."

Riley grinned, his eyes shining with relief. "You'd have to catch me first."

Anna leaned against the doorframe, her arms still crossed but her posture softening. "Take it slow," she urged. "There's no rush."

Bryan nodded, his gaze fixed on the far wall. "One step at a time," he muttered, more to himself than anyone else.

With Riley at his side, he moved cautiously across the room. Each step was a battle, his movements deliberate and shaky. The floorboards creaked softly beneath him, a testament to the quiet effort filling the space. When he finally reached the far wall, he rested his hand against it, his chest heaving with exertion.

"Not bad," he muttered, more to himself than anyone else.

"Not bad?" Riley echoed, his voice brimming with pride. "That was awesome! You went, like, a hundred miles!"

Bryan smirked, his lips quirking despite his exhaustion. "Felt like it."

Anna crossed the room, stopping a few feet away. Her eyes glistened with unshed tears as she took in the scene. "You need to sit down before you overdo it."

Bryan met her gaze, his expression softening. "Just needed to know I could still do it."

Anna nodded slowly. "You can."

Bryan reached out, his hand trembling slightly as he rested it on Riley's shoulder. "Couldn't have done it without my spotter."

Riley beamed, puffing out his chest. "Told you I'm the best."

Bryan let out a quiet breath, his voice softer now. "Yeah, you are."

Anna moved to his side, helping him back to the couch. He sank into the cushions with a relieved sigh, and Riley climbed up beside him, curling into his side without hesitation.

For a moment, the three of them sat together in silence, the weight of the past few days finally lifting just enough to allow a flicker of hope. Outside, the sun dipped below the horizon, casting long shadows across the quiet street. The world beyond the safe house was still uncertain, still dangerous.

But for now, in this fragile moment, they had each other. And that was enough.

***

The Boston FBI office loomed over the city like a fortress, its cold, brutalist architecture an unsubtle reminder of the power it housed. Inside, the air was sterile, thick with the faint scent of industrial cleaner and the distant hum of fluorescent lighting. To most, it would feel oppressive—a calculated labyrinth of authority and control. To Bryan, it was laughably predictable.

He let his escort lead him deeper into the building, through unmarked hallways and past unyielding doors. At last, they stopped at an interrogation room. The space was as uninspired as Bryan expected: beige walls scuffed from years of use, a scratched metal table bolted to the floor, and a single overhead light that cast stark, unflattering shadows. In the corner, a camera blinked with a small red light, its attempt at subtlety undercut by its conspicuous placement.

Bryan walked in and sat down without hesitation, his movements slow but deliberate. His hand absently turned his wedding ring as his gaze swept the room. He knew the setup—had written it into countless stories over the years, down to the fluorescent glare and the faint aroma of stale coffee clinging to the air.

They think they're in control, he thought, leaning back in the chair. They think this room, this setup, gives them power. But intimidation only works on people who don't know the game. And I've played this game a hundred times—on the page and in my head.

His eyes flicked to the camera, and for a moment, he let a faint smirk cross his lips. Nice try, it seemed to say.

Two agents entered, the heavy door clicking shut behind them. The first, Agent Stone, looked as if he'd been plucked from a law enforcement recruitment poster. His sharp suit, slicked-back hair, and predatory gaze radiated arrogance. His smirk as he looked Bryan over was that of a man who thought he'd already won. The second agent, Michaels, was a stark contrast: rumpled suit, thoughtful eyes, and a demeanor that projected quiet professionalism. He didn't need to puff himself up. If Stone was the showman, Michaels was the tactician. Bryan made a mental note to keep an eye on him.

"Mr. Jensen," Michaels began, his voice calm as he set a file down on the table and opened it. "I'm Agent Michaels. This is my partner, Agent Stone. You understand why you're here?"

Bryan nodded, his expression neutral. Michaels glanced at the file as he continued. "You've done a remarkable job staying off the radar over the years. Quiet town, private life, pen name. And yet, somehow, you end up here."

Bryan leaned back, his voice steady. "Funny how life works, isn't it?" His gaze flicked to the camera again, a hint of amusement dancing in his eyes.

Stone interrupted with a sneer, pulling a magazine from the file. With a dramatic flourish, he slammed it onto the table. The glossy cover featured a photo of Anna kissing Bryan, the headline above it screaming with tabloid sensationalism. Stone crossed his arms and leaned back, waiting for a reaction.

"What's funny to me is this," he said, his smirk widening. "A cozy little photo shoot with the neighbor, huh? I guess that kiss wasn't just about being neighborly."

Bryan's eyes flicked to the magazine. His expression remained unreadable, his voice calm but firm. "A misunderstanding," he said. He looked up at Stone, his tone even. "My agent... soon-to-be former agent was greedy. The photographer was nosy. That's the only story here."

Stone wasn't deterred. Smirking, he leaned forward. "And yet both men are dead now. How do you explain that, Mr. Jensen? What does it mean?"

Bryan paused, tilting his head slightly as if considering the question. "I guess it means they're no longer alive, right?" he said finally, his tone sincere. "And I don't have to worry about a messy breakup. Mike was really, really emotional."

Stone blinked, momentarily thrown by the blunt reply. Bryan leaned back again, his face a picture of innocent sincerity as the silence stretched.

"You know what I mean," Stone said finally, irritation creeping into his voice. "Don't play games with me."

"No," Bryan said, his voice sharpening. "I know exactly what you mean. But let me remind you—you're the FBI. Isn't figuring out stuff like that supposed to be your job?" He crossed his arms, his gaze sharpening. "Or is this your new approach? Asking stupid questions, hoping for stupid answers?"

Stone stiffened, leaning in closer. "You're awfully defensive, Jensen. Makes me wonder if you're not as innocent as you're trying to look."

Bryan didn't flinch. Instead, he placed his hands on the table and rose slowly, his movements deliberate. "Defensive? No," he said, his voice dropping. "I'm just tired of wasting my time."

He stepped toward Stone, his gaze unflinching. "Maybe you should think about what pushing the wrong button on a man who's lost his family, been tortured by a gangster, and barely survived might get you." He gestured toward Michaels with his bandaged hand, flexing his fingers deliberately. "Or maybe you need a cup of coffee. I'll let you know when to call the ambulance for your partner here." A faint smirk tugged at his lips. "But don't take too long. He might not make it."

"All right, that's enough," Michaels said, standing abruptly. His voice was firm but calm. "Mr. Jensen, sit down. Agent Stone, back off. Now, let's all try to remain professional, shall we?"

Bryan slowly retook his seat, his voice measured. "Professional? Fine. But keep pushing, and I'll have a team of the most expensive lawyers in the country crawling so far up your chain of command's ass that they'll see what they're eating before it passes their teeth."

Stone flushed, his smirk faltering as Bryan delivered the final blow. "And you?" Bryan added, leaning back. "You'll be lucky to find a job sweeping gym floors at that fancy-ass college where you got gentleman C's."

Visibly shaken, Stone stiffened in his seat, his attempts at control crumbling. Michaels, however, adjusted smoothly, steering the conversation back to the facts with measured precision.

Bryan twisted his wedding ring absently as he leaned back, his gaze flicking briefly to the camera. You're playing catch-up, he thought, the faintest trace of a smile lingering on his lips.

***

Anna sat at the cold metal table, her hands twisting a tissue into shreds as she tried to calm her racing thoughts. The chair beneath her felt deliberately uncomfortable, the hard edges pressing into her back. Despite the neutral beige walls and the faint hum of fluorescent lights overhead, the room felt oppressive. She tried not to think about Riley— alone, somewhere in another room. That was the real reason her stomach churned.

When the door creaked open, two agents stepped inside. The first, a man with a calm demeanor and sharp eyes, introduced himself as Agent Carmichael. The second, a woman with a no-nonsense expression and a brisk tone, wasted no time.

"I'm Agent Carter," the woman said, her voice clipped as she pulled out a chair across from Anna. "Let's start simple. How long have you known Bryan Jensen?"

Anna straightened slightly, keeping her tone steady. "Several months. We're neighbors."

Carter didn't blink as she jotted something down in a notebook. "Neighbors? That's all?"

Anna caught the hint of suspicion in the question and folded the mangled tissue in her lap. "Yes," she said firmly. "He's been… a good friend to me and my son. Nothing more."

Without a word, Carter reached into her folder and slid a magazine across the table. Anna's heart sank as her eyes landed on the glossy cover. The photo of her kissing Bryan was plastered beneath a screaming headline she didn't bother to read.

"This doesn't look like 'just neighbors,' Mrs. Sokoloff. Care to explain?"

Anna drew in a slow breath and held Carter's gaze. "That photo was taken out of context. It's not what you think."

"Oh?" Carter leaned forward; her pen poised over the notebook. "So, you're telling me this photo, which looks like a kiss between two very familiar people, doesn't mean anything?"

Anna's grip on the tissue tightened. "It was a moment of gratitude—nothing more," she said, her voice cooling. "Bryan has been kind to us—especially to my son. But if you're trying to make it something else, you're wasting your time."

Carmichael, who had remained silent, tapped his pen lightly against the notebook. His gaze lingered on Anna, studying her intently. She glanced at him briefly before looking away, unsettled by his quiet scrutiny.

***

The interrogation room was frigid, a thin vent above the door pushing cold, stale air into the small, windowless space. Riley's sneakers tapped softly against the tiled floor as he sat in a chair far too large for him. His legs swung slightly, the steel table before him reflecting the glare of the single overhead light. Beige walls, chipped paint, and the faint tang of industrial cleaner gave the room the same charm as a dentist's office.

Riley wasn't impressed. This wasn't his first time being in a room that screamed authority. He'd spent more than a few hours in the backrooms of his father's clubs—places with more smoke, more noise, and more actual danger. This? This was just another room with people who thought they were smarter than they really were.

The door clicked open, and Riley tilted his head slightly, his expression blank. The agent who stepped in wasn't what he expected. She was young, in her early twenties, maybe 5'7", 115 lbs., with a soft smile and carefully styled blonde hair. Her green eyes were piercing sharp and screamed, 'Intelligent.' She carried a notebook in one hand and, in the other, a Klondike bar still wrapped in crinkly plastic.

"Hey, Niko," she said brightly, her voice warm and friendly. "I'm Agent Scott. Thought you might like a snack."

Riley's eyes flicked to the ice cream. He didn't trust her, but he wasn't about to turn down ice cream. "Sure," he said with a shrug. "Why not?"

Scott walked over and set the treat in front of him, her smile never faltering. Riley grabbed it and tore the wrapper open, taking a big bite. The vanilla and chocolate were cold on his tongue, a small comfort in the sterile room. He didn't say thank you, didn't acknowledge her effort. Instead, his sharp eyes locked on her as he chewed.

"So," Scott began, settling into the chair across from him, "I just want to ask you a few questions. Nothing serious. Sound good?"

Riley chewed slowly, letting the silence stretch before swallowing. "First of all, Lady, only my piece of shit father called me 'Niko.' I prefer 'Riley," he said, his tone dripping with mock sincerity, "and if you're gonna try to bribe me into talking to you, you're gonna need more than ice cream."

Scott chuckled softly, crossing her legs and leaning in slightly. "Noted, and it's not a bribe, 'Riley.' I'm just trying to make this easier for you. You've been through a lot, haven't you?"

He shrugged, taking another bite. "Maybe. But you're barking up the wrong tree if you think I'm gonna cry in my dessert." He paused, his eyes narrowing slightly. "And if we're gonna talk about Bryan, don't put him in the same class as my 'father.'" His tone shifted, colder now, and the words carried weight. "My father was a vicious bastard who wanted me dead. Bryan's not him. Not even close."

Scott blinked, caught off guard by the venom in his voice. "All right," she said carefully. "Fair enough."

Riley leaned back, licking a bit of chocolate off his thumb. "You know, though," he said, his voice lightening, "a cute thing like you could probably get more out of a guy if you undid a couple of those buttons. Didn't they teach you that at FBI school?" He bobbed his eyebrows, grinning like a cartoon character. "Just saying."

Scott froze mid-smile, her pen pausing over her notebook. "Wow," she said, her voice tight. "You're a bold one, aren't you?"

Riley tilted his head, his grin widening. He lifted his arm—the one not holding the ice cream—and, using his index finger, made a lazy circular motion as if twirling an invisible lasso. "Stand up and turn around."

Scott hesitated, her eyes narrowing. "Excuse me?"

"You heard me," Riley said, taking another slow bite of the ice cream, his smirk daring her to follow his lead. His eyes sparkled with mischief, the finger still making slow, deliberate circles in the air as though it were the most natural thing in the world.

Scott stared at him, but curiosity got the better of her. She stood slowly and turned in place, her movements stiff and deliberate.

When she faced him again, Riley tilted his head, his expression thoughtful. "Nice," he said, drawing the word out. "Could lose a couple of pounds, but nice. We could use you on the floor."

Scott's jaw tightened, and her cheeks flushed. "Excuse me?" she snapped, her friendly veneer cracking.

"You know... at one of my father's clubs," Riley smirked, leaning forward now, his tone teasing and sharp. "But lose the bra," he added, motioning with his hands toward his chest. "Make the 'girls' pop. The room's cold enough—might as well work it."

Scott's mouth opened, but no words came out for a moment. Her hand clenched the pen so tightly it squeaked against the notebook. "You're unbelievable."

Riley leaned back in his chair, tossing the ice cream wrapper onto the table. "Fifty bucks if you'll lick my toes," he added casually, his grin widening.

Scott's face went from pink to red in an instant. "Excuse me?" she hissed.

Riley tilted his head innocently. "What? Too low? Fine. A hundred. Do you take a card? I'm out of cash right now."

The silence that followed was deafening, save for the slight tap of Scott's pen against the table. Her hand trembled slightly as she jotted something down, muttering to herself. "You little—"

"—And a temper, too," Riley interrupted with a knowing grin. "Yowzah. You've got it all, toots."

\*\*\*

When Scott left the room, she stormed into the observation area, her face still flushed. She slammed her notebook onto the counter, glaring at the screen, which showed Riley leaning back in his chair, completely unbothered.

"That kid..." she began, her voice tight.

"What now?" Michaels asked, glancing up from his own notes.

Scott pointed at the screen as if Riley could somehow feel it. "He told me to unbutton my blouse, said I'd do great in one of his father's clubs, then had me stand up and turn around like a damn showgirl. After that, he told me to lose a few pounds and my bra. Oh, and then he offered me fifty bucks to lick his toes. And when I didn't reply, he raised it to a hundred, as if it were a negotiation."

The room went silent for a beat before Carter burst out laughing. "You're kidding."

"I wish I were," Scott snapped. "Then, when I started to push back, he asked if I'd take a credit card!" She ran a hand through her hair. "He's impossible."

Carter leaned back in her chair, wiping tears from her eyes. "God, I love this kid."

Michaels nodded slowly, his eyes still on Riley. "He's not intimidated by us. He's running circles around you."

As the agents filed out of the observation room, Scott hesitated by the door. She glanced down at her notebook, then over her shoulder toward the monitor. Her brow furrowed slightly, and she gave her hips a quick glance. "Lose a few pounds, my ass," she muttered under her breath.

She froze, realizing exactly what she'd just done. Her lips pressed into a thin line, and she sighed heavily. "Dammit," she muttered as she stalked out of the room. "He got me."

***

Bryan sat in a stiff, uncomfortable chair near the lobby's far wall, his hands resting on his knees. The faint hum of fluorescent lights overhead blended with the occasional murmur from a receptionist typing away behind the desk. The air smelled faintly of industrial cleaner, a scent Bryan had come to associate with places like this—cold, calculated, and impersonal.

His jaw clenched as his eyes remained fixed on the double doors leading back to the interrogation rooms. Patience wasn't his strong suit, and after hours of waiting, he could feel it wearing thin.

Finally, the doors swung open, and Anna emerged, her expression tight but composed. Behind her, Riley strolled out, hands in his pockets, a smug grin plastered across his face. Bryan stood, meeting them halfway.

Anna sighed, brushing a stray strand of hair from her face. "I think they're done with us."

"You okay?" Bryan asked, his voice low and steady, though his eyes flicked toward Riley with quiet concern.

"Fine," Anna replied quickly, though the clipped edge in her voice betrayed otherwise.

Bryan shifted his focus to Riley, whose grin had somehow grown even wider. The kid practically bounced on the balls of his feet, the picture of nonchalant mischief. "How'd it go, kid?"

Riley shrugged, his tone light. "I think she's got the hots for me." Riley glanced at Anna. "Don't worry, Mom; I was a complete gentleman."

Bryan blinked, completely thrown, as Anna froze mid-step. "What?"

Riley bit into his smirk, playing up his innocence. "What can I say? I'm irresistible." He paused for dramatic effect, then motioned in front of his chest with his hands. "Nice rack, too."

Anna's sharp gasp cut through the sterile air of the lobby. "Riley!" she hissed, her voice a mix of shock and exasperation.

Riley turned toward her; eyebrows raised as though her reaction was completely uncalled for. "What? It's not like I'm wrong. And hey, I didn't say anything bad. You'd have to see it under the right lighting, but trust me, she's got enough to work with."

Anna's mouth dropped open, her composure crumbling. "What are you talking about?!"

Riley shrugged again, completely at ease. "She could work the floor. Like the girls at the clubs. I mean, she doesn't have their moves yet, but give her some time. She could pull it off."

"Pull what off?!" Anna's voice rose an octave, her hands clenching into fists at her sides.

"Working the floor," Riley explained as if that clarified everything. He gestured vaguely with his hand as though Anna should know exactly what he meant. "You learn to spot it after a while. It's all about attitude and angles."

Anna's jaw moved, but no words came out. She looked at Bryan for help, but he was just as dumbfounded, his mouth half-open as though he were struggling to find words. Riley, unfazed, stuffed his hands back into his pockets and strolled toward the front entrance, pushing the glass doors open with a casual swagger.

Bryan finally recovered, turning to Anna. "Did he just—?"

"—Yes," Anna snapped, cutting him off, her face flushed with disbelief.

Bryan opened his mouth to say more, but the sound of tires crunching against pavement interrupted him. A car pulled up to the curb outside, and Detective Browning climbed out of an unmarked sedan. His suit was slightly rumpled, and his tie was loosened, but his sharp eyes took in the trio with practiced efficiency.

"Everything good?" Browning asked, his voice neutral but probing as his gaze moved from Anna to Bryan and then toward the doors Riley had just gone through.

Before either could respond, Riley stuck his head back through the doorway, grinning like he'd just won the lottery. "Yeah, we're good. You're late, though. I was just telling 'em about my new girlfriend." He jerked a thumb over his shoulder. "Agent Scott. Nice gal. Thinks I'm cute. Nice rack, too. Could probably kill it on the floor with a little practice."

Browning froze mid-step, his head tilting slightly. "Wha... what?"

"Don't worry," Riley said with a wink. "I'll let her down easy." With that, he disappeared back outside, leaving the doors to swing shut behind him.

For a moment, silence hung in the air. Bryan, Anna, and Browning exchanged baffled looks as the absurdity of Riley's statement sank in. Finally, Browning broke the silence, muttering under his breath, "What the hell kind of circus is this?"

Bryan exhaled heavily, rubbing the bridge of his nose. "You get used to it," he muttered, his voice resigned.

Anna shot him a glare. "I'm not sure I want to."

Browning shook his head as he headed for the door. "Well, let's hope the kid doesn't get us all arrested on charm alone."

Outside, Riley was already waiting by the car, arms crossed and a smug grin lighting up his face. "Come on, lovebirds," he called, motioning impatiently. "Let's roll!"

## CHAPTER 6 - RETURN TO HAVENWOOD

The late afternoon sun cast long shadows over the quiet streets of Havenwood as Bryan's truck rumbled into the driveway. Behind it, Browning's sedan pulled up, the dust from the long drive settling around them.

Browning stepped out first, stretching with a grunt. He glanced toward the truck, concern flickering across his face as Anna hurried to the passenger side.

Bryan sat slumped in the seat, pale and drawn, his beard thicker than before, his hair unruly. Recovery had taken its toll, but the fight still burned in his eyes.

"I'll get the chair," Browning muttered, pulling it from the truck bed with a practiced ease. The wheels creaked as he unfolded it.

Anna reached for Bryan's arm. "Almost there," she murmured.

Riley hovered nearby, his grip tightening on his sketchpad. He hadn't spoken much during the ride, but he'd refused to sit anywhere but beside Bryan.

"All right, big guy," Browning said, positioning the chair. "Let's do this."

Bryan inhaled sharply as he shifted his weight. Pain shot through him, but he gritted his teeth. Browning moved quickly, hooking an arm under Bryan's shoulder to ease him into the chair.

"Easy now," Browning said. "No heroics."

Bryan smirked faintly. "Never liked running anyway."

Anna reached for the chair, but Browning waved her off. "I got him."

They reached the front steps. Riley frowned at the small but undeniable obstacle.

"How do we get him up there?"

Anna bit her lip. "We'll manage."

Browning sighed. "All right, Jensen, you think you can stand long enough?"

Bryan nodded. "Not much choice."

Between Browning's steady grip and Anna's careful guidance, they maneuvered Bryan up the steps. By the time they reached the door, all of them were winded.

The front door swung open, revealing destruction. Browning stilled, his grip tightening on the wheelchair. The air inside was stale, laced with the metallic tang of dried blood and the acrid sting of burnt wood.

Anna stepped in first, Riley at her side. The living room lay in ruin. The couch was overturned, stuffing spilling out like entrails. Broken frames littered the floor, but one remained—hanging lopsided yet untouched, its presence defiant amidst the wreckage.

Bryan exhaled slowly as Browning wheeled him inside. His eyes swept over the damage, his shoulders sagging. Silence settled like a heavy blanket.

"Well," Browning muttered, scratching the back of his neck. "Home sweet home?"

No one laughed.

Anna moved further in, running her fingers over the broken remnants of a coffee table. Riley bent down and retrieved something from the debris—a toy soldier, scuffed but intact. He studied it before glancing at Bryan.

"It's not that bad," he said softly. "We can fix it."

Anna met Bryan's gaze. No words were needed. She moved to his side, resting a hand on his shoulder.

"We're home."

Bryan's fingers brushed hers. "Yeah. We are."

Browning cleared his throat. "I'd stick around, but you've got enough on your plate."

Anna gave a tired smile. "Thank you, Detective."

"Just Matt," he said. "And don't thank me yet. Still gotta figure out what the hell happened here." He looked at Bryan. "I'll check in later."

Bryan nodded. "Appreciate it."

Browning hesitated, eyes lingering on the tilted family photo before he stepped outside. The door clicked shut behind him.

Silence returned, broken only by the creak of wood as Riley moved to sit beside Bryan. Anna knelt before them, her hands on Bryan's knees.

"No matter what," she whispered, "we're here."

Bryan's gaze drifted to the family photo—the one thing left standing. He let out a slow breath. "Yeah," he murmured. "We're here."

***

The house loomed in the fading light. Bryan hesitated at the threshold, fingers hovering over the doorknob. His breath hitched, and for a moment, he seemed lost. Anna placed a steadying hand on his arm.

Bryan pushed the door open.

The foyer was untouched, but the living room was worse. The warmth that once lived there had been stripped bare. The TV lay shattered. Books, DVDs, and shattered frames littered the floor. The couch was torn apart. Bryan's armchair—a place of solace—stood ruined.

Then Anna saw the family portrait. Pristine, untouched above the fireplace.

Her breath hitched.

She remembered the night she'd stood on Bryan's porch, asking to come inside. His refusal had stung, but now, as she took in the wreckage, she understood. This wasn't just damage. It was grief made manifest.

She turned away from the portrait, nausea curling in her gut. How had he survived this? How had she judged him so quickly?

"This is bad," Riley whispered.

Bryan moved toward the kitchen doorway, then stopped abruptly. His body went rigid. His breathing quickened.

Anna followed his gaze. The kitchen was a wreck—the table was overturned, and dishes were shattered. Blood smeared on the walls.

Bryan's breath hitched. "No," he whispered, voice breaking. "Not again," Bryan rasped, the walls closing in.

"Bryan," Anna said, gripping his arm. "It's okay."

"I... can't... can't," he gasped. "I can't go... in there."

His knees buckled. Anna caught him, her voice sharp. "Riley!"

"I got it!" Riley darted inside, dragging a chair over. "Here."

Bryan collapsed into it, head in his hands. His breath came in ragged gasps.

"You're okay," Anna murmured. "You're safe."

Riley hovered nearby, worry deepening his frown. "Is he... gonna be okay?"

Anna nodded. "Good job, Riley." She turned back to Bryan. "We'll get through this."

Bryan stared at the floor. Shadows of memories clawed at him. The blood. The pain. The betrayal.

Anna cupped his face, forcing him to look her in the eyes. "Bryan," she said, her voice steel-wrapped in warmth. "You survived. We're fixing this. Together."

His breathing slowed. His shoulders loosened.

Riley crouched beside him. "You're tough," he said. "Superhero tough."

Bryan let out a breath—half laugh, half sigh. "Not sure about that, kid."

Anna smiled through her tears. "Well, we are."

For the first time in weeks, Bryan let himself believe it.

***

Outside, the sun dipped lower, casting long shadows over the yard. The journey ahead was uncertain, but as Bryan sat between Anna and Riley, he felt the faintest flicker of hope.

They would rebuild—together.

***

The three of them sat there, surrounded by the destruction, a stark reminder of what they had endured. But for the first time, they faced it together.

Outside, the sun dipped lower, casting long shadows across the yard. The journey ahead was daunting, but as Bryan sat between Anna and Riley, he felt the faintest flicker of hope. They would rebuild—brick by brick, moment by moment. Together.

***

The walk to the house was silent. Bryan's arm rested heavily on Anna's shoulders, his steps faltering. His weight bore down on her, but she didn't complain. She kept her head down, her eyes fixed on the path ahead, determined to get him to safety.

Riley trailed behind them; his hands jammed into his pockets. The sight of Bryan like this—so broken—left a knot in his stomach. He wanted to say something, crack a joke, or lighten the mood, but the words wouldn't come.

They reached the house, its facade dark and silent, the windows reflecting the deepening twilight. Anna paused at the front door, her hand trembling as she reached beneath the doormat. The key was still there, rusted slightly but solid.

She unlocked the door and pushed it open. The air inside was stale, tinged with the faint scent of abandonment. Shadows stretched long across the floor. The house was as eerily quiet as she remembered.

Anna guided Bryan inside, avoiding the kitchen altogether. She led him to the bedroom she had once called her own, the room untouched since the night she'd fled in terror. The bed was still made, though the sheets were dusty, and the air carried the faintest memory of lavender from an old sachet hanging by the window.

"Let's get you lying down," Anna said softly, her voice steady despite the storm raging inside her. Bryan didn't resist. He sank onto the bed, his head falling back against the pillow. His eyes stared blankly at the ceiling, unseeing.

Riley lingered in the doorway, his small hands gripping the frame. "Is he... gonna be okay?" he asked, his voice barely above a whisper.

Anna tucked a blanket around Bryan, brushing his damp hair back gently. "He just needs rest," she said, her tone firmer than she felt. "Stay with him, okay? Don't let him be alone."

Riley nodded, his wide eyes flicking between Anna and Bryan. "What about you?"

"I'll be right back," Anna said, forcing a small smile. "I just need to take care of something."

***

Anna moved through the house with purpose, though her heart raced with every step. Each room she passed seemed to echo with the ghosts of that night—Taylor's betrayal, Bryan's desperation, Alexi's arrival. When she reached the kitchen doorway, she stopped, her breath catching at the sight before her.

The back door was ajar, the wind stirring the curtains in faint, ghostly waves. The chair that had once held Taylor stood nearby; its ropes still coiled in place like a grim monument to the chaos that had unfolded. Bloodstains streaked the floor, dark and sticky against the faded tiles, leading in jagged trails toward the living room and back door. The table, overturned with one leg splintered, jutted awkwardly into the space like a broken limb.

This had been the epicenter of everything. The moment Taylor had turned on them. The moment Bryan had acted with terrifying decisiveness to save her and Riley. The moment their lives had changed forever.

Anna's chest tightened as the memories threatened to overwhelm her, but she forced herself to square her shoulders. She couldn't let this house remain frozen in that night. It wasn't just a crime scene; it was where they had lived, loved, and fought to survive. She wouldn't let Taylor's shadow linger here any longer.

133

Taking a deep breath, she stepped into the room and closed the back door, the click of the latch reverberating like a gunshot in the silence. She turned toward the mess, hesitating only briefly before grabbing a rag from the counter and dampening it under the faucet.

Her hands trembled as she knelt and began scrubbing the bloodstains. The rag came away red almost immediately, and she wrung it out under the faucet, watching as the water turned a pale pink before draining away. Her shoulders shook with every stroke, but she didn't stop. She couldn't. Every motion felt like reclaiming a piece of herself, of Bryan, of Riley.

"Mom."

The quiet voice broke through the stillness, and Anna froze, her hands clutching the rag tightly. She turned her head to see Riley standing in the doorway, his small figure silhouetted against the dim light of the hall. His wide eyes swept the room before landing on her hunched form, his face twisting with concern.

"I told you to stay with Bryan," Anna said, her voice trembling as she swiped at her tear-streaked face. "He needs you right now."

"He's okay for now," Riley said, stepping into the room, his sneakers squeaking faintly on the tiles. "But you're not."

Anna's hand stilled mid-scrub, her shoulders tensing. "I'm fine," she said, her tone brittle. "I just... I need to clean this up."

Riley moved closer; his gaze unflinching as he knelt beside her. He reached out, taking the rag from her hands, his small fingers brushing against hers. "You don't have to do it alone," he said softly, his voice steady despite the quiver beneath it.

Anna stared at him, her resolve crumbling under the weight of his words. Her tears flowed freely now, each one a release of the tension and fear she'd been holding inside. "Riley..." she whispered, her voice breaking as she pulled him into her arms.

Riley let her hold him, his small frame strong and unwavering. "It's okay," he murmured, his words muffled against her shoulder. "You've got me, Mom. We'll do it together."

When Anna finally pulled back, her eyes were red and puffy, but there was a glimmer of determination in them. "Thank you," she said, her voice hoarse but sincere.

Riley nodded, handing her another rag from the counter. "Let's finish this," he said simply, his tone matter-of-fact.

They worked in silence, side by side. Anna scrubbed the bloodstains while Riley focused on the smaller debris. Together, they cleared away broken glass, righted the overturned table, and uncoiled the ropes from the chair. Riley's hands trembled as he dropped the ropes into a trash bag but he said nothing, only glancing once at Anna before returning to his task.

When the floor was clean and the chair had been moved to the corner, Anna took a step back to survey their work. The kitchen wasn't perfect, it would never be perfect—but it no longer felt like a crime scene. It felt like a place that might, one day, hold warmth again.

***

Anna placed a hand on Riley's shoulder and squeezed it gently. "You're amazing, you know that?" she said, her voice steady now, filled with quiet pride.

Riley grinned up at her, his eyes bright despite the exhaustion etched into his young face. "I learned from the best," he said, his tone teasing but sincere.

Anna chuckled softly, brushing her hand through his hair. "I don't know what I'd do without you."

"You're stuck with me," Riley said, squeezing her hand. "No matter what."

Anna's heart swelled with love and gratitude as she hugged him tightly. In that moment, she knew that no matter how long the road ahead might be, they would walk it together.

And they would be okay.

# CHAPTER 7 - A PLEA FOR HELP

The parking lot outside the small grocery store was nearly empty, save for a few scattered cars sitting under the afternoon rain shower. Anna shifted Bryan's truck into park and turned to Riley, who sat in the passenger seat, swinging his legs absently.

"Okay," Anna said, her voice steady but tired. "Stay put, alright?"

Riley nodded, but his gaze was already wandering. His eyes landed on the ice cream parlor next door, its brightly painted sign a sharp contrast to the weathered buildings around it. He said nothing, simply unbuckling his seatbelt as Anna stepped out of the truck.

Inside the grocery store, Anna quickly became engrossed in her task. Armed with Bryan's credit card, she moved methodically through the aisles, filling the cart with cleaning supplies, disinfectants, trash bags, and anything else she thought might help salvage the wreckage they had left behind. Her focus narrowed, her mind occupied by lists and worries.

\*\*\*

Inside the truck, the cabin felt unnaturally still, save for the occasional pop of the cooling metal and patter of rain on the windshield. Bryan sat slumped in the passenger seat, his hands resting limply on his thighs. His eyes stared straight ahead, unblinking, fixed on nothing. He wasn't asleep, but he wasn't present either.

Riley sat in the driver's seat, his small hands resting on the steering wheel, mimicking Bryan's usual posture. He glanced sideways, hoping for some kind of acknowledgment. "Hey, Bryan," he said softly, testing the waters. "Want me to teach you some tricks? I know how to spin the wheel really fast."

No answer. Bryan didn't even blink.

Riley shifted uncomfortably, drumming his fingers against the wheel. "Okay, okay. Maybe not. But hey, I'll make you a deal—if I'm ever driving this thing for real, you can't get mad at me for going fast. I mean, not too fast. Just, you know, a little fast."

Still nothing. Riley's stomach tightened. He leaned back, letting out a soft sigh. "You're not even listening, are you?"

The silence felt heavier now, as if the truck's cabin were closing in. Riley glanced toward the grocery store, then back at Bryan. "I'll be right back," he said, more to himself than to Bryan. When there was no reaction, Riley made his decision.

*** 

The ice cream parlor door jingled as Riley stepped inside, the cheerful sound a sharp contrast to the rain hammering the sidewalk outside. The warm air enveloped him, carrying the scents of vanilla, chocolate, and freshly baked cones. He stood just inside the door, his small frame dripping with rain, water pooling around his sneakers, which squeaked faintly with every movement.

The parlor had been lively only moments before. Families, young and old, along with small cliques of teenage girls and young women, filled the booths. Laughter and conversation echoed through the space as spoons clinked against bowls, blending with the hum of the ice cream freezer.

One of the young women, seated near the window, caught Riley's entrance with a quiet glance. She stood out, even among her peers, with fiery red-orange hair that fell in soft waves over her shoulders, catching the muted light of the afternoon. Her emerald-green eyes flicked briefly to the boy at the door before returning to her melting sundae. A delicate silver chain rested lightly against her neck, a small jade pendant swaying faintly as she shifted in her seat.

Around her, the other women murmured in hushed tones, their attention shifting like the rest of the room to the drenched boy standing in the doorway.

The room fell silent the moment Riley stepped inside.

Heads turned, eyes locking onto him. Conversations halted mid-sentence. Even the steady rhythm of the ice cream scoop scraping against frozen tubs ceased. The cheerful atmosphere evaporated, replaced by a tense, watchful stillness.

Riley hesitated for a moment, the weight of their stares pressing down on him. His hair hung in wet strands across his forehead, water dripping from his jacket onto the polished floor. He squared his shoulders and walked toward the counter; each step punctuated by a faint squeak of his soggy sneakers.

Genevieve's gaze flickered back to him as he moved. Her emerald eyes narrowed slightly, and her fingers absently traced the edge of her sundae dish. She didn't speak, but the subtle crease between her brows deepened. Her posture, relaxed yet attentive, set her apart from the quiet unease radiating from the other women in the room.

Behind the counter, Mrs. Harper stood frozen, her sharp blue eyes fixed on Riley. Her hand gripped the edge of the counter, knuckles pale against the polished surface. She wiped at her apron, a practiced motion that betrayed a flicker of discomfort as she watched him approach.

"What can I help you with, son?" she asked, her voice polite but cautious, carrying the same tension that hung over the room.

Riley swallowed hard, his throat dry despite the rainwater clinging to him. "My mom told me," he began, his voice trembling slightly but growing stronger with each word, "that if I'm lost, I should find a mom. Any mom. And she'll help me."

Mrs. Harper's brows knitted together, her lips parting as though to respond, but no words came. Her eyes softened briefly before she caught herself, her expression hardening once more.

"Ma'am," Riley continued, his voice louder now, cutting through the oppressive silence, "I know how you feel about me, my mom, and Bryan. But I'm standing here, an outsider, and I'm telling you—I'm lost. My mom is lost. And Bryan..." His voice broke briefly before he regained his composure. "Bryan's not okay."

He turned, his rain-soaked figure twisting to face the room. His eyes, wide and glistening, swept over the women sitting at the booths. "I'm asking for help. My mom and Bryan need it. I'm begging you... all of you... any of you."

For a moment, no one moved. No one spoke. The silence pressed down on Riley like the rain had outside, heavy and unrelenting.

Genevieve shifted slightly, her gaze lingering on Riley as the tension in the room thickened. Her fingers stilled on the edge of her dish, and for a fleeting moment, her emerald eyes flickered with something that almost resembled understanding.

A few women exchanged uneasy glances. One looked away entirely, pretending not to see him. A child's spoon clattered to the floor, the sound impossibly loud in the stillness.

Riley's shoulders slumped. His small fists unclenched at his sides, his fingers trembling as he wiped at his face, smearing rainwater with the tears he refused to let fall.

Behind the counter, Mrs. Harper's hand twitched against the edge of the counter, a tiny gesture of indecision as her gaze followed him.

Without another word, Riley turned and walked out, his sneakers squeaking faintly with every step. The bell jingled as the door closed behind him, the sound almost mocking in its cheerfulness.

***

The rain fell in heavy sheets, soaking Anna as she stepped out of the grocery store. She juggled an overstuffed basket filled with cleaning supplies, her eyes scanning the parking lot. Her gaze landed on the truck, and panic flared in her chest when she saw the empty passenger seat.

"Riley!" she called, her voice sharp and edged with fear. Dropping the basket onto the wet pavement, she sprinted toward the truck, her heart pounding in her ears.

Halfway there, she spotted him trudging through the rain, his head bowed, his small frame hunched against the downpour. Relief flooded her, followed swiftly by a wave of frustration.

"Riley!" she shouted, her voice cracking. "What were you thinking? You scared me half to—"

She stopped short as she reached him. His hair hung in limp strands across his forehead, and his hands were trembling. His eyes, rimmed red and filled with weariness far beyond his years, locked onto hers.

Without a word, Anna dropped to her knees and pulled him into her arms. The rain soaked through her clothes, chilling her to the bone, but she didn't care.

"Oh, baby," she murmured, her voice breaking. "What happened?"

Riley clung to her, his small hands clutching at her jacket. "I went for help," he whispered.

Anna pulled back slightly, her hands framing his face as she searched his expression. "Help?" she echoed, her brow furrowing. "Riley, what do you mean—"

She froze as movement behind Riley caught her eye.

Several women, holding umbrellas against the rain, approached cautiously. At their center was Mrs. Harper, her apron damp but her expression resolute. Flanking her were the others, their faces a mixture of guilt and determination.

Among them was the fiery-haired young woman with emerald-green eyes, her rain-dampened hair catching faint highlights even in the gloom. She lingered toward the back, her expression unreadable as she scanned the scene.

Riley turned, following Anna's gaze. He glanced back at her, his voice small but steady.

"I went for help," he repeated.

Mrs. Harper was the first to speak, her voice hesitant but steady. "Anna, isn't it?" she began, her hands twisting the edges of her apron. "We... heard what your son... Riley, isn't it? We heard what he said. And he's right. We've been... wrong."

Anna blinked, her emotions warring between gratitude and disbelief. Riley pressed closer to her side, his hand gripping hers tightly.

Mrs. Harper stepped forward, her expression softening. "We want to help," she said firmly, glancing back at the other women for support. "However we can. Cleaning, cooking, watching Riley—whatever you need."

The other women nodded, murmuring quiet agreements. One stepped forward with a tentative smile. "We're sorry it took us this long to see it."

Anna felt the sting of tears in her eyes. She looked down at Riley, then back at the women. "Thank you," she said, her voice thick with emotion. "We... we need it."

Mrs. Harper nodded; her expression resolute. "Then let's get started."

***

The women helped Anna recover the cleaning supplies from the rain-soaked pavement and carry them to the truck. Several lingered near the passenger-side window, glancing at Bryan's motionless figure inside. Their faces darkened with guilt, the weight of his condition sinking in alongside the impact of Riley's desperate plea.

As Anna settled Riley into the truck and climbed into the driver's seat, she paused, looking at Mrs. Harper and the others. "Thank you," she said again, her voice quiet but heartfelt.

Mrs. Harper placed a hand on Anna's arm, meeting her gaze. "You're not alone anymore."

For the first time in weeks, as the truck pulled away, Anna felt the faintest glimmer of hope.

***

The house loomed before them, a crumbling relic of its former self. The rain had stopped, and shadows stretched across the yard as the late-afternoon sun dipped lower, casting an eerie light over the boarded-up windows and weathered façade. For the women of Havenwood, it was their first glimpse inside Bryan's house—what had once been a home was now an artifact of anguish.

Anna led the group up the cracked path to the front door, clutching the keys tightly. She hesitated, glancing back at the women who had followed her here after Riley's plea. Among them, Mrs. Harper stood nearest, her apron still damp from the rain, while Genevieve lingered toward the back, her fiery hair gleaming faintly in the dim light.

Anna slid the key into the lock, her hands trembling slightly. She took a steadying breath before turning the handle. "I'll warn you," she said softly, "it's bad."

The door creaked open, and the women stepped inside.

***

The foyer offered no reprieve, but the living room hit them like a physical blow.

The space was frozen in chaos, its destruction vivid and raw. Torn cushions spilled their stuffing across the floor like entrails. Shelves that once held books and keepsakes now stood empty; their contents strewn haphazardly. Pages of novels fluttered faintly in an unseen draft. A toppled coffee table lay on its side, one leg snapped clean off, while the television lay shattered nearby, its broken screen reflecting jagged shards of light.

"Gods above..." one woman whispered, her voice barely audible.

The witches moved slowly, their footsteps tentative on the warped floorboards. The air was heavy, thick with something unseen yet suffocating.

"What happened here?" another woman murmured, her gaze darting nervously around the room.

"This isn't just destruction," Mrs. Harper said quietly, her expression unreadable as her eyes scanned the devastation. "It's torment."

Genevieve remained silent, her emerald eyes flicking over the room with quiet precision. Her gaze lingered on a family portrait above the fireplace—untouched amidst the wreckage. The smiling faces of Bryan, Ashley, and Brianne seemed almost cruel in contrast to the devastation surrounding them.

"She left this," Genevieve murmured, her voice low. "Why?" Her fingers brushed the edge of the frame, as though touching it might reveal the answer. The untouched glass felt cold beneath her fingertips, a stark contrast to the storm of chaos surrounding it.

Anna felt a chill creep up her spine as her eyes locked on the portrait. It wasn't just fear—it was something heavier, a force pressing down on her chest. She swallowed hard, forcing herself to look away.

"It wasn't just anger," Genevieve said softly. "It was punishment."

"Punishment? For what?" one of the women asked.

"An act of kindness," Anna whispered.

The weight of her words sank into the room. The women exchanged glances; their expressions heavy with a guilt that couldn't be spoken aloud. They had turned their backs on him, each in their own way, and now they stood in the ruins of a life they had quietly abandoned.

*** 

Riley stood at the doorway to the kitchen, his hand gripping the frame tightly. He hadn't said a word since they arrived, but his silence spoke volumes. His shoulders were taut, his breaths shallow as his eyes fixed on the threshold as if crossing it would shatter him entirely.

Anna moved to his side, her voice gentle. "Riley, baby, you don't have to go in."

"I can't," he whispered, his voice hoarse.

Mrs. Harper stepped forward, placing a hand on Anna's shoulder. "We'll handle it," she said firmly. She motioned to the others, and they hesitated only briefly before stepping past Riley into the kitchen.

The destruction here was no less harrowing. Chairs lay overturned, their legs splintered, while the table had been pushed violently against the wall, its surface gouged with deep scratches. Broken dishes littered the floor, their jagged edges glinting in the fading light. A sour smell lingered; the remnants of long-spoiled food added an unsettling layer to the scene.

Genevieve crouched near the wall, her fingers tracing faint scratches in the wood. Her expression remained calm, but her emerald eyes darkened slightly. "Whatever happened here... it left its mark," she said softly.

The air shifted abruptly as one of the women neared a door at the back of the kitchen. She stopped short, her breath catching as an unnatural chill seeped through the air.

'That's it, isn't it?" Genevieve whispered, her voice tight.

Anna followed her gaze, her stomach knotting as her eyes landed on the basement door. The wood looked ordinary, but the space around it seemed darker somehow, with shadows that were deeper and more menacing.

Genevieve moved closer, her emerald eyes narrowing. "There's something..." she began, her voice trailing off. She didn't need to finish. The oppressive energy radiating from the door was palpable, even to those who lacked the ability to wield magic.

Mrs. Harper placed a hand on the doorframe but immediately drew back, her fingers trembling. "It's strong," she said, her voice shaking. "Whatever happened down there... It's still echoing."

Riley stood frozen near the kitchen doorway, his small frame tense as he stared at the door. His face was pale, his hands trembling slightly. "That's where it happened," he said, his voice barely audible.

Genevieve glanced at him; her expression unreadable. His slight frame seemed too fragile for the weight of this house's history, yet he stood firm, his eyes steady on the door. Something about him drew her in, a thread she hadn't expected to find in an outsider.

Anna moved quickly to Riley's side, wrapping an arm around his shoulders. "It is," she said softly. "But you don't have to go near it."

Genevieve knelt by the door, her fingers hovering just above the surface of the wood. "This isn't just residual," she murmured. "It's alive. Whatever was unleashed here, it hasn't left." She glanced up at Anna, her expression grim. "No wonder he couldn't face this place."

Mrs. Harper straightened, her hands curling into fists. "We're not leaving this like it is," she said firmly. She turned to the others. "We'll deal with it. But carefully."

The witches returned to the living room, their faces pale but resolute. Mrs. Harper clapped her hands, breaking the silence. "Let's get to work," she said, her tone leaving no room for argument.

Anna blinked, surprised. "You... you don't have to—"

"—We're here, aren't we?" Mrs. Harper interrupted gently. Her blue eyes softened. "Riley asked us for help. And we're not leaving until it's done."

The others nodded, some murmuring quiet agreements. Even Genevieve, who had remained distant throughout, stepped forward, her jade pendant gleaming faintly. "This place has suffered enough," she said, meeting Anna's gaze. "Let's start fixing it."

Anna blinked back the sting of tears. These women, who had once viewed her and Riley with such suspicion, now moved with purpose through the wreckage. It wasn't just the house they were mending—it was something deeper, something she hadn't realized needed fixing.

*** 

The women worked in near silence, and their movements were efficient and deliberate. They avoided the basement door, though its presence loomed like a dark specter. Broken furniture was removed, walls were scrubbed, and what little remained intact was carefully salvaged.

As the sun dipped below the horizon, the house began to take on a semblance of order. It was far from whole, but it was no longer a place of torment. For the first time, it felt as though something better might grow from the ruins.

## CHAPTER 8 - INTO THE STORM

The conference room at the Boston FBI Field Office was tense, the air thick with unspoken frustration. The hum of the air conditioning did little to cut through the oppressive atmosphere as agents filed in, their expressions grim. The long table was cluttered with files, photographs, and printouts—remnants of a failed investigation.

At the head of the table stood Special Agent in Charge Phillips, her posture stiff, her eyes sharp with displeasure. Her suit was immaculate, but her expression was anything but composed. The silence before she spoke was deliberate, her gaze sweeping over the agents like a blade.

"Let's recap," she said, her voice low and cutting. "Bryan Jensen. Anna Sokoloff and her son, Niko. Three interviews. Three subjects. And what do we have to show for it?" She let the question hang before slamming a folder onto the table. "Nothing! Not a damn thing."

She turned her gaze to Agent Michaels and Agent Scott, who sat uncomfortably at the table. "Michaels. Scott. You were supposed to bring in actionable intelligence. What I got instead was a circus act. Care to explain?"

Michaels cleared his throat, shifting in his seat. "Ma'am, Jensen is... not an ordinary subject. He's calculated. Reserved. He knows exactly how to answer without revealing anything.

Scott, still smarting from her encounter with Riley, muttered under her breath, "The kid's worse."

Phillips snapped her attention to Scott. "Speak up, Agent."

Scott hesitated but straightened in her chair. Niko Rilej—'Riley' Sokoloff—he's manipulative. Plays dumb, but he's sharp as hell. He twisted every question I asked back on me. And that mouth—he knows how to get under your skin."

A chuckle rippled through the room before Phillips's glare silenced it. "So, a ten-year-old ran circles around you?" She exhaled sharply. "And Jensen?"

Michaels hesitated. "He's good, ma'am. Never raised his voice. Never let us get to him. He's hiding something—he's just better at it than most."

Phillips clicked a remote, and Jensen's dossier appeared on the screen. His stoic face stared back at them.

"Bryan Jensen. Or, as the literary world knows him, Alan Hoyle, a best-selling author. Twenty-one novels. Multiple movie adaptations. Net worth? Low nine figures." A murmur spread through the room. "Yet he lives like a hermit in a Victorian deathtrap in a town without a Starbucks."

Another slide.

"Orphaned at twelve. Fast-tracked through school. Studied across Europe. Organized crime specialist. Fluent in multiple languages. Lands at Harvard, then—vanishes."

Click. Anna's face appeared.

"Anna Sokoloff. Formerly Mitchell. WITSEC participant. Hunted by Alexi Sokoloff. Moves to Havenwood. And who does she wind up next door to? Bryan Jensen."

Click. Riley.

"Niko 'Riley' Sokoloff. Ten years old. Outwitted an international crime syndicate. Top of his father's most-wanted list. Oh, and the kid who turned one of our own into a punchline."

Laughter erupted, but Phillips silenced it with a look. The next slide displayed satellite imagery of Havenwood.

"Population: 3,014. No real estate turnover in decades. No crime. No economic activity beyond local crafts. But get this—satellite images don't match. Landmarks shift. Structures change. Either there's a glitch, or this town has secrets."

Agent Carter raised a hand, holding up a black notebook. "Found this at Jensen's. I sent it to NSA contacts. They threw AI at it. Nothing. It's a cipher they can't crack."

Phillips's eyes narrowed. "Scott. Michaels. Get ready. You've got work to do."

***

The FBI sedan cut through the misty rain on Route 2. Michaels drove, Scott flipping through a thick file.

"Bryan Jensen," she muttered. "Best-selling author. Recluse. Survived a full-scale assault by Alexi Sokoloff and ten of his men."

Michaels smirked. "Self-defense, right?"

Scott snorted. "Self-defense? He bludgeoned one to death with a bat. And let's not forget—he shot Alexi Sokoloff. In the eye."

Michaels raised an eyebrow. "In the eye? Coroner confirms that?"

Scott's voice dropped. "No. When they went back for Sokoloff... his head was missing."

Michaels glanced at her. "Missing?"

"Gone," she confirmed. "And both mother and son swear they saw it happen."

Michaels exhaled. "If his head's missing, how does the gunshot story hold up? What did they see?"

Scott stared out at the blurred trees. "That's what we're here to find out. Because whatever took Sokoloff's head... wasn't Bryan Jensen."

***

The FBI sedan rolled slowly down Havenwood's main street, the agents taking in the scenery. The rain-washed air carried a faint chill, and the town seemed to have stepped out of a postcard from a bygone era. A single stoplight marked the intersection ahead, and beyond it, neatly maintained buildings nestled amid the dense, shadowy forest. The street was quiet, save for the occasional rumble of an old truck passing through.

The car pulled to a stop in front of the Havenwood Police Station, a modest brick building with a small, faded sign identifying it. It was the kind of place you could drive past without noticing if you weren't looking for it.

Agent Scott stepped out first, her sharp heels clicking against the wet pavement. She pulled her trench coat tighter around her and glanced at the single window of the station. A neatly handwritten sign hung in the glass:

"Out for coffee."

Scott blinked, glancing back at her partner, Agent Michaels, who had stepped around the car to join her.

"Out for coffee?" she said, her tone laced with disbelief. "Is this guy serious?"

Michaels leaned into peer through the window, spotting a utility belt hanging neatly from a hook on the wall. The holstered pistol and handcuffs gave the impression that the station wasn't exactly bustling with activity.

"Looks like it," Michaels replied with a smirk. "Small-town life, huh?"

Scott glanced around, spotting a diner a short walk down the street. A hand-painted sign reading "Mary's Diner" swung gently in the breeze above the door. Through the wide front windows, they could see a handful of patrons sipping coffee and chatting.

"Guess we'll find him there," Scott said, already walking toward the diner. Michaels followed, adjusting his jacket against the chill in the air.

\*\*\*

The bell above the door jingled as the agents stepped inside, and the hum of conversation abruptly stopped. Heads turned toward them—mostly older men in worn flannel shirts and caps, sitting at the counter or in booths. Their eyes lingered on the agents' crisp suits and polished shoes, marking them as outsiders immediately.

Behind the counter, a waitress —a young woman with blonde hair and a kind, yet weathered, face— paused mid-pour, her coffee pot in hand. Through the order window, a short-order cook glanced up briefly before returning to his grill.

In one of the corner booths, a man in his late forties or early fifties nursed a steaming cup of coffee, his uniform consisting of jeans, a flannel shirt, and a faded bomber jacket. He looked up at the agents, his expression amused, as though he'd been expecting them.

"That's gotta be him," Scott muttered under her breath as they walked over to the booth. Michaels nodded, letting her take the lead.

"Chief Edwards?" Scott asked as they reached the table.

Edwards set his coffee down and smiled warmly. "That's me. But I'm just 'Officer' Edwards. No need for a 'Chief' here. From the looks of ya, you two must be DIS," he said.

Both Michaels and Scott pulled out their FBI credentials, holding them up.

Edwards paused, studying the badges for a moment before a grin tugged at his lips.

Michaels quipped, "Mulder and Scully, right? Yeah, we get that a lot..."

Scott rolled her eyes. "No, we don't."

But Edwards furrowed his brow, the grin faltering. "Mulder and Scully? I'm not following. Is that some kind of code?"

Michaels blinked. "You know... The X-Files. Aliens? Conspiracies?" When Edwards didn't react, Michaels leaned back in mild disbelief. "FBI agents running around solving weird cases?"

Edwards gave him a blank look. "Sorry, never heard of it."

Michaels narrowed his eyes slightly. "You're joking, right?"

Edwards shrugged. "Can't say I am. Havenwood doesn't get much in the way of television out here. Never has. Guess we missed that one."

The agents exchanged a quick glance, Michaels' face flickering with confusion and a hint of suspicion. "You're telling me you've never seen the X-Files? It's been a thing since the '90s."

Edwards chuckled, standing and grabbing his coffee. "'Fraid not, Agent Michaels. But it sounds like I'd enjoy it—maybe if I ever get the chance to watch this TV of yours."

He gestured to the open seats across from him. "Go ahead, sit. I'll guess you're here to follow up on recent events."

Scott and Michaels shared another quick look before sitting down. "That's right," Michaels said, shifting back into professionalism. "We're Agents Michaels and Scott. We wanted to introduce ourselves and touch base before we started asking questions."

Edwards nodded appreciatively. "Glad to see someone remembers how to play nice. Most federal agents barge in as if they own the place."

Scott's mouth opened slightly, but no words came. She glanced at Michaels, who gave her a shrug, clearly as baffled as she was.

"Come on," Edwards continued, motioning toward the door. "Let's head to the station. I'll show you around."

As they followed him, Edwards gestured toward the station visible down the street. "I left my badge and gun back at the office. Can't exactly look the part of Chief of Police without 'em, can I?"

He turned, grabbed his coffee, and headed for the door. "Would you like a cup of coffee while we're at it?"

Scott shook her head politely. "I'm good, thanks."

Michaels shrugged. "I'll take one if you're offering."

The waitress stepped in with a smile, handing Edwards a to-go cup and pouring another for Michaels. Edwards tipped an imaginary hat to her and thanked her before leading the agents toward the door.

Following Edwards, Scott elbowed Michaels lightly in the arm and murmured, "Mulder and Scully? Really?"

*** 

The three walked down the quiet street, the faint smell of rain lingering in the air. Edwards strolled with the ease of someone who knew every inch of the town, his mug in hand. "Beautiful place, isn't it?" he said, glancing at the agents. "City folks come through now and then, usually just passing through. They always say the same thing: 'Man, you could get lost in a place like this.'"

Scott glanced around at the quaint storefronts and the towering forest in the distance. "Can't argue with that," she said, though her tone was guarded.

Edwards chuckled. "Havenwood grows on you. Not much crime, not much trouble. But every now and then, something big rolls through. Guess you're here because of that."

Michaels studied him as they walked. "We're here because things don't add up. And because someone wanted us to pay attention to this town."

Edwards nodded knowingly but said nothing more until they reached the station. He unlocked the door, flipped the sign to "Open," and held it open for the agents.

***

The interior of the station was as quaint as its exterior—a single desk with a manual typewriter sitting prominently in one corner, alongside a landline phone that looked as if it hadn't been replaced in decades. A rotary phone hung on the wall nearby, paired with a scanner that gathered more dust than it was used. A coffee pot gurgled faintly in one corner, its glass carafe filled with dark, steaming liquid, while an old-school radio softly played a country song in the background.

Next to the desk stood a filing cabinet, its drawers slightly dented but functional, with a bulletin board above it pinned with faded wanted posters, handwritten notes, and the occasional outdated flyer advertising events like "Havenwood's Summer Festival."

Edwards walked over to the wall, clipped on his belt, and secured his gun. "There," he said, smiling. "Now I'm official."

The agents glanced around, taking in the simplicity of the place. Scott raised an eyebrow. "This is it? No cells, no backup?"

Edwards shrugged, taking a leisurely sip of his coffee. "Don't need much. Havenwood's quiet. Most of the time, anyway."

Michaels smirked. "Most of the time?"

Edwards's smile faded slightly, his voice lowering a notch. "Well, let's just say the past year has been a little more exciting than usual. I've got my theories about why, but I'm guessing that's what you're here to figure out."

Scott folded her arms, her gaze sharp. "It is. And we'll need your cooperation."

Edwards nodded, his expression serious now. "You've got it. Just remember—you're guests here. We take care of our own, but we don't like outsiders stirring things up without cause."

Scott and Michaels exchanged a look, their silent communication suggesting caution. Havenwood was already living up to its reputation for being insular. They would have to tread carefully.

***

The agents followed Edwards down Havenwood's quaint main street, their polished shoes tapping softly against the aged brick sidewalk. Edwards strolled ahead, coffee cup in hand, his easy demeanor a stark contrast to the agents' alert, calculating presence. The gentle rustling of wind through the trees and the occasional chirp of a bird punctuated the quiet, idyllic setting.

"You know," Edwards began, his tone light and conversational, "before all this mess, we didn't have any trouble in this town. No graffiti, no jaywalking, no kids tee-peeing houses, nothing. Havenwood's the kind of place people dream about when they say they want to live somewhere peaceful."

Agent Scott's sharp eyes scanned the surroundings, noting the carefully maintained storefronts and the faint buzz of activity from the town's residents. They passed the Havenwood Fine Woodworks shop, its sign proudly proclaiming, "Custom Creations—Locally Made." Behind its large windows sat finely crafted furniture, its elegant designs hinting at a deep tradition of craftsmanship.

"That's the big industry around here?" Michaels asked, gesturing toward the woodworking shop.

Edwards nodded. "Yep. Keeps the town afloat. Been here for generations. Folks come from all over to order pieces—tables, cabinets, chairs. Havenwood's craftsmanship is well-known. Keeps everyone employed, keeps the town quiet."

Scott tilted her head slightly. "Impressive. But a town this small can't survive on just furniture."

Edwards shrugged. "Maybe not in the big city, but we're different out here. People don't need much. We're self-sufficient. Got everything we need. Outsiders? They don't tend to stick around for long."

Scott and Michaels exchanged a glance. Michaels pressed him. "You mean the incident involving Bryan Jensen?"

Edwards paused mid-step, taking a slow sip of his coffee before replying. "Let's just say things got complicated when them outsiders moved in next door. That whole mess turned this quiet little town upside down. And Jensen? Well, he's been a part of the town for years, but he's always kept to himself. Never any trouble, though."

"And now?" Michaels asked, his tone pointed.

Edwards turned to face them; his expression thoughtful. Behind him, the stately brick building of the Havenwood Town Hall stood proudly, its weathered sign a testament to its age. "Now, we're just trying to pick up the pieces. You're here to find answers, right? Maybe you'll find some. But let me give you a piece of advice—don't go digging too deep. This town's got its own way of doing things, and we take care of our own."

Scott studied him, her gaze sharp and unyielding. "We appreciate the advice, Chief."

Edwards tipped his head, gesturing toward the building. "Come on. The mayor's waiting."

***

The shift in Edwards' tone when mentioning Bryan was subtle, but it wasn't lost on Scott. Her sharp instincts picked up the slight hesitation, the careful wording. It was clear Edwards wasn't saying everything he knew, but he wasn't going to give them more without a reason.

For the people of Havenwood, Bryan had always been an outsider—someone they tolerated but never truly accepted. Edwards' polished demeanor masked the town's true feelings: Bryan's presence was only ever begrudgingly accepted because of Ashley. Her death had unraveled even that thin thread of acceptance, leaving Bryan as a tolerated inconvenience.

Yet, Edwards didn't hint at any of this. His words painted Havenwood as a tight-knit, idyllic community—no need to let federal agents get a whiff of the town's deeper secrets.

***

Edwards led them inside the Town Hall, its interior as unassuming as the rest of the town. The wood-paneled walls were adorned with black-and-white photographs of Havenwood through the decades—loggers posing beside felled trees, children playing outside the old schoolhouse, and a picture of the original woodworking shop's founding.

The receptionist, a middle-aged woman with a welcoming smile, waved them through. "Mr. Harper's expecting you," she said.

Edwards knocked lightly on a wooden door with a small brass plaque that read "Mayor's Office." A deep voice called out, "Come in."

The mayor's office was modest but well-kept, with a large oak desk dominating the center of the room. Behind it sat Mr. Harper, a tall man with a full head of silver hair and the kind of presence that immediately commanded attention. His piercing blue eyes swept over the agents as he stood, extending his hand.

"Agents," Harper said warmly. "Welcome to Havenwood. I'm Mayor Harper."

Scott shook his hand firmly. "Agent Scott, and this is Agent Michaels. Thanks for meeting with us."

Harper gestured to the chairs in front of his desk. "Of course. Please, sit. Can I offer you anything? Coffee, tea?"

"No, thank you," Scott said politely, taking a seat.

Michaels settled in beside her, his sharp eyes scanning the room. "We're here to follow up on the recent incidents involving Bryan Jensen and Anna Sokoloff."

Harper nodded, his expression grave. "Yes, I assumed as much. It's been a difficult time for everyone involved. Bryan's a good man, and the Sokoloffs have been through enough. I hope you're not here to make things harder for them."

Scott's gaze was steady. "We're here to get answers, Mr. Harper. Nothing more, nothing less."

Harper leaned back in his chair, folding his hands across his chest. "I respect that. But Havenwood's a tight-knit community. We value our privacy. I'd hate for this investigation to disrupt our way of life any more than it already has."

Michaels leaned forward slightly. "Mayor Harper, with all due respect, people have died. Organized crime is involved. This isn't just about Havenwood anymore."

Harper's jaw tightened, but he nodded. "I understand. And I'll do what I can to help. Just keep in mind—this town looks out for its own. I hope you'll do the same."

***

Inside the small, antiquated police station, Michaels sat at the lone desk, flipping through a sparse collection of handwritten incident reports and yellowed files. The cramped room smelled faintly of stale coffee and old wood, its walls adorned with faded community notices and decades-old mugshots.

"This place barely qualifies as a station," Michaels muttered, holding up a handwritten note in loopy cursive. "Look at this— 'Missing cat: Found by Mrs. Harper.' Is this the most action this place has ever seen?"

Scott paced nearby, scanning the bulletin board dotted with outdated reminders and a few missing pet posters. "You said earlier things got 'complicated' when the Sokoloffs moved in," she said, turning toward Edwards, who was filling his coffee pot at a corner station. "Care to elaborate?"

Edwards took his time, setting the pot down before turning to face her. "You've got to understand something, Agents. This town doesn't do 'complicated.' That mess with Sokoloff? It was a storm in a place not built for storms. Break-ins, gunfire, people getting hurt... and worse. Havenwood isn't made for that kind of trouble."

Michaels leaned back in his creaky chair, his arms crossed. "And Jensen? He just happened to be at the center of it all?"

Edwards met his gaze, unfazed. "Bryan Jensen was defending his home. If someone came after your family, what would you do?"

Scott tilted her head, her voice measured. "Well, who killed the others? Werewolves?"

The room fell silent. The faint gurgle of the coffee pot was the only sound as Edwards shifted, clearly uncomfortable. "I don't know what you're talking about."

Michaels raised an eyebrow, his tone laced with disbelief. "Really? Because the reports we've seen mention multiple attackers torn apart by what looked like animals. However, according to the wildlife registry, there is nothing in this area that could have done that."

Edwards shrugged, his voice calm but evasive. "Coyotes, maybe. Sometimes, wolves wander down this way. You'd have to ask Fish and Game."

Scott stepped closer, lowering her voice. "What about Alexi Sokoloff? You must have heard what they found—or didn't find—when they went back for his body."

Edwards's expression hardened, his jaw tightening. "You're asking the wrong person."

## CHAPTER 9 - THE DIVIDE

Edwards drove the agents down the narrow, winding road leading to the outskirts of Havenwood. Dense trees flanked the route, their overhanging branches creating a natural canopy that muted the late afternoon sunlight. The occasional rustle of leaves and the distant call of a bird punctuated the stillness.

The road ended at a small cul-de-sac, where three houses stood in a line, each separated by a buffer of untamed forest. Two of the homes were unoccupied, the one nearest the road still bore the scars of the Sokoloff incident, with boarded-up windows and caution tape fluttering in the breeze. At the far end of the cul-de-sac sat Bryan's house, an imposing Victorian that seemed to brood under the weight of its peeling paint and sagging porch.

The car came to a stop, and Edwards gestured toward the house. "There's your man," he said, stepping out of the car. The agents followed, straightening their coats against the brisk wind.

Bryan stood on the porch, one hand in his jacket pocket, the other clutching the cane that supported him, his posture tense as he watched the trio approach. Anna lingered just inside the doorway; her expression wary. Riley peeked out from behind her, curiosity evident on his face.

Edwards gave a casual wave. "Bryan, these folks need a word."

Bryan's jaw tightened, and he stepped forward, his boots creaking on the weathered boards. Bryan extended his hand and shook each of their hands in response.

"Agents, I'd like to say it's nice to see you again, but to be honest, it isn't," he said, his tone clipped.

Michaels wasted no time, pulling out his notepad. "Mr. Jensen, we need access to the trail leading to the other house on your property. The one where the Sokoloff incident occurred."

Anna stepped out onto the porch, putting herself between the agents and Bryan, her arms crossed protectively. "Why do you need to go out there?" she asked, her tone sharp.

Scott met her gaze evenly. "It's standard procedure, ma'am. We need to examine the scene ourselves and piece together what happened."

Anna's frown deepened. "We've told you everything there is to know. There's nothing else to find out there."

Riley leaned against the doorframe, muttering just loud enough to be heard. "Except for the creepy stuff."

Bryan shot him a warning look. "Riley, not now."

Michaels pressed forward. "Mr. Jensen, this is your property, and we're asking for your permission. We're not here to disrupt your lives, but we have a job to do."

Bryan hesitated, his gaze shifting to Anna. She shook her head slightly, her unease evident, but Bryan sighed, running a hand through his hair. "Fine," he said reluctantly. "I'll take you."

Anna's voice tightened. "Bryan, you don't have to do this."

Bryan turned to her, his voice calm but firm. "It's better if I do."

Riley perked up. "Can I come?"

"No," Bryan said immediately, his tone leaving no room for debate. "You stay here with your mom."

Bryan nodded curtly, then descended the porch steps and followed the group toward the car.

*** 

The dirt trail leading to the house cut through the forest like a scar, its edges overgrown with moss and tangled roots. The air was heavy with the earthy scent of damp leaves and decaying wood, and the faint rustle of unseen wildlife added to the eerie atmosphere. The agents followed Bryan in silence, with Edwards bringing up the rear, his hand resting casually on his holstered sidearm.

"This property is massive," Scott remarked, her sharp eyes scanning the trees. "You own all this?"

Bryan didn't look back. "Inherited it. Along with everything else."

Michaels glanced at Edwards. "Quiet town. Big secrets."

Edwards didn't respond, his expression neutral as he walked.

The group came to a stop at the edge of a clearing, where the remnants of Ashley's house loomed like a specter. The structure had succumbed to years of neglect, its roof sagging and its windows broken. Nature had begun reclaiming it, with vines creeping up the walls and moss overtaking the steps.

"This is it," Bryan said flatly, gesturing toward the house. "Whatever you're looking for, you won't find it here."

Scott stepped forward, her boots crunching on the overgrown path. "We'll be the judge of that."

Michaels followed, his eyes sweeping the area. "Let's see what this place is hiding."

Bryan stood back with Edwards, his posture rigid. "Do what you need to do," he said, his tone hard. "But do it before dark."

Scott turned to him; her brow furrowed. "Why's that?"

Bryan's expression was unreadable, but his voice carried a weight that made even Edwards glances at him. "Because this is private property, and unless you have a search warrant, I want you off it before nightfall."

The agents exchanged a glance but didn't press further. As they moved toward the house, Bryan lingered at the edge of the clearing, his gaze fixed on the treeline as though he were expecting something, or someone, to emerge.

As the agents moved toward the dilapidated remains of Ashley's house, Michaels paused, glancing back at Bryan.

"You've lived here longer than we have, Mr. Jensen. Maybe you should come inside with us, give us your perspective."

Edwards stiffened, his hand brushing instinctively against his holstered sidearm. "Now, hold on just a second. That's not a good idea. Bryan's been through enough with this place—"

"—It's fine, Ed," Bryan interrupted, his voice calm but firm. His eyes locked on Edwards, a subtle message passing between them. "I'll guide them back when we're done."

Edwards hesitated, his easygoing façade slipping for just a moment as his gaze flicked between Bryan and the agents. "You sure about that?" he asked, his tone laced with unspoken meaning.

Bryan nodded, his face unreadable. "What do I have to worry about? You're from the government... you're here to help." Bryan eyed the two agents. "Yeah. I'll handle it."

Scott tilted her head, watching the silent exchange with keen interest. "We appreciate it, Mr. Jensen," she said, her tone polite but pointed. "It's always helpful to have someone familiar with the area."

Edwards's jaw tightened, but he forced a smile, tipping his hat slightly. "Well, if you insist. Just remember, it gets dark quickly out here. Best not to linger."

"We won't," Bryan said, his voice low.

Edwards gave Bryan one last hard look before turning and walking back down the trail, his footsteps fading into the quiet of the forest.

\*\*\*

As they stepped into the shadowy interior of the house, the agents could feel the oppressive weight of the place, both

170

literal and metaphorical. Dust motes swirled in the beams of sunlight filtering through broken windows, and the air was thick with the scent of mildew and decay.

Bryan followed them in, his expression carefully neutral. "What exactly are you hoping to find in here?" he asked, his tone almost casual.

Michaels glanced around, his flashlight cutting through the dim light. "Clues, Mr. Jensen. Maybe answers."

Bryan crossed his arms, leaning lightly against the doorframe as though to distance himself from the room. "Answers to what?"

Scott shot him a sidelong glance. "Why don't you tell us?"

Bryan didn't flinch, his gaze steady. "If I had anything else to give, don't you think I'd have given it to you already?"

The floorboards creaked ominously beneath their feet as Bryan led the agents into the house, their flashlights cutting through the gloom. The air was thick with dampness and decay, the scent of rot blending with the faint metallic tang of old blood. Shadows stretched and twisted in the corners, cast by the fading daylight filtering through broken windows.

"Watch your step," Bryan said, his voice steady but low. He gestured to a gaping hole in the center of the living room floor. "One of 'em fell through there. Didn't make it."

Scott peered over the edge, her flashlight revealing jagged planks and debris below. "Christ," she muttered. "How did this place not collapse under all that fighting?"

"Wasn't any fighting, just some falling," Bryan said tersely. "Luck? Or, a lack of it, depending on your point of view."

Michaels examined the structural damage, noting the splintered wood and smeared handprints along the edge of the hole, evidence of a desperate, failed attempt to hold on. He whistled low. "This wasn't a fight. It was a war."

Bryan didn't respond, moving toward the staircase. "Bannister's unstable," he warned. "Stick close to the wall, and don't lean too hard on anything."

The agents followed him up, the staircase groaning with each step. Bryan's grip on the railing was firm, his limp pronounced as he climbed. The second floor was worse— holes in the ceiling let in shafts of dim light, illuminating shattered picture frames and scattered debris.

"This place is a death trap," Scott muttered, more to herself than anyone else.

"It was," Bryan said, leading them down the hallway. His tone was flat, detached, as though recounting someone else's story.

The door at the end of the hall was ajar, its frame splintered from what was clearly a violent entry. Bryan pushed it open with his cane, stepping aside to let the agents enter.

The upstairs room was a study in chaos. Bloodstains marred the floorboards, dark and smeared, forming a macabre map of the final confrontation. A broken chair lay in the corner, its shattered pieces stained red. The outline of where a body had fallen was faint but unmistakable, surrounded by the faded remains of hastily discarded medical supplies—gauze, empty syringes, and a bloodied pair of scissors left behind in the chaos of the SWAT evacuation.

"This is where it ended," Bryan said, leaning against the doorway. His face was impassive, but his eyes were sharp, watching the agents take it all in.

Scott crouched near the largest bloodstain, running her gloved fingers along the edge. "This is where Sokoloff died?"

Bryan nodded. "Dropped him right there."

"And you?" Michaels asked, gesturing to another bloodstain trailing toward the doorway.

"Collapsed after," Bryan said. "Lost a lot of blood. SWAT got me out before it got worse."

Scott rose, her flashlight playing over the jagged walls and shattered furniture. "This wasn't self-defense. This was survival."

Bryan's jaw tightened, but he said nothing.

Michaels crossed his arms, his eyes narrowing. "You took on Alexi Sokoloff and his men. Killed him. And yet, you lived to tell the tale. Why is that, Mr. Jensen?"

Bryan met Michaels' gaze evenly. "Because I had no choice."

Scott's eyes flicked to Bryan; her expression thoughtful. "And the rest of his men? The ones who didn't fall through the floor. What happened to them?"

Bryan's mouth twitched, his gaze drifting toward the broken window at the far end of the room. The wind whispered through the cracks, carrying with it the faint scent of pine and damp earth.

Finally, he spoke, his tone measured. "Have either of you ever lived in a wooded area?"

The agents exchanged a glance, taken aback by the unexpected question. Neither answered.

Bryan smirked faintly. "Didn't think so. Let me ask you something else. Ever seen an animal's remains in the woods?"

Scott's brow furrowed. "What does that have to do with—"

"—You haven't," Bryan interrupted, his voice cutting cleanly through the room. "And you know why? Because nature cleans up after herself. An animal... or a human... dies out here, and it becomes part of the circle of life. Nature doesn't waste. That's a human ideal."

His words hung heavy in the air; the oppressive silence of the house swallowed the faint echo of his voice. He turned his sharp gaze back to the agents, his tone quiet but laced with finality. "So, if you're wondering what happened to the assholes you can't find... ask Mother Nature. If she's in a good mood, she'll let you know. Piss her off..."

Michaels straightened slightly, his eyes narrowing, while Scott's jaw tightened, her expression unreadable. The implications of Bryan's words weren't lost on either of them, but neither was willing to press him further—not yet.

Bryan adjusted his cane, his voice taking on a new edge, quiet but steeped in foreboding. "Well, you heard Officer Edwards' warning. We need to get out of here before darkness falls. Unless you really want to know what happened to those 'poor, unfortunate souls.'"

The agents exchanged a glance, their unease palpable. Michaels gave a half-smile that didn't reach his eyes. "We'll take your word for it."

Bryan turned, heading for the stairs without another word, leaving the agents to process his chilling remark in the oppressive silence of the room. The fading daylight seemed to dim further as if the house itself was urging them to leave.

Scott leaned against the doorway of the upstairs room, her arms crossed. "Mr. Jensen, if you would, could you walk us through what happened that night? In your own words."

Bryan remained standing near the damaged banister, his hand resting on his cane. His gaze drifted to the window, where the late afternoon light filtered through the fractured glass.

"Anna and I fought," he began, his voice low and steady. "Over the magazine cover. Things were said, and we went our separate ways. I went back inside my house."

Michaels took out his notepad. "What kind of things?"

Bryan's jaw tightened, but he didn't look at the agent. "Things that didn't matter in the end. A few minutes later, maybe half an hour, she knocked on my door. We talked. Cleared the air. She told me they were going to be relocated. Asked me to have dinner with her and Riley. Sort of a... going-away-slash-thank-you-slash-apology-thing."

Scott raised an eyebrow. "And you agreed?"

Bryan nodded, his eyes narrowing slightly. "Yeah. I did… Right before we sat down, I stepped outside to toss a loaf of burnt bread. She burns things… a lot." A faint, wry smile flickered across his face, then faded. "That's when I heard the gunshot."

His gaze darkened, and he looked back at the agents. "I turned around and saw Taylor waving a gun at Anna and Riley. I got the jump on her from behind. Got her… got her weapon. When we questioned her, she confessed to working with Alexi and stated that they were on their way."

Michaels leaned forward slightly. "What did you do next?"

"I sent Anna and Riley out here." Bryan gestured vaguely toward the forest beyond the window. "To this house. Told them to wait until it was safe."

"And you?" Scott asked.

Bryan's grip on his cane tightened. "I went back to my house. And I waited."

Michaels's pen paused mid-note. "Waited for what?"

Bryan lifted his hand, holding up three fingers, "For them to come."

No reply.

"I got one of them before they got me," Bryan said, his voice growing quieter. "And… well, you know the rest."

Scott's gaze sharpened. "No, we don't. How did you get from your basement to here, Mr. Jensen? In your condition?"

Michaels glanced at Scott before adding, "We've reviewed the medical reports. With those injuries, it doesn't add up."

Bryan's lips pressed into a thin line; his eyes distant. "Funny what love motivates you to do, isn't it?" His tone carried an edge that made even Scott pause.

"Love?" Scott repeated. "You told us you were just friends."

Bryan's gaze dropped to the bloodstained floorboards. For a long moment, he said nothing. Then, softly, almost as if speaking to himself, he replied, "I guess I didn't realize it until just now."

Michaels scribbled a note. "And then?"

Bryan gestured vaguely to the bloodstains on the floor. "I was here. Alexi was dead. I was bleeding out."

Michaels stepped closer; his expression skeptical. "That's a lot of blanks for someone who came out on top against a man like Sokoloff. Are you saying you don't remember the details of how you killed him?"

Bryan's jaw tightened, and he leaned heavily on his cane. "I vividly remember every second of getting sixteen of my bones broken, two of my fucking fingers cut off, and pulling the trigger. I remember his body hitting the floor. The rest... not so much."

Scott's voice took on a more probing tone. "And the others? The men outside your house? Torn apart by what looked like animals—what about them?"

177

Bryan's gaze snapped to hers, sharp and unyielding. "I wasn't in any position to see what happened outside. I was too busy trying to stay alive."

Scott didn't flinch, her eyes narrowing. "Convenient."

Bryan's knuckles whitened as he gripped his cane, his voice dropping low. "You think it's convenient? Have you ever been gutted, Agent Scott? Ever have your bones shattered while someone laughs at you? If so, you'd know that survival isn't convenient. It's cruel. It's messy. And it doesn't leave room for taking notes."

The air hung heavy; Scott's expression unreadable as Michaels stepped closer to her side.

"Trauma does strange things to memory, Mr. Jensen," Michaels said, snapping his notepad shut with a sharp click. "But the truth has a funny way of surfacing."

Bryan's lips quirked with a humorless smile, his gaze steady. "Then I guess we'll both be surprised when it does."

Michaels turned toward the door, gesturing for Scott to follow. "We've seen enough for now. Let's head back."

Scott lingered, her eyes scanning the room one last time before landing on Bryan. "This story isn't over," she said softly, her tone carrying both a warning and a promise.

Bryan didn't reply, his attention drifting back to the bloodstained floor.

As the agents stepped into the hallway, Michaels leaned slightly toward Scott, his voice a murmur. "He's hiding something."

Scott glanced back at the doorway, her jaw tightening. "No kidding."

Bryan remained where he stood, listening as their footsteps faded. The house creaked around him, its oppressive silence returning. He exhaled slowly, the weight of the moment pressing down on him.

Finally, he muttered to himself, his voice barely audible in the empty room. "If only you knew."

*** 

The storm battered them as they emerged from the woods, rain lashing in sheets and wind howling through the trees. Willow branches clawed at the trio, and the air was alive with debris—leaves, twigs, and loose gravel spinning in chaotic spirals.

"Where's the house?" Michaels shouted over the roar; his shoulders hunched against the wind as he squinted through the rain.

"Straight ahead," Bryan said, his voice calm, almost too calm. He moved with purpose, his steps sure and steady, while the agents stumbled behind him, struggling to keep up. The faint glow of porch lights appeared ahead, cutting through the storm's fury.

Anna stood waiting on the porch, her hair whipping around her face. She clutched the railing for balance, her other hand brushing damp strands from her eyes. "Everything alright?" she called, her voice barely carrying over the wind.

Bryan stepped onto the porch, nodding. "Fine."

The agents exchanged a look, both visibly shivering as they struggled to shield themselves from the elements. Michaels folded his arms tightly across his chest, his fingers clutching at the fabric of his sleeves. "Fine doesn't exactly cover it," he said, his tone sharp despite the chattering of his teeth.

Scott shook the rain from her coat, brushing water from her face as she adjusted her stance to avoid the spray of wind-blown rain off the porch roof. Her gaze flicked back to the trees, then to Bryan. "That was... something else," she muttered again, though this time her words carried more weight.

***

The rain hammered the roof, and the wind rattled the beams as Scott and Michaels stepped onto the porch, drenched and shivering. Michaels's boots scraped against the slick wood as he glanced uneasily toward the driveway, where their car was nearly submerged in a growing puddle.

"You'll be driving nowhere in this weather," Anna interjected, pointing across the cul-de-sac. "There's a spare house there—dry and warm. You can stay until morning."

Scott hesitated, glancing at Michaels. She pulled her collar tighter against the wind, her brow furrowed in doubt. "Appreciate the offer, ma'am, but—"

"—No 'but,'" Anna said, cutting him off firmly. She shifted closer to the railing for stability, her hair whipping around her face again. "The roads are a mess, and driving at night isn't safe. It's not a big deal."

Bryan, standing to the side as if unfazed by the storm raging around him, added in a measured tone, "She's right. Better to wait until morning."

The wind howled louder, rattling the porch's wooden beams and sending a spray of rain through the gaps in the roofline. The agents exchanged a glance. Michaels shifted his weight, his boots scraping against the slick wood. He exhaled sharply, defeated. "Alright. Thanks. We'll take you up on that."

Scott gave a reluctant nod, brushing a drenched strand of hair from her face. "Yeah. A fresh start in the morning sounds good."

Anna's tone softened as she opened the door to the warm glow inside. "Good. Come on in. Dinner's almost ready. You should eat before you head over."

Another gust whipped around them, sending a cascade of water down the porch steps. The storm wasn't relenting, and as the agents followed Anna inside, the safety and warmth of the house felt like a reprieve they hadn't realized they needed.

***

By the time Edwards parked his patrol car outside the Town Hall, the rain was coming down in sheets. The wipers had done little more than smear the water across the windshield, and the relentless downpour drummed on the vehicle's roof like a warning. He grabbed his hat and stepped out, pulling it low to shield himself against the wind. The storm tugged at his coat, snapping it against his legs as he climbed the stone steps, slick with rain pooling in the uneven cracks.

181

The warm interior of the Town Hall offered an instant reprieve, but the building couldn't entirely escape the storm. The windows rattled in their frames, a low, rhythmic creaking that accompanied the occasional thud of wind-driven rain. The sound reverberated through the otherwise quiet space, a constant reminder of the tempest outside. Inside, Mayor Harper sat at his desk, leaning over a stack of papers, his frown deepening with every passing second. Across from him, Ed Jones lounged in a chair, his posture deceptively relaxed, yet his presence was commanding. His polished shoes tapped faintly against the wooden floor, a metronome to the storm's chaotic rhythm.

"Officer Edwards," Harper said, looking up from his papers. His voice carried over the drumming rain, steady but tight. "You've got some explaining to do."

Edwards shook the water from his hat and then hung it on the stand. His boots left damp prints on the worn floorboards as he stepped forward. "Mayor. Mr. Jones."

Jones's smile was faint, almost patronizing. "Officer Edwards," he said smoothly. "I trust you've had an eventful day."

Edwards kept his expression neutral. "Two FBI agents showed up this morning. Scott and Michaels. They said they were following up on loose ends from their investigation."

Harper straightened slightly in his chair, his tone clipped. "And?"

"They wanted to ask questions about Bryan Jensen and the other two outsiders," Edwards replied, pausing for a moment as if weighing his next words. "Mr. Jensen ended up guiding them into the woods—to the house behind his property."

At the mention of the house, Harper leaned back, his brow furrowing deeply, while Jones's fingers tightened briefly on the armrest of his chair. The room seemed to grow colder, as if the storm outside had crept in through the cracks.

Jones's voice, smooth but edged, broke the silence. "The house? That was... bold."

Edwards met Jones's gaze evenly, his tone measured. "He figured it was better to show them something than let them wander around on their own."

Harper raised an eyebrow, his voice steady but tinged with concern. "And? How'd it go?"

"I'm told they came back in one piece," Edwards said carefully, his gaze flicking toward the window as if checking for confirmation from some unseen source. "Bryan even offered them the use of one of the spare houses for the night because of the rain."

Jones leaned forward slightly, his voice dropping as if to lend weight to his words. "You're telling me Bryan Jensen— an outsider—took federal agents into the woods, into the house, and now they're staying in Havenwood?" He shook his head slowly, a faint smirk tugging at the corner of his mouth. "That's reckless."

The wind howled outside, rattling the windows harder as Harper cut in, his tone firm. "Bryan has done nothing but keep those agents from digging deeper. If you've got another solution, Ed, I'm all ears."

Jones rose, his movements deliberate, adjusting his cuffs with a precision that felt calculated. "Let's hope your faith isn't misplaced, Mayor. The woods aren't exactly forgiving."

The storm seemed to punctuate his words, a powerful gust slamming rain against the windows with enough force to make the glass shudder. Jones turned toward the door, pausing briefly to glance back at Harper. His polished shoes echoed faintly on the floor as he said, "If anything happens—"

"It won't be because of Bryan," Harper called after him, his voice unwavering.

Jones didn't respond. A flash of lightning briefly illuminated his silhouette as he stepped into the hallway. The heavy door thudded shut behind him, and the sound of his retreating footsteps faded into the howling wind.

The room fell silent, save for the steady rhythm of rain against the windows and the faint creaking of the old building as it weathered the storm. Harper sighed, rubbing his temples. "Keep an eye on those agents, Edwards. Make sure Bryan doesn't get dragged into anything worse than he already is."

Edwards nodded; the weight of the conversation settled heavily on his shoulders. "Will do, Mayor."

As he stepped out into the storm, the rain struck him with renewed force, soaking through his coat in seconds. The wind roared louder, carrying with it a feeling Edwards couldn't shake—a sense that the storm wasn't the only thing bearing down on Havenwood tonight.

*** 

184

By the time Edwards returned to his patrol car, the windows of Bryan's house glowed warmly in the rain. Inside, the clink of plates and muffled voices painted a picture of calm, though Edwards knew better. Whatever storm was brewing in Havenwood, this house was at its center.

***

The dining room was warm and inviting, a stark contrast to the storm raging outside. Scott and Michaels sat at the table; their damp jackets draped over nearby chairs. Steam rose faintly from the fabric as it dried, mingling with the comforting aroma of Anna's stew. Riley darted in and out of the room, setting plates with a mix of eagerness and care, the rhythmic clinking of dishes filling the quiet moments between conversations.

"Careful with that, Riley," Bryan said from the doorway, his tone calm but carrying the faintest trace of affection.

"I've got it!" Riley said, his small hands trembling slightly as he balanced the last plate. He set it down with exaggerated care, then turned toward Scott, grinning like he'd just completed a daring mission.

Scott watched the boy with a faint smile, her usual guarded demeanor softening despite herself. She wasn't accustomed to these domestic moments, which felt so unremarkable yet impossibly intimate.

Michaels leaned toward her; his voice low. "Not quite a family, but not strangers either."

Scott nodded, her gaze drifting toward Anna and Bryan. Anna was at the counter, ladling stew into bowls with practiced care. Bryan leaned casually against the doorway,

185

his arms crossed loosely, though his eyes followed Riley with quiet attentiveness. There was a weight between the two adults, something heavy and unspoken that connected them, whether they acknowledged it or not.

Scott thought back to their earlier conversation with Bryan, to the moment his mask had slipped just enough for them to glimpse what lay beneath.

"You'd be surprised what you'll do for those you love."

The words lingered in her mind, reverberating now as she watched the three of them. Whatever had happened to these people—whatever had brought them together, had forged something stronger than any shared history she'd ever encountered.

"This is more than just circumstances," she muttered under her breath, barely audible. Michaels glanced at her, raising an eyebrow but saying nothing.

Riley broke the silence, grinning as he turned to Scott. "Bryan taught me how to throw a baseball. Wanna see?"

Scott chuckled, leaning back in her chair. "Maybe in the morning, kid."

Riley, clearly delighted, winked at her and blew a quick kiss her way before darting off toward the kitchen. Scott blinked, doing a double-take as her face flushed a deep pink. Michaels let out a low chuckle, shaking his head. "Smooth," he muttered under his breath.

Bryan, watching from the doorway, smirked faintly. Anna caught Riley as he dashed past, her disapproving look softened by a twitch of amusement. "Riley, what did I say about bothering our guests?" she chided lightly.

"I wasn't bothering her," Riley said, feigning innocence. "She liked it."

Michaels chuckled again, and even Scott's lips quirked upward despite herself. For a moment, the room felt lighter, the storm outside a distant echo.

As dinner wound down, the comforting clatter of spoons against bowls mingled with the sound of the storm outside. Riley, his plate wiped clean, suddenly slipped away from the table. Anna noticed his absence but let it slide—until she spotted him moments later in the living room, crouched by the front door.

"Riley, what are you doing?" Anna asked, her voice carrying an edge of suspicion.

"Nothing!" he said quickly, his back still turned.

"Riley..." she said, drawing the word out as she approached. When she came closer, she gasped. Sitting in Riley's lap, as calm as you please, was a sleek, auburn-furred cat with striking green eyes. The creature purred loudly, its tail flicking in satisfaction as Riley scratched behind its ears.

"Riley Sokoloff!" Anna said sharply. "Why is there a cat in this house?"

Riley flinched but held his ground, cradling the cat protectively. "You said—" he began, his voice rising in defense. "—You said if we ever had a house, you'd think about letting me have a cat. Well, guess what? This is a house."

Anna blinked, caught off guard. "I—what? That's not the point! You can't just drag animals in here without asking, especially without asking Bryan! This is his house."

Riley shot her a pleading look before turning his gaze to Bryan, who had walked into the living room, curious about the commotion. "Bryan?" Riley said, his voice filled with the kind of hope that only a kid could muster. "Can I keep her? She's just a cat. She won't take up much space, and she's nice—I promise!"

Bryan looked at Riley, then at the cat, who seemed to be eyeing him with an unnervingly intelligent gaze. For a moment, he hesitated, but the sheer desperation in Riley's expression was enough to sway him.

"You know, Riley, taking care of a cat is a big responsibility," Bryan said, his voice calm but with a faint twinkle in his eye. "You sure you're ready for that?"

"I am!" Riley said earnestly. "I'll feed her and everything. I swear!"

Anna sighed, looking between Riley and Bryan. "You're really going to let him keep her?" she asked, exasperated.

Bryan shrugged. "I don't see the harm. Besides," he added, a small smile creeping onto his face, "it's not every day you find a cat this friendly in a storm."

Riley grinned triumphantly, hugging the cat closer. "Thanks, Bryan! You're the best."

"Just make sure she stays out of trouble," Bryan said, ruffling Riley's hair as he turned back toward the dining room.

Anna threw her hands up. "Fine," she said, defeated. "But don't come crying to me if she scratches the furniture."

Riley ignored her, already whispering to the cat as he stroked her fur. "See? I told you it'd be fine." He paused, tilting his head thoughtfully as he studied her. "Now, what do I call you?"

The cat blinked slowly, her green eyes fixed on him with a calm, almost expectant gaze. Riley's face lit up as inspiration struck. "Geez, you're cute. That's it—you're 'Gee!'"

The cat's ears twitched slightly, and her tail swished as though in approval. Riley beamed, pressing his cheek against her fur. "Gee. It's perfect."

***

As the rain turned into a steady, unrelenting downpour, Michaels stepped outside for a cigarette. Scott lingered near the window, her gaze fixed on Bryan and Riley, who were tidying the table together. She wasn't entirely sure what to make of him—this man who seemed so ordinary on the surface yet carried the weight of a thousand secrets.

Scott folded her arms and leaned against the windowsill. "You see the way he looks at them?" she asked quietly, not looking at Michaels.

Michaels exhaled a plume of smoke, his expression thoughtful. "Yeah. As if he'd do anything to keep them safe."

Scott nodded. "And they look at him like he already has."

The two agents fell silent, their roles as investigators momentarily overshadowed by something far more human. Scott let the thought sit uneasily in her mind. This wasn't what they'd come here for. Facts were her foundation, and yet no amount of evidence could account for what she saw in this house—a family forged by survival, whether they realized it or not.

## CHAPTER 10 - GENEVIEVE

The storm outside continued its relentless symphony, the rain tapping against the windowpane in a soothing rhythm. Inside Riley's room, the air was still heavy with the lingering warmth of the day and the faint, earthy scent of the rain-soaked world outside. A single shaft of moonlight spilled through the window, cutting across the room like a silver thread, illuminating Riley's bed, and the auburn-furred cat curled up beside him.

Riley absently ran his fingers through Gee's soft fur, his hand moving in slow, rhythmic strokes. The sound of her purring, deep and resonant, filled the small space, wrapping around him like a cocoon. "You know, Gee," he murmured, his voice low and contemplative, "you're the only one I can really talk to. You never judge me. You just... listen."

He paused, his fingers stilling as a wave of unspoken thoughts threatened to rise to the surface. *Sometimes I feel like I don't belong. Not here, not anywhere. But you make it easier. As long as you're around, things don't feel so... heavy.*

Gee's green eyes blinked up at him, her gaze steady and piercing, as though she understood every word. Riley chuckled softly, shaking his head. *If you could talk, you'd probably tell me I'm being a dumb kid.*

Gee stood suddenly, her movements fluid and deliberate, and padded to the edge of the bed. Riley frowned, propping himself up on his elbows. "Gee? What's wrong?"

She stopped in the beam of moonlight, her silhouette outlined in silver. The air in the room shifted, charged with energy, Riley couldn't quite name. Then, without warning, her form began to shimmer. Riley's breath caught as he watched, his heart pounding in his chest.

It was like watching a dream unfold—surreal and mesmerizing. The ripple of light moved over her, and fur gave way to smooth, porcelain skin. Her limbs elongated, her feline grace transforming into the unmistakable elegance of a woman. Within moments, she stood before him—not a cat, but a striking, ethereal figure with fiery red hair cascading over her shoulders and emerald-green eyes that locked onto his.

Riley froze, his body stiff with shock and a flicker of something else, something unfamiliar and electric. "Gee?" he whispered, his voice barely audible.

She tilted her head, her lips curving into a small, knowing smile. "It's still me, Riley," she said, her voice soft and melodic, carrying a warmth that seemed to seep into his very bones.

Riley's wide eyes darted across her face, her hair, her form, as though trying to reconcile the impossible. "You're... not a cat," he managed, his voice cracking slightly.

Gee stepped closer, her movements slow and deliberate, her gaze never leaving him. The mattress dipped under her weight as she knelt on the bed, bringing herself level with him. Her hand rose, hovering for a moment before brushing gently against his cheek. The touch was featherlight, but it sent a shiver down Riley's spine.

"You've always seen me, Riley," she murmured, her voice low and intimate. "Even when you didn't realize it."

Riley's breath hitched as he stared into her eyes, the world around him narrowing to just the two of them. Her touch was steady, grounding him even as his mind raced to process what was happening. He felt vulnerable yet safe, his heart pounding in a way that was both exhilarating and terrifying.

Gee leaned in slightly, her face so close he could feel the warmth of her breath. Riley's pulse quickened, his senses heightened as he caught the faint scent of something floral and wild, like a spring meadow after rain. Her eyes searched his, her expression unreadable but charged with an intensity that made his chest tighten.

"You're not scared," she observed, her lips barely moving.

Riley swallowed hard, his voice a shaky whisper. "A little. But you're still Gee, right?"

"Always," she replied, her lips curving into a smile that was both reassuring and mysterious. "And I'll always be here for you."

She lingered for a moment longer, her hand resting against his cheek, her eyes holding his. Then, slowly, she began to shift again. The transformation was fluid, almost hypnotic, as her fiery hair receded into fur and her form grew smaller. Within moments, the cat was back, her green eyes still locked onto his as she padded closer and curled up beside him.

Riley let out a soft laugh, his chest still tight with the lingering weight of the moment. "You're... something else, Gee," he muttered, his voice tinged with awe.

Gee's purring resumed, louder than before, vibrating against his side as she nestled closer. Riley reached out, his hand resting gently on her fur, the tension in his body easing as the familiar warmth of her presence enveloped him.

As his eyes drifted shut, a small smile played at the corners of his lips. For the first time in a long time, he felt like he wasn't alone, not really. And that was enough.

***

Agent Scott stirred quietly, the soft creak of the floorboards under her bare feet muted by the oversized shirt she'd hastily pulled on over her sleepwear. The house was still, save for the faint snoring from Michaels' room. She glanced at the coffee maker, briefly considering starting a pot, but a movement outside the window caught her attention.

Through the rain-speckled glass, Riley was making his way toward Bryan's truck, a spring in his step despite the wet grass underfoot. Scott paused, her mind racing. Alone, unsupervised, and curious—a golden opportunity. She quickly ensured her Glock-19 was secure at the small of her back, hidden beneath the fabric of her shirt, before quietly slipping out the door.

The crisp morning air bit at her exposed legs as she crossed the cul-de-sac, her steps deliberate to avoid splashing into puddles. Riley turned just before reaching the truck, his expression morphing from surprise to suspicion as Scott intercepted him.

"Morning," she said casually, stuffing her hands into her pockets. "You're up early."

"So are you," Riley replied, his tone sharp for a boy his age.

Scott smiled, ignoring the bite in his words. "The storm finally let up. I thought I'd stretch my legs."

Riley smirked, crossing his arms. "You're not here to stretch your legs. What do you really want?"

She chuckled softly, leaning against the truck. "Okay, you got me. I wanted to ask you a couple of questions."

Riley's grin widened. "You sure? It didn't go so great for you last time, did it?"

Scott's cheeks flushed, but she held her ground. "Honestly? No. But that was then. I thought maybe we could take a walk, talk... You know, off the record."

Riley tilted his head, his sharp eyes narrowing. "Yeah, but we aren't 'just friends,' are we?"

"Are you afraid of me, Riley?" Scott countered, her tone playful.

Riley's smirk faded. "You? No. But, I am afraid of what my mom will do after she finds out I went walking with someone who doesn't trust us. You bet your butt I am."

Scott laughed lightly, raising her hands in mock surrender. "I won't tell if you don't. And I promise to be nice."

Riley studied her for a long time, his young features betraying an uncanny maturity. Finally, he shrugged. "Fine." He started walking down the road toward town, but stopped when Scott spoke again.

"I was thinking about a walk in the woods."

Riley hesitated, then turned toward the trailhead, his face unreadable. Without another word, they disappeared into the shadows of the trees.

***

The trail was damp and muddy, their footsteps muffled by the loamy ground. Drops of condensation fell intermittently from the canopy above, mingling with the soft calls of birds and the rustling of leaves. They walked in silence for a while, the natural rhythm of the forest settled between them.

"So," Riley said finally, his voice cutting through the quiet. "What do you want to ask me?"

Scott glanced at him, choosing her words carefully. "I wanted to hear your version of what happened the night of the incident."

Riley hesitated but kept walking. "I already told you."

"No," Scott pressed, her tone steady but insistent. "You spent most of that interview interviewing me for a job at a strip club."

Riley giggled, his boyish grin briefly returning. "Yeah, that was fun."

"Fun for you, maybe not so much for me."

Riley stopped suddenly, turning to face her. "It was a lesson, Agent."

"A lesson?" she asked, folding her arms.

"Yeah," Riley said matter-of-factly, "something I thought they'd have taught you at FBI school."

"And that would be?"

"Never prejudge a person. You went in there thinking I was just a scared little kid."

Scott blinked, caught off guard. Riley's smirk grew as he continued. "I stripped you bare, rolled you in baby oil, and sent you back naked for all the world to see."

Scott opened her mouth to respond, but stopped short. The look in Riley's eyes—sharp, unrelenting—told her everything she needed to know. This wasn't just a kid. This was a boy who had grown up in the unforgiving world of his father's criminal enterprise, surrounded by brutal lessons and survival instincts most adults couldn't fathom.

"Didn't your parents ever tell you not to play in the street?" Riley asked, his tone lighter now. "You'll get run over."

Scott swallowed, recovering quickly. "Where'd you pick this stuff up?"

"Does it matter?"

Scott shrugged. "No. You're right. I underestimated you."

"No," Riley corrected, his voice calm but firm. "You disrespected me. There's a difference."

Scott nodded slowly, filing the lesson away. "Noted."

They walked in silence again, the tension between them easing slightly. Finally, Riley stopped near the edge of a clearing. "So, what do you want to know?"

Scott hesitated. "How did your mother, father, and you manage to survive that night?"

Riley's expression hardened. "First of all, the man you're talking about isn't my father. He's my dad. Alexi Sokoloff was my father."

"I'm sorry," Scott said softly. "I didn't know there was a difference."

"Well, there is... two minutes and a drunken grunt can make any thug a 'father.' It takes sacrifice, commitment, and love to make a 'dad.'" Riley bent down, pulling off his shoe and sock. He turned his heel toward Scott, revealing a series of burn scars covering his soles. "My 'father' did this to me."

Scott gasped, instinctively reaching out before pulling her hand back. Riley put his sock and shoe back on, his movements deliberate. "My 'dad'... Bryan Jensen died in front of me. After saving us from my 'father.'"

He stood, brushing dirt off his hands, and started walking again, leaving Scott frozen in place. His words echoed in her mind, stark and raw.

"Don't ever sell my dad short again. Ever." Riley said without looking back.

*** 

They walked in silence for what felt like hours, the dense woods muffling the world around them. The path was overgrown in places, with roots snaking across it like forgotten veins. The occasional rustle of leaves or snap of a twig sent faint echoes through the stillness.

When they reached the trailhead near Ashley's house, Riley stopped abruptly, his stance rigid.

"You wanna go back inside, don't you? Find something you and your partner missed. Make some brownie points?" he asked, his tone unreadable.

Scott hesitated. "If I could, yes."

Riley crossed his arms, staring directly into Scott's eyes. "Quid pro quo."

"Excuse me?" Scott replied, her tone sharp, almost reflexive.

"Don't insult my intelligence, Lady," Riley snapped, his voice cutting through the stillness like a blade.

Scott's lips pressed into a thin line. She narrowed her eyes. "Name it."

"Why were you looking at me the way you were last night?" Riley asked, his voice quieter now but no less intense.

Scott stiffened, caught off guard. "I wasn't—"

"—Fine, let's go," Riley said, turning on his heel and heading back toward the trailhead.

"Wait a second—" Scott started after him, but Riley suddenly wheeled around, jabbing a finger in her direction.

"—You lie to me again," he growled, "and good luck finding your way back. Maybe they'll find you. Maybe they won't."

The threat landed like a thunderclap. Scott froze, her breath catching in her throat.

It took a moment for the full weight of his words to settle. Her mind raced. We've been walking for what seemed like hours. But then the pieces fell into place: yesterday, it had only taken half an hour to hike out here. The woods, impossibly dense and unyielding, seemed to stretch endlessly now. Riley's casual threat of abandonment wasn't just bluster—it was chillingly plausible. Her pulse quickened as she remembered Bryan's cryptic warning: Nature cleans up after herself.

Scott cleared her throat, forcing calm into her voice. "Alright. No more lies."

Riley didn't move; his gaze was fixed on hers, as if he were weighing her sincerity. Finally, he nodded. "Trust and respect are earned," he said flatly, stepping closer. "You're doing it again—lying, disrespecting, and thinking... damn it... that I'm just a kid."

Scott blinked, startled by the sudden edge in his voice.

"You've no idea what I've gone through just to survive," Riley continued, his tone sharper now, his eyes blazing with an intensity far beyond his years. "And that's dangerous."

Scott's mouth opened slightly, but no words came. Riley leaned in closer, his voice dropping to a low growl. "Underestimating me is dangerous. You think I was toying with you in Boston? Sure, to a point. But I was also being honest."

He gestured sharply at her, his expression hardening. "You. Your figure. All of you from head to toe—it's an asset. One you're wasting."

Scott stiffened, unnerved by the boy's piercing insight.

"If you want to be the best you can be," Riley continued, his tone unrelenting, "then dig deep. Learn what your assets are and how to exploit them to your advantage. Because judging someone like me? Assuming you know me?" He paused, stepping even closer, his voice like a cold blade. "It's insulting. Under the right circumstances, it'll get you killed."

For a moment, Scott could only stare, her heart pounding. There was no trace of the child she thought she'd been dealing with. Every word he said seemed to peel back another layer, exposing something darker, sharper—a survivor forged in fire.

Scott cleared her throat, forcing calm into her voice. "Alright. No more lies."

"Okay. I saw you with your mom and Bryan," Scott began, her voice carefully measured. "I saw the way you looked at them. And it made me wonder how you got to be... you."

Riley's brow twitched slightly. "Go on."

"And what would you be like... what would..." Scott hesitated, searching for the right words.

"What kind of man I'd grow up to be?" Riley finished for her, a faint smirk tugging at the corner of his lips.

Scott shifted uncomfortably, realizing how thoroughly the boy had read her thoughts. She nodded slowly.

Riley suddenly sighed, breaking the tension. His expression softened, his voice calm. "Good answer. Fine. Come on, but you'll have to hold my hand."

Scott frowned, trying to shake off the lingering chill of his words. "I don't need—"

Her protest faltered when she caught a flicker of something in Riley's eyes. Fear. It was so fleeting, so carefully hidden, that for a moment she thought she imagined it. But it was there—raw and vulnerable, a glimpse of the boy buried beneath the survivor.

And just as quickly, it was gone, replaced by the mask of cool composure he'd worn since the start of their walk. Yet that fleeting moment stayed with her, a silent revelation: Riley was afraid, not for himself, but for her. He's risking something, she realized. Maybe everything.

"You don't have to be afraid," Riley interrupted, his voice now eerily soothing. "I'm not doing this for me. I'm doing it for you. And my dad."

Scott's gaze dropped to the small, weathered charm clutched in Riley's other hand. A talisman of some kind, she guessed, though its significance escaped her. She hesitated, then took his outstretched hand.

"Hold tight," Riley said, his voice low. "So, they don't come for you."

"They?" Scott asked, her voice barely above a whisper.

"The Shadows," Riley replied softly.

Her grip tightened instinctively, icy fear coiling in her gut despite herself.

They resumed their walk, but the silence between them felt heavier now. Riley's hand was steady, his steps deliberate, and Scott couldn't shake the feeling that he was leading her, not to a house, but into something far darker than she had anticipated.

As the treeline thinned and the looming silhouette of the house came into view, Scott's mind churned. Riley's words stayed with her, echoing louder with each step: You don't have to be afraid... I'm doing this for you.

And now, layered beneath that thought, was something new: What was he afraid of?

It was unsettling, the way he said it, not like a child trying to reassure an adult, but like a man delivering a promise—and perhaps, a warning.

\*\*\*

The house loomed like a dark sentinel, its crumbling frame barely held together by time and the ravages of decay. The closer they got, the colder the air seemed to become. Scott found herself gripping Riley's hand tighter, though she didn't want to admit it. Riley stopped just shy of the threshold, his head tilting as if listening for something.

"Last chance to back out," he said without looking at her.

Scott shook her head. "I'm not backing out."

Riley sighed, then stepped inside, pulling her with him. The air inside the house was heavy, thick with the scent of mildew and something else—something metallic, almost coppery. Dust motes floated lazily in the weak beams of light streaming through broken windows. The floorboards creaked under their weight, and the faint echo of their footsteps seemed to stretch unnaturally far.

Riley stopped near the base of the staircase, his eyes scanning the shadowy corners of the room. "Stay close, do everything... and I mean everything I tell you, and above all else... don't touch anything," he whispered.

Scott nodded, her eyes darting to the jagged hole in the floor near the center of the room. The edges of the wood were splintered, and dark stains marred the planks around it. She swallowed hard, her hand instinctively brushing the Glock at her back.

"This way," Riley said, tugging her toward the stairs.

As they ascended, the wooden steps groaned in protest. Riley moved carefully, avoiding certain boards with an uncanny awareness of their fragility. Scott followed his lead, her grip tightening as they climbed. At the top, Riley paused, his gaze fixed on the door at the end of the hallway.

"It happened there," he said softly, pointing to the shattered doorway.

Scott glanced at him. "What happened?"

Riley's voice was barely audible. "Everything."

He led her down the hall, each step feeling heavier than the last. When they reached the doorway, Riley hesitated before pushing it open. The room beyond was a chaos of broken furniture and bloodstained floors. The outline of a body was still faintly visible, a macabre reminder of what had transpired there. Scott shivered; the air was colder here than anywhere else in the house.

Riley stepped inside, his eyes scanning the room with an expression that was far too old for his years. "This is where my dad died," he said, his voice steady but hollow. "And where my father lost."

Scott's chest tightened. She wanted to say something—anything—but no words seemed adequate.

Riley turned to her, his face pale. "You wanted to know about the Shadows, right?"

Scott nodded cautiously. "Yes."

Riley's gaze flicked to the corners of the room, where the shadows seemed to stretch and twist unnaturally. "They're unlike anything you've seen before. They don't just hide in the dark. They are the dark. They watch. They wait. And when you're alone, they come for you."

Scott's hand went to the Glock at her back, her fingers brushing the grip. "Have you seen them? The Shadows?"

Riley nodded slowly. "I've seen them. Felt them. They tried to take me once... but my dad wouldn't let them."

Scott frowned. "How did he stop them?"

Riley hesitated, his hand clutching the talisman tighter. "You wouldn't believe me if I told you."

"Try me."

Riley looked at her, his young face shadowed by memories far too heavy for him to bear. "He became one of them... just long enough to save me."

The words hung in the air, heavy and suffocating. Scott stared at him, trying to make sense of what he was saying. "What do you mean, 'became one of them'?"

Riley's grip on her hand tightened. "It's better if you don't know. They can hear when you talk about them. And they don't like it."

Scott's heart skipped a beat. She glanced around the room, her eyes searching the corners where the darkness seemed to ripple unnaturally. "Riley... we should leave."

He nodded, his voice trembling. "Yeah. We shouldn't have come in."

***

They turned back toward the hallway, but as they descended the stairs, the air grew colder. The faint sounds of the forest outside seemed to fade, giving way to an oppressive silence. Riley's grip on Scott's hand became almost painful.

"Riley?" Scott whispered. "What's wrong?"

"Shhhh," Riley hissed, his eyes darting around the room. "They're here."

Scott froze, her other hand reaching for her Glock. The room darkened inexplicably, as though the sunlight filtering through the broken windows had been snuffed out. Then she saw them—pairs of faintly glowing eyes emerging from the corners, their shapes indistinct but unmistakably menacing.

Her breath caught. "What the hell—"

"—They're not going to stop," Riley whispered urgently. "Come on!"

He yanked her toward the door, but the Shadows moved faster, their forms coalescing into a writhing mass that surged toward them. Scott pulled her Glock, firing a shot into the dark shapes. The sound echoed unnaturally in the space, but the bullet passed harmlessly through as though the Shadows weren't even there.

"Damn it!" Scott growled, her heart racing.

"Hold on!" Riley shouted, pulling the talisman out. He held it aloft, and it began to glow with an intense, otherworldly light. The Shadows recoiled, their shapes splintering and dissipating like smoke in the wind.

Scott shielded her eyes against the brightness, her ears ringing from the shot. When she looked back, the Shadows were gone, leaving only the oppressive silence behind.

Riley stood in the center of the room, clutching the talisman tightly. His face was pale, his breath coming in short gasps. "We shouldn't have gone in," he said softly, not looking her in the eye.

***

The forest seemed brighter as they emerged from the house, but the tension lingered in the air. Riley walked ahead, his steps hurried, while Scott followed in stunned silence.

"What the hell were those things?" she asked finally.

"I don't know," Riley replied, his voice weary. "And I don't want to know."

Scott glanced at him, her mind racing with questions, but something in his tone stopped her from asking. Instead, she said quietly, "Thank you. For saving me."

Riley stopped, turning to face her. His young face was stern, resolute. "Bryan saved me first. And my mom. He gave everything... his life... To keep us safe. You don't get to treat him like he's the bad guy."

Scott nodded, her voice soft. "I won't."

Riley studied her for a moment, then held out his hand. "Good. Now let's get out of here."

Scott took his hand without hesitation, and together, they walked back toward the safety of the trail, the house fading into the shadows behind them.

***

The trail stretched before them, dappled with the faint light filtering through the treetops. Despite the brightness, an eerie stillness hung in the air, broken only by the crunch of their footsteps on the damp forest floor. Riley walked a step ahead, his grip on the talisman still firm, as though releasing it might undo whatever fragile balance they'd managed to restore.

Scott quickened her pace, matching his stride. "You're holding that thing like your life depends on it."

Riley glanced at her, his face unreadable. "Sometimes it does."

Scott frowned, studying the worn object in his hand. "What is it, really?"

"A Ward," Riley said.

Scott raised an eyebrow. "A Ward of what?"

Riley nodded; his expression far too serious for someone his age. "Protection. It keeps them away."

"The Shadows?"

He didn't respond immediately, his eyes scanning the trees as though expecting something to emerge. Finally, he said, "Yeah. Them... and other things."

Scott's curiosity burned, but she kept her questions measured. "Who gave it to you?"

Riley hesitated. "Someone who cares."

Scott's lips pressed into a thin line. "Not Bryan?"

Riley stopped walking and turned to face her. "No. Bryan didn't need one. He was one."

The words struck her harder than she expected. Scott opened her mouth to respond, but Riley turned away, resuming his brisk pace down the trail.

\*\*\*

The forest around them seemed to grow quieter with every step, the sounds of birds and rustling leaves fading into an oppressive stillness. Scott couldn't shake the feeling that they were being watched. She glanced over her shoulder but saw nothing out of the ordinary.

"Does it always feel like this out here?" she asked, her voice low.

"Like what?" Riley replied without looking back.

"Like something's following you."

Riley shrugged. "Sometimes 'it' is."

Scott's stomach tightened, but she pushed down the unease. "You seem awfully calm about that."

"I've had practice," Riley said matter-of-factly. "Besides, they don't like the light."

Scott glanced at the talisman in his hand, its faint glow barely visible in the daylight. "That thing must be pretty special."

"It's not just the Ward," Riley said, his tone softening. "It's what's behind it. The person who made it... they put their strength into it. Their will to protect."

Scott's brows furrowed. "And who was that?"

Riley's lips twitched into a small, fleeting smile. "Someone who knew what was out here long before you did."

***

The trail forked ahead, one path leading back toward the houses and the other veering deeper into the woods. Riley hesitated, his eyes scanning the darker path.

"This way," he said, pointing toward the denser trees.

Scott hesitated. "That doesn't look like it leads home."

"It's a shortcut," Riley assured her. "Trust me."

Scott frowned but followed. The foliage thickened as they moved off the main trail, branches clawing at her clothes and hair. Riley maneuvered through the undergrowth with practiced ease, his small frame slipping through tight spaces where Scott had to push and duck.

The air grew cooler, the shadows deeper. Scott's hand instinctively brushed the Glock at her back, her senses on high alert.

"How much farther?" she asked.

"Not far," Riley replied, his voice unusually quiet. "We'll be out soon."

Riley suddenly halted, holding up a hand. Scott froze, her heart pounding. She scanned the woods around them but saw nothing unusual.

"What is it?" she whispered.

Riley didn't answer immediately. His head tilted slightly, as if he were listening. Then, without turning, he said, "We need to go faster."

Scott frowned. "Why? What's—"

"—Just trust me," Riley interrupted, grabbing her hand and pulling her forward. His grip was tight, almost urgent.

Scott's breath quickened as she stumbled after him. The forest seemed to close in around them, the shadows deepening unnaturally. The faint glow of the Ward in Riley's hand flickered as if straining against an unseen force.

"Riley, what's going on?" she demanded, her voice sharper than she intended.

"They're coming," he whispered, his voice trembling.

Scott's blood ran cold. "Who's coming?"

Riley glanced back at her, his eyes wide and filled with something she hadn't seen before—fear. "The ones who don't stop."

***

The woods behind them seemed to come alive with movement—shadows shifting, branches cracking, the sound of something large and unnatural moving swiftly through the trees. Scott drew her Glock, her eyes darting wildly as her training kicked in.

"Keep moving!" Riley shouted, his voice breaking the growing din.

Scott's grip on his hand tightened as they sprinted through the underbrush. The world around them blurred into a mess of dark shapes and snapping branches. She could hear them now—whispers, low and guttural, growing louder with every step.

Riley suddenly veered to the left, pulling her off the faint trail and into the thickest part of the woods. "This way!"

Scott followed without question, her lungs burning as they crashed through the undergrowth. The whispers grew louder, almost deafening, as if the forest itself were speaking.

A sharp, guttural sound erupted behind them, and Scott glanced back just in time to see a writhing mass of shadows surging toward them. She fired a shot, the sound ringing out like a thunderclap, but the bullet passed harmlessly through the darkness.

"Damn it!" she hissed.

"Don't stop!" Riley yelled, dragging her forward. "The Ward's the only thing keeping them back!"

Scott's mind raced. What the hell were these things? And how had Riley been living with this nightmare?

\*\*\*

As they burst into a small clearing, Riley came to a sudden halt. He turned to face the oncoming shadows, raising the Ward high above his head. Its faint glow flared into a blinding light, bathing the clearing in a golden radiance. The shadows recoiled, their forms splintering and dissipating with anguished shrieks that sent shivers down Scott's spine.

Scott shielded her eyes, her breath coming in ragged gasps. When she lowered her hand, the shadows vanished, and the forest fell eerily silent once more.

Riley, sweat pouring down his young face, stood in the center of the clearing, clutching the Ward tightly, his small frame trembling. "We're safe... for now."

Scott holstered her Glock, her hands shaking slightly. "What the hell were those things?"

Riley didn't answer immediately. He lowered the Ward, its light fading back to a faint glow. "I told you," he said quietly. "The Shadows."

Scott stared at him, her mind struggling to reconcile what she'd just seen. "And the Ward?"

Riley met her gaze, his expression unreadable. "The only thing between us and them."

They made their way back in silence, the oppressive weight of the encounter settling over them like a shroud. When they finally reached the edge of the woods, Scott felt an almost overwhelming sense of relief as Bryan's house came into view.

Riley stopped just short of the open clearing, turning to face her. "You're going to keep this to yourself, right?"

Scott nodded slowly, still processing everything. "Yeah. I'll keep it quiet."

Without another word, Riley turned and walked toward the house, leaving Scott standing at the edge of the woods, the talisman heavy in his hand.

They reached a small clearing where the light from the Ward began to fade back to its faint glow. Riley paused, his breathing steady despite their frantic run. Scott, on the other hand, leaned against a tree, trying to catch her breath.

Riley lowered the Ward slowly as its light faded, the clearing growing dimmer. He stood in the center, his chest rising and falling with deep, measured breaths, his knuckles white around the talisman. Scott leaned against a nearby tree, her hands on her knees as she tried to catch her breath.

"That... was insane," she managed between gasps, her voice tinged with both awe and fear. Her eyes drifted to the small object in Riley's hand. "And that thing... what is it, really?"

Riley glanced at the Ward, his expression tightening. He hesitated, his fingers curling protectively around it, before finally speaking. "Bryan gave it to me when he thought... he wouldn't make it. Told me to keep it safe, for me and my mom."

Scott straightened; her curiosity piqued. "What does it do?"

Riley's lips pressed into a thin line. "It keeps us safe. It's more than just a Ward—it's... him. Like carrying a piece of him wherever I go."

Scott's gaze softened as she studied the boy, his small frame radiating a quiet strength far beyond his years. "That's a hell of a gift."

Riley's grip on the Ward tightened, his voice quiet but firm. "It's not just a gift. It's a promise."

Scott smiled faintly, trying to lighten the mood. "Think I could borrow it sometime? Just in case of emergencies?"

Riley turned to her, his green eyes sharp and unwavering. "You don't borrow something like this. You keep it safe, or you don't touch it at all."

The weight in his words left Scott momentarily speechless. She nodded slowly, sensing the depth of what he'd just said. "Fair enough."

Riley tucked the Ward back into his pocket, his movements deliberate. "Come on," he said, starting toward the trail. "We shouldn't stick around."

Scott followed, her mind lingering on the boy's quiet conviction and the meaning behind the Ward. It wasn't just an object; it was trust, sacrifice, and love, all wrapped into one small, glowing symbol. And for Riley, it was everything.

Riley smirked faintly, his eyes sharp as he scanned the forest around them. "Told you."

Scott straightened, her adrenaline still coursing through her. "You really don't know what those things are?"

Riley shrugged, the smirk fading. "I know enough. I know they're not something you want following you home." He paused, then turned to her, his expression suddenly serious. "Speaking of which… I need you to do me a favor."

Scott raised an eyebrow. "A favor? After you just dragged me into the middle of whatever the hell that was?"

Riley tilted his head, considering her words. "Yeah. And I also kept you alive, so… quid pro quo."

Scott snorted softly. "Quid pro quo? Again? Where'd you learn that?"

"Really? Movies. Old gangster flicks." Riley's lips twitched into a small smile. "But I mean it. I need your word."

Scott hesitated, folding her arms. "Alright. What's the favor?"

Riley leaned closer, his voice dropping to a conspiratorial whisper. "One, you don't tell anyone—anyone—what just happened out here. Not your partner, not Bryan, not even my mom."

Scott frowned. "Not even Bryan? He might—"

"—He doesn't need to know," Riley interrupted firmly. "Trust me, he's got enough on his plate."

Scott studied him, noting the uncharacteristic tension in his posture. "Alright. And what's the second thing?"

Riley hesitated, glancing away for a moment. Then, with a mischievous glint returning to his eye, he leaned in and whispered something into Scott's ear. At first, her expression shifted from shock to mild amusement, and finally to a wry smile.

"Really?" she asked, crossing her arms. "That's your big request?"

Riley straightened, his grin widening. "Yep. You said, quid pro quo, didn't you?"

Scott sighed, shaking her head. "Alright. But you'd better hold up your end of the deal when the time comes."

"Deal," Riley said, extending his hand.

Scott looked at the boy, shaking her head again, but she took his hand. "You're a piece of work, you know that?"

Riley just winked. "You ain't seen nothin' yet."

***

The faint glow of the Ward grew stronger as they approached the trailhead leading back toward Bryan's house. Riley's steps slowed as the forest around them grew lighter, the oppressive darkness finally loosening its grip.

Scott glanced down at him, her earlier irritation giving way to curiosity. "You've been carrying that thing for a long time, haven't you?"

"Ever since Bryan gave it to me," Riley said, his tone quieter now. "He told me to keep it safe. To never let it go."

Scott studied the small object in his hand, realizing for the first time the weight of its significance. "He gave it to you to protect you and your mom, didn't he?"

Riley nodded. "Yeah. But it wasn't just about protection. It was… like giving me a piece of himself. Like he was saying, 'If I can't be there, this will be.'" He hesitated, his voice softening. "It's more than a Ward. It's him."

Scott swallowed hard, the boy's words resonating in a way she hadn't expected. "Bryan must care about you a lot."

Riley looked up at her, his expression unguarded for the first time. "He's my dad. He told me so."

Scott's heart tightened, hearing the raw emotion behind those words. "He's lucky to have you, Riley. You're lucky to have each other."

Riley's smirk returned, though it didn't quite reach his eyes. "Yeah, well, don't forget that when you're grilling him later."

Scott chuckled softly, shaking her head. "I'll keep that in mind."

***

The trees thinned as they reached the edge of the forest, Bryan's house visible just ahead. Riley slowed, releasing Scott's hand and tucking the Ward safely into his pocket. Scott's eyes lingered on the house, the morning light casting it in an almost serene glow.

"You're gonna keep your promise, right?" Riley asked, his voice cutting through her thoughts.

Scott turned to him, nodding. "Yeah. Your secret's safe with me."

Riley studied her for a moment, then gave a small, satisfied nod. "Good."

They crossed the clearing together, the tension from their journey through the woods gradually dissipating. But Scott knew the questions would linger—about the Shadows, the Ward, and the boy who carried more weight than any ten-year-old should. For now, though, she let them rest, focusing instead on the bond they'd forged in the heart of the forest.

As they approached the house, Scott glanced down at Riley, unable to shake the feeling that she'd only just begun to scratch the surface of the mystery that was Havenwood— and the people who called it home.

# CHAPTER 11 - HAVENWOOD

Agent Scott stepped quietly through the front door of the small house she and Michaels were staying in, shutting it behind her with a deliberate softness. The morning light filtered through the gauzy curtains, illuminating the modest living room and casting long shadows across the worn hardwood floor. Scott exhaled, her hand brushing against the cool metal of her Glock tucked safely at the small of her back.

The sound of shuffling feet pulled her attention to the adjoining kitchen, where Michaels, still in sweats and a rumpled T-shirt, appeared, scratching at his stubbled jaw. He blinked at her, his expression caught somewhere between annoyance and curiosity.

"Early start?" he muttered, heading straight for the coffee pot.

"Couldn't sleep," Scott replied, keeping her tone casual as she shrugged off her coat and draped it over the back of a chair.

Michaels paused, glancing over his shoulder. "That's funny, considering you looked dead to the world when I turned in. Something on your mind?"

Scott busied herself with tidying up the small table, avoiding his gaze. "Just needed some air. Figured I'd get a feel for the place."

Michaels poured himself a cup of coffee, his sharp eyes narrowing slightly. "That all?"

"Relax," she said, shooting him a faint smirk. "Not everything's a conspiracy, Michaels."

He sipped his coffee, clearly unconvinced but unwilling to press further. "Alright. Since you're up and moving, how about breakfast? Diner food sounds good to me."

Scott nodded, her expression neutral. "Let's get it over with."

***

The bell above the door jingled as Scott and Michaels stepped into Mary's Diner. The scuffed linoleum floors and wooden booths bore the weight of decades, and the air was thick with the scent of fried bacon and brewed coffee. Conversation halted the moment the agents entered, replaced by a heavy, uneasy silence.

Scott adjusted her jacket, her expression calm but alert. Michaels surveyed the room with the detached air of someone accustomed to walking into hostile spaces. A middle-aged waitress behind the counter paused mid-pour, her smile faltering.

"Morning," Michaels offered, his tone polite but firm.

The waitress hesitated, then nodded toward the booths. "Anywhere's fine."

The agents exchanged a glance before sliding into a booth near the window. The hushed murmurs resumed, though every glance in their direction carried an undercurrent of distrust.

"Friendly crowd," Michaels muttered, unfolding the menu.

221

"They've heard about us," Scott replied, her tone low. "Small towns don't keep secrets from each other—just from outsiders."

Their waitress approached, notepad in hand, her eyes darting between the two. "What'll it be?"

"Two coffees, black," Michaels said. "And whatever's hot on the griddle."

As the waitress walked away, Scott scanned the room. A wiry man at the counter pretended not to watch them; his head angled just slightly too far in their direction. At a nearby table, a burly man openly glared. Scott met his gaze, unflinching, until he shifted uncomfortably.

"They're not subtle," she murmured.

"They don't have to be," Michaels replied, taking a sip of the steaming coffee that had just been delivered. "We're not exactly blending in."

Scott's gaze sharpened. "Notice the waitress? Too nervous for a diner worker."

"She knows who we are. Just doesn't want to end up in the crossfire," Michaels said, his tone casual. "And the guy at the counter?"

"Eavesdropping," Scott replied. "Poorly."

The atmosphere thickened further when the door jingled again.

\*\*\*

The agents looked up as a sharp-dressed man walked through the door, his polished shoes incongruous against the diner's worn floor. Edward Jones, his tailored suit pristine, glanced around before spotting them.

"Here we go," Michaels muttered.

Jones ordered a coffee and approached their booth with a smile that didn't quite reach his eyes. "Agents. Edward Jones, Attorney at Law. I was hoping we'd cross paths."

Scott's expression hardened. "The same Edward Jones who survived the incident at Boston General?"

Jones's jaw tightened briefly before his smile returned. "That's correct. Quite the ordeal."

"Please, join us," Scott said, gesturing to the empty seat across from them.

Jones slid into the booth, placing his coffee cup on the table with calculated precision. "I imagine you've found Havenwood... enlightening."

"We're still gathering information," Scott replied, her tone neutral.

Jones leaned back, his smile faint. "Havenwood is a fascinating place. Stories get passed down here, and those stories have a way of lingering."

Scott tilted her head slightly. "Speaking from experience?"

Jones's chuckle was low, almost self-deprecating. "Let's just say I've learned that Havenwood isn't always what it seems."

"And you're here to share your wisdom?" Michaels asked, leaning forward.

Jones took a deliberate sip of his coffee. "Let me offer some advice. There's an abandoned house in the woods behind Bryan Jensen's property. It holds… significance."

Scott's expression didn't waver. "How so?"

Jones's gaze drifted to the window, where the trees loomed dark and silent. "Strange things happen there. Things that can't be explained. If you want answers about Havenwood—or Jensen—that's where you'll find them."

Michaels smirked faintly. "Generous of you to point us in the right direction."

"Just civic duty," Jones said with a small smile. "But be careful. Havenwood doesn't take kindly to outsiders poking around."

Jones stood, adjusting his jacket. "Good luck, Agents."

As he walked away, Scott's fingers tapped lightly against the table.

"Well," Michaels said dryly. "That was subtle."

"He's pushing us toward the house," Scott said, her voice low. "Whatever's there, it's what he wants us to see."

"Do you think it's a trap?"

"Maybe. Or maybe he wants to keep the heat off himself. Either way, we proceed on our terms."

***

The sign above the shop read "Havenwood Fine Woodworks" in elegant script, its simplicity belying the intricate craftsmanship within. Agents Scott and Michaels stepped out of their car, the crisp air carrying the faint scent of wood shavings and varnish.

Michaels's shoe landed squarely in a puddle, soaking his pant leg. He muttered a curse, shaking off the water as Scott smirked.

"Welcome to the countryside," she quipped, heading toward the heavy oak door.

Inside, the shop was a blend of artistry and industry. The showroom displayed ornate tables, chairs, and cabinets, each piece a testament to generations of skilled craftsmanship. The soft hum of machinery emanated from the workshop beyond.

Behind a small reception desk sat a young woman with auburn hair; her features were neat but unremarkable, in contrast to the grandeur of her surroundings. Her name tag read Kendra. She offered the agents a professional smile.

"Good morning," Kendra said brightly. "How can I help you?"

Scott stepped forward, presenting her badge. "Agent Scott, FBI. This is Agent Michaels."

Kendra blinked in surprise, her smile faltering for a moment. "The FBI? Wow. What brings you to Havenwood?"

Scott kept her tone even. "We're here to speak with the owner or supervisor about some routine questions. Would they be available?"

"Of course." Kendra rose, gesturing toward the office. "Mr. Marston is in the back. I'll let him know you're here."

As Kendra stepped away, Michaels nudged Scott's arm with his elbow, tilting his head toward a different corner of the showroom.

"Look at that," he said, sotto voce.

Scott followed his gaze, expecting to see another intricate piece of furniture. Instead, she spotted her.

Genevieve stood at the far end of the showroom, her fiery red-orange hair catching the light as if it had been polished. Dressed in a fitted leather jacket and skinny jeans, she held two wooden bowls in her hands, inspecting them with meticulous care. Her emerald-green eyes flicked over the craftsmanship, her expression one of approval. She turned the bowls slightly, revealing delicate carvings of vines and flowers etched along their rims.

Michaels didn't bother hiding his interest, his gaze lingering too long on her feline-like grace.

"Eyes up, Michaels," Scott said sharply, her voice low but firm.

He coughed and looked away, trying to compose himself. "Just... appreciating the scenery."

"Uh-huh."

Genevieve appeared oblivious to the exchange, but as she set the bowls on the counter, her lips quirked in the faintest hint of a smile.

Kendra returned with Henry Marston, a rugged man in his mid-fifties. His handshake was firm, his demeanor cautious. "Agents. What can I do for you?"

As Scott began explaining their inquiry, Genevieve moved toward the counter to make her purchase.

"I'll take these," she said softly to Kendra, her voice carrying a melodic lilt.

Michaels's attention wavered again, his focus shifting toward her. Genevieve tilted her head slightly, her red hair cascading over one shoulder, and gave him a glance—just enough to make Michaels' clear his throat and look away.

Kendra began ringing up the bowls, her movements brisk but professional. "Beautiful pieces, aren't they?" she asked.

Genevieve's smile widened, though she didn't respond. As she reached into her bag to pay, her gaze shifted momentarily to Scott, and her smile took on a knowing edge.

"Lovely day for a drive, don't you think, Agent Scott?" she murmured, her tone casual but laced with something almost playful.

Scott froze, startled. She didn't remember introducing herself to this woman.

Before she could respond, Genevieve collected her bowls, gave Michaels a faint nod of acknowledgment, and strolled out of the shop, the doorbell jingling softly in her wake.

*** 

In a dimly lit study lined with leather-bound books and heavy curtains, Ed Jones leaned back in his chair, a faint smile tugging at his lips. The amber glow of whiskey swirled lazily in his glass, catching the light from a single desk lamp.

A quiet knock disturbed the stillness. A young man entered hesitantly; his hands clasped tightly in front of him. "Sir, the agents were at the diner this morning."

Jones arched an eyebrow, his smile deepening. "Yes, I know. And?"

"They were asking questions."

Jones chuckled softly, setting his glass on the desk with a gentle clink. "About Jensen. About the woods. Naturally. Outsiders always think they can uncover Havenwood's secrets."

The young man shifted uneasily, his eyes flicking nervously to the edges of the room, where the shadows seemed to ripple faintly, alive with movement. A chill brushed past his cheek, and he took a small step back toward the door. "Do you want me to...?"

"No." Jones's voice cut through the air, smooth but firm. "Let them sniff around. Curiosity is a leash, and we'll pull it when the time is right."

The man nodded quickly, his movements stiff, and then retreated to the door. "And Jensen?"

Jones's smile vanished, his expression sharpening like a blade. "Leave him to me. For now."

As the door closed, Jones leaned forward, steepling his fingers beneath his chin. The shadows along the edges of the room thickened briefly, a faint ripple traveling through them like a breath. The temperature dropped imperceptibly, and a whisper of cold air brushed past his cheek.

"Soon," he murmured, his voice barely audible. "Soon, they'll see."

Jones rose, walking to the far wall. Placing his palm against a hidden panel, he pressed inward. A section of the wall slid open with a low hiss, revealing a secret chamber—a small, pitch-black room barely visible except for the faint glimmer of a raised dais at its center. On the dais stood a single candle, black as obsidian.

***

In the chamber, Jones struck a match and lit the black candle. The flame hissed to life, casting warped shadows that danced along the walls like living things. The air grew colder with each flicker, carrying the scent of sulfur and something darker, older.

Jones began to chant, his voice low and guttural, the syllables twisting the air around him. The shadows responded immediately, rippling and coalescing into a swirling void. From its depths, eyes emerged pinpricks of light, cold and ancient, like distant stars.

The young man's earlier hesitation lingered faintly in the room, as though absorbed by the shadows themselves. Jones's chant grew steadier, his tone commanding yet calm. "The woods. Tonight. Watch them. If they stray too far, remind them of their position."

The void pulsed faintly, its glowing eyes narrowing as though in comprehension, before dissipating into nothingness. The oppressive cold lifted, leaving behind a silence so complete it seemed to press against the walls.

Jones exhaled slowly, his lips curling into a cold, satisfied smile. "They'll learn," he murmured, his voice barely above a whisper. "They always do. Eventually."

The shadows retreated into the corners of the chamber, their movements fluid yet unnerving, as if reluctant to leave. Jones's gaze followed them, his expression pensive.

The candlelight flickered as he closed his eyes. The stillness of the room no longer felt like a victory but like the echo of something far older—a lesson forged in survival.

And what a price it was, he thought, as his mind drifted.

## CHAPTER 12 - GREGOR VASILEVIĆ

The reek of brine and unwashed bodies clung to the air like a second skin, saturating the cramped quarters of the ship.

Gregor Vasilević—no, not Gregor. Not here. Here, he was a nobody, a face in the crowd of desperate souls fleeing persecution. For the first time in centuries, he was nameless; identity stripped away like the fine silks he'd once worn as a prince among his kind.

He adjusted the tattered bonnet on his head, the fabric scratchy against his scalp. Beneath the ill-fitting dress, his chest was bound tightly to mimic a woman's form. The woolen shawl scratched at his skin, but the discomfort was secondary. Survival demanded this indignity.

The child in his arms screamed again, its shrill wail cutting through the cacophony of voices and the endless creak of the ship's hull. People glared at him—or rather, at her, the young mother he pretended to be. Gregor forced a tremble into his lips, cast his gaze downward, and muttered soothing nonsense to the infant.

"Poor dear," one woman muttered nearby, shaking her head. "Alone with a babe in these times. God help her."

Gregor wanted to retch. The baby was not his. It had been plucked from its cradle in the chaos of his flight. A motherless child for a desperate mother, he'd reasoned. The babe's cries had masked his escape through the shouting mob, its small warm weight providing a shred of credibility to his disguise as he fled toward the harbor.

Now it was dead weight—a liability. It would serve its purpose for only so long.

The ship lurched, and Gregor tightened his grip on the child. The stench of vomit rose from somewhere in the hold, mixing with the salty air. He fought the urge to gag, his jaw tightening as the familiar sting of humiliation surged through him.

He was Gregor Vasilević. A prince of the blood. A warlock of noble lineage. He had walked among kings and queens, whispered in their ears, and swayed their hearts with the power of his words. And now? Reduced to this—to rags, to deception, to this wailing parasite.

A sudden hush fell over the crowded hold as two men descended the steps, their boots loud against the wooden planks. Sailors. Their eyes, bloodshot and leering, swept over the huddled masses. One of them—a burly man with a crooked grin and a stink of rum—pointed at him.

"Here now," he slurred, his grin widening. "A fine lass, all alone. What say you, Jakob?"

The other sailor chuckled darkly. "Aye, fine indeed. Pretty little thing."

Gregor's grip on the child tightened instinctively. "I am not well," he said, pitching his voice higher, soft, pleading. "Please, leave me be."

The sailors ignored his words, stepping closer. One reached out, grabbing his shawl and yanking it away. "Let's see your face, girl."

Gregor's heart thundered in his chest as the shawl fell away, revealing his angular features. The sailor's grin faltered, confusion flickering across his face.

"What the—?"

Gregor didn't let him finish. His free hand shot forward, fingers curling into a claw. A surge of energy pulsed through him, his old instincts rising unbidden. The sailor's throat closed mid-gasp, his eyes bulging as he clawed at an invisible force.

The other sailor cursed, stumbling backward, but Gregor's power flared again. The man slammed into the wall of the hold, pinned by unseen hands. His mouth opened in a silent scream as Gregor squeezed the air from his lungs.

Then he stopped.

No. Not here. Not now.

Releasing his grip on the sailors, Gregor cast a quick glance around the hold. The passengers were too afraid to move, too stunned to cry out. He shifted the wailing child in his arms, letting its cries break the spell of silence. Muttered prayers and murmurs filled the space.

The sailors scrambled back up the stairs, their courage broken. Let them whisper of witches and curses. Let them spread their fear. It would keep them away.

For now.

***

The ship reached open water under the cover of darkness, the sea stretching endlessly in all directions.

Gregor stood at the ship's railing, the child still in his arms. Its cries had dwindled to soft whimpers, its small body trembling against him.

It was no longer needed.

With a calm precision that belied his inner turmoil, Gregor unwrapped the makeshift sling that held the child close. He looked down at it—a tiny, helpless creature. Its wide, teary eyes stared up at him, uncomprehending.

"You served your purpose," Gregor whispered, his voice devoid of emotion.

And with that, he released the child over the edge of the ship. It disappeared into the black waves below, the sound swallowed by the endless roar of the ocean.

Gregor turned away, his expression unreadable as he adjusted his bonnet and shawl. He moved back toward the hold, his steps steady. He had survived. He had endured. He would rebuild.

And one day, he would take back what was his.

***

The bell above the door jingled softly as Scott and Michaels stepped out of the woodcraft shop and into the late afternoon haze. The air was crisp, with the faint scent of sawdust lingering in the breeze. Michaels adjusted his tie, his gaze flicking toward the tree line in the distance.

"Friendly place," he said dryly, unlocking the sedan with a chirp.

Scott followed him to the car, her pace measured. "Friendlier than you, apparently. I thought I'd have to pull you off the floor after that little encounter back there."

Michaels frowned. "What are you talking about?"

"Come on," Scott said, sliding into the passenger seat and smirking. "Next time, keep your eyes in your sockets and your tongue off the ground. You're going to end up tripping somebody."

Michaels flushed. "It wasn't like that."

"Uh-huh." Scott's smirk widened as she buckled her seatbelt. "Pretty sure you'd have carried those bowls out to her car if she'd asked."

"I would not," Michaels protested, starting the engine.

"Right," Scott replied, the word dripping with sarcasm. "Glad to know your professionalism is intact."

Michaels sighed, pulling the car onto the main road. "Can we move on?"

"Gladly." Scott leaned back in her seat, but the hint of amusement lingered on her face.

As the sedan rumbled along the quiet street, Michaels cleared his throat. "So... about the house in the woods."

Scott's smirk vanished. "We covered that already."

"Not really," Michaels countered. "Jensen, the locals, even that lawyer—everything keeps pointing back there. It's the common denominator, Scott. We should check it out."

Scott's fingers drummed against the door handle as she stared out the window. "And what exactly do you think we're going to find? It's an abandoned house."

"Which makes it perfect for hiding things," Michaels said, glancing at her. "Or for whatever these people don't want us to see."

"We've already been warned about going near it," Scott replied flatly.

"That's why we go after dark," Michaels said, his voice light but firm. "No one's watching, no one's following. Jensen, the kid, the woman—none of them will even know."

Scott's jaw tightened. "And if something happens?"

"Then we write it up in the report," Michaels replied with a shrug. "We're investigating. It's what we do."

Scott's gaze stayed fixed on the horizon; her expression unreadable. Convincing him to drop the idea without tipping him off about her earlier visit was impossible. She would have to let it play out—and be ready for whatever came next.

"Fine," she said, at last, her voice carefully neutral. "But if this goes sideways, it's on you."

Michaels grinned; his confidence unwavering. "Relax. What's the worst that could happen?"

Scott didn't reply, but the tension in her shoulders spoke volumes as they drove on, the woods looming ever closer.

## CHAPTER 13 - WAIT UNTIL DARK

The woods were deathly silent, the kind of quiet that pressed against the ears and amplified every rustle, every breath. Scott and Michaels moved cautiously, their flashlights cutting thin beams through the oppressive darkness. Their steps were deliberate, but even the crunch of leaves beneath their boots sounded too loud, like an uninvited intrusion.

As they approached the clearing, the atmosphere grew heavier. The air turned colder, biting against their skin and causing their breaths to form faint white clouds that dissipated quickly into the night. Michaels shifted uncomfortably, rubbing his hands together to fight the chill.

"Quiet out here," he muttered, his voice barely above a whisper.

"Too quiet," Scott replied, her eyes darting to the edges of the path. The beam of her flashlight jerked slightly in her grasp, her knuckles tightening.

The trees opened suddenly into a wide clearing, revealing the house—a hulking, decayed silhouette against the dim moonlight. Its jagged roof and broken windows gave it the look of a creature lying in wait.

But the house wasn't the first thing they noticed.

A dense, knee-deep mist rolled across the clearing, glowing faintly under the moonlight. The vapor seemed alive, swirling and rippling with each step they took, refusing to settle even in the absence of wind.

"What the hell is that?" Michaels asked, stopping at the edge of the mist. His flashlight beam cut into it but revealed nothing below.

Scott's gaze swept the clearing, her unease growing. "Keep moving," she said, her voice low and firm.

Michaels hesitated before stepping forward, his boot sinking into the mist. The vapor parted reluctantly around his leg before closing again, leaving no trace of his step.

"I don't like this," Michaels muttered, his bravado slipping. "Not one bit."

"Neither do I," Scott admitted, her tone unusually sharp.

They pushed forward slowly, the mist swirling more intensely the closer they came to the house. Overhead, a cloud passed across the moon, plunging the clearing into near-total darkness. The silence grew oppressive, each breath loud in their ears.

Then came the sound—a faint rustling, soft and deliberate.

Scott froze, her flashlight jerking toward the sound. "Did you hear that?"

"Yeah," Michaels whispered, his voice tight. "What was it?"

Scott didn't answer, her attention locked on the shifting mist. As the moonlight returned, the clearing lit with a ghostly glow, and her stomach turned. Swirls in the vapor moved with purpose, circling their feet like something unseen was gliding just beneath the surface.

Michaels exhaled sharply. "Jesus... What's down there?"

"I don't know," Scott replied, her voice tight.

The rustling sound came again, louder this time, followed by the faintest scrape of something moving across the wood. Scott's flashlight darted toward the porch of the house, but nothing moved.

The air felt thicker now, heavier. Scott's fingers tightened around the grip of her sidearm. "We need to turn back," she said, her voice barely above a whisper.

"Too late for that," Michaels muttered. His usual confidence was gone, replaced by the growing realization that this was a mistake.

The mist swirled more violently, coiling and uncoiling like tendrils reaching for them. The faint rustling grew louder, joined by a low, guttural growl that reverberated through the clearing.

"Scott..." Michaels said, his flashlight shaking in his grip.

"I know," she replied tersely. "Stay close. Keep your light moving."

The clouds passed over the moon again, and the clearing fell into darkness. The rustling grew louder and closer, until it surrounded them completely.

Scott felt her breath hitch as a faint shimmer moved through the mist—a ripple, too large to be natural.

"Move," she commanded, her voice firm despite the pounding in her chest.

Michaels didn't argue. They began backing toward the house, their footsteps slow and deliberate. The mist shifted with them, swirling in lazy circles as if taunting them, reminding them it could close in at any moment.

"Scott," Michaels whispered again.

"What?"

"We shouldn't have come here."

Scott didn't reply. The look in her eyes said it all: he was right.

Another growl echoed through the clearing, this one deeper, closer. The house loomed behind them like a waiting maw, but it was the only thing offering even the illusion of safety.

"Inside," Scott said, her voice tight with urgency.

They stepped onto the porch, the wood creaking under their weight. The growling stopped, replaced by a deafening silence.

Scott's hand rested on the doorknob, her pulse racing. Behind them, the mist continued to swirl, the faint shimmer of something large moving just out of sight.

Without a word, she pushed the door open, the hinges groaning in protest. They stepped inside, the darkness swallowing them whole as the door creaked shut behind them.

\*\*\*

The living room was bathed in a warm, golden glow from a single lamp on the side table. The storm that had raged earlier was now a gentle drizzle, its soft patter against the windows blending with the occasional creak of the old house. The room smelled faintly of pine wood and the lingering aroma of dinner.

Riley sat cross-legged on the plush rug in the center of the room, his attention divided between the small tower of building blocks he was half-heartedly assembling and the cat nestled in his lap. Gee, her auburn fur sleek and glistening in the lamplight, stretched lazily before settling against him, her emerald eyes half-lidded in contentment.

The soft rhythm of her purring filled the quiet space, a soothing counterpoint to the tapping rain. Riley scratched behind her ears absentmindedly, his fingers tracing the line of her neck.

Upstairs, muffled voices filtered through the ceiling. Bryan and Anna were talking—low, indistinct words carrying the natural cadence of adults sorting through the ordinary business of life. The warmth of their conversation added to the house's cocoon-like tranquility.

Riley yawned, his eyelids drooping. He glanced at the staircase, wondering if Anna would be mad if he stayed up just a little longer. "What do you think, Gee?" he murmured. "Think I can stay awake?"

Gee didn't respond, her body slack and at ease against him. The calm of the house was almost hypnotic, every sound and flicker of light reinforcing the feeling of safety. Riley leaned his head back against the edge of the couch, closing his eyes for a moment.

Then Gee shifted.

Her ears twitched first, her emerald eyes snapping open. Her body tensed against Riley's lap, the gentle purring ceasing mid-vibration. Riley blinked, startled by the sudden change.

"What's wrong, girl?" he asked, his voice soft.

Gee's gaze snapped toward the staircase. Her fur bristled slightly, her tail flicking once, twice, before she leapt from Riley's lap with a silent grace.

"Gee?" Riley called after her, watching as she landed soundlessly on the wooden floor and padded toward the staircase. She moved with purpose, her movements precise and fluid, her head tilted slightly as if listening to something only she could hear.

The house seemed to hold its breath. Even the rain against the windows quieted.

Riley stood, his brows knitting in confusion. "Where are you going?"

Gee, didn't pause. She ascended the stairs, her auburn tail disappearing over the top landing. Riley hesitated, then followed, his socks muffling his steps against the worn wood.

By the time he reached his room, Gee was already there. She slipped inside, her body low and purposeful as she made her way to the window. It was ajar, letting in the faint scent of damp earth and rain.

With a final glance back at Riley, her emerald eyes catching the light like small, glowing orbs, Gee leapt onto the sill and disappeared into the night.

The room felt suddenly emptier without her. Riley stepped closer to the window, peering out into the darkness, but saw only the faint shimmer of raindrops in the moonlight.

"Gee?" he whispered, his voice barely audible.

The night gave no answer, but the distant woods seemed alive, their dark canopy pulsing faintly with a hidden energy.

***

The forest was restless, its stillness a lie. Beneath the thin veil of chirping crickets and the occasional hoot of an owl, something darker thrummed—a low, almost imperceptible hum that made the air feel heavier.

Gee moved like a shadow, her auburn fur a streak of motion against the dark underbrush. Her paws landed silently on the damp earth, her every movement fluid and purposeful. The mist that lingered low to the ground swirled around her legs as she darted through it, her emerald eyes glowing faintly in the faint moonlight.

The trees whispered as she passed, their skeletal branches seeming to reach for her. The path ahead was bathed in intermittent light as clouds drifted across the moon, casting fleeting shadows that moved like specters in her periphery.

She didn't slow. The pull was undeniable—a sharp, urgent whisper at the edge of her senses. Something unnatural lay ahead, a wrongness that made her fur bristle and her instincts scream.

The forest itself seemed to push back, its once-familiar paths feeling alien, hostile. The rustling leaves grew louder, shifting like a collective breath. Somewhere in the distance, a branch snapped with a sharp crack that echoed unnaturally, the sound bouncing and twisting until it seemed to come from all sides.

Gee hesitated for the briefest of moments, her ears flattening as her head turned sharply toward the noise. Her body tensed, muscles coiled as if ready to strike or flee. The mist swirled around her, forming faint, swirling patterns as though it, too, was alive and watching.

Then came the growl—a deep, guttural sound, faint but unmistakable. It reverberated through the forest, low and menacing, vibrating in her chest. Gee's pupils narrowed to slits, her tail flicking once before she bolted forward.

The forest grew darker as she neared her destination, the moonlight struggling to pierce the thickening canopy of branches. The crickets had gone silent now, leaving only the sound of her movement and the rhythmic pulse of her heart pounding in her ears.

Ahead, the clearing loomed, the house at its center a blackened silhouette against the dim light. Gee slowed slightly, her body hugging the ground as she approached. The mist was denser here, swirling with deliberate, unnatural patterns that coiled like snakes at the edges of the clearing.

Her senses burned with urgency; her gaze fixed on the faint glow of flashlights cutting through the mist near the house. The agents were there, unaware, vulnerable.

She slipped into the shadows, her auburn fur vanishing as if it had been swallowed by the night. The last glimpse of her was a faint glimmer of her emerald eyes reflecting the light, before the darkness claimed her entirely.

The forest stilled once more, holding its breath.

***

The air inside the house was stale, thick with the scent of mold and rot. Dust hung in the moonlight that filtered through the jagged holes in the roof, creating faint beams that crisscrossed the darkened interior.

Scott and Michaels stood back-to-back in the center of the room, flashlights off, their breaths shallow. The faint creak of the house settling echoed like a warning in the silence.

"You good?" Michaels whispered, his voice tight.

"Define 'good,'" Scott muttered, her hand gripping her sidearm tightly. Her eyes darted upward, following the shifting shadows cast by the faint moonlight.

The clouds outside thickened, further dimming the light. With each passing second, the room grew darker, the beams from the roof holes fading until the space was cloaked in an oppressive gray.

"Stay sharp," Scott hissed, her voice barely audible.

Then, something moved.

A ripple passed over the remaining sliver of moonlight— a shape that didn't belong. Scott's eyes narrowed, her gut twisting. She turned her head slowly upward, her breath catching as she saw them.

The shadows weren't just on the walls; they were descending. Silent and deliberate, they lowered themselves from the beams above like spiders on invisible threads, their forms twisting unnaturally in the faint light.

"Scott?" Michaels's voice was sharp with unease.

"Don't move," she whispered, her voice low and firm. Her heart pounded in her chest as the shadows drew closer, their movements fluid and predatory.

Her grip tightened on her gun.

"Scott?" Michaels repeated, panic creeping into his voice.

"RUN!" Scott shouted, spinning and firing. The muzzle flash illuminated the room in stark bursts, revealing the full extent of the descending figures—elongated, humanoid shapes with empty voids where faces should have been.

Michaels bolted for the door as Scott fired again, her shots tearing through the shadows with no visible effect. The air grew colder, and the growls from the figures deepened into an otherworldly roar.

"Move!" she screamed, turning and sprinting after Michaels.

The two agents barreled through the narrow hallway, their flashlights bobbing wildly as they ran. The entrance loomed ahead, but the oppressive darkness seemed to close in around them, the house itself becoming a labyrinth of shadows.

Michaels threw open the door, the wood splintering under his weight as he stumbled out into the clearing. Scott was close behind, her chest heaving as she skidded to a stop beside him.

Behind them, the house was silent once more, the shadows retreating into its depths.

***

The warm light of the living room contrasted starkly with the chaos unfolding in the woods. Bryan descended the staircase, his hand brushing the worn wooden banister as he called out to Anna.

"I'll grab it from the truck," he said casually.

Anna appeared at the top of the stairs, carrying an empty coffee mug. "Don't forget your coat," she teased lightly. "I don't need you catching a cold."

Bryan sighed, smirking faintly. "Yes, Mom."

Anna rolled her eyes, following him down the stairs as Riley appeared in the hallway, rubbing his eyes.

"Hey, I thought you were already in bed," Anna said, smiling at him.

"I'm not tired," Riley muttered, his gaze shifting to the floor.

Bryan opened the front door, stepping onto the porch and pulling it closed behind him. The faint drizzle tapped against the roof as he made his way toward the truck.

Inside, Anna headed toward the kitchen but stopped mid-step when Bryan reentered the house. He checked the key hanger by the door, then patted his pockets, frowning.

"Anna, have you seen the truck keys?" he asked casually.

"No, I thought you had them," she replied, setting her mug on the counter.

Bryan shook his head, muttering to himself as he checked his coat pockets.

Anna hesitated, her eyes narrowing as she turned to Riley. "Wait... weren't you outside this morning?"

Riley stiffened, his hand drifting to his pocket. "Uh... yeah, I was."

Bryan looked up from his search, his brow furrowed. "What does that have to do with—"

"—Riley," Anna interrupted, her tone sharper. "What are you talking about?"

"The keys," Riley stammered. "They must've slipped out of my pocket when—"

"—When what?" Anna asked, stepping closer.

Riley swallowed hard, glancing toward the stairs leading to his room. "When we went for a walk."

Anna's confusion deepened, but before she could press him further, the distant sound of rapid gunfire shattered the quiet.

The unmistakable staccato of bullets echoed through the night, sharp and insistent.

Bryan froze, his eyes widening. "Shit!" he hissed, yanking the door open.

"Bryan!" Anna called after him, but he was already gone, bolting into the night.

*** 

Gee halted mid-stride; every muscle taut as her senses sharpened. Her emerald eyes widened, pupils dilating in the dim light. The distant echo of gunfire sliced through the silence, pulling her attention toward the old house in the woods. Without hesitation, she sprang forward, a blur of auburn fur weaving through the tangled underbrush. Her movements were a seamless blend of power and grace, each stride propelling her faster as she raced against unseen threats.

*** 

Near the decrepit house, Agents Scott and Michaels sprinted with every ounce of strength they had left. Their breaths came in ragged gasps, the cold air burning their lungs. The forest seemed to conspire against them—roots snagged at their feet; branches clawed at their faces. Behind them, the Shadows moved leisurely, almost playfully, their dark forms gliding over the mist-covered ground.

"Don't look back!" Scott shouted, pushing herself to keep pace.

Michaels glanced over his shoulder despite the warning, his eyes widening at the sight. "They're still coming!"

The mist swirled around their ankles, thickening as if trying to pull them down. The once-faint rustling grew into a cacophony of whispers, enveloping them.

***

At the trailhead, Bryan charged into the forest, his heart pounding in his chest. He pushed himself hard, feet pounding against the damp earth. But his body, still recovering from previous ordeals, began to protest. His vision blurred, and a sharp pain lanced through his side.

He stumbled, collapsing onto his hands and knees. Gasping for breath, his muscles convulsed, and a familiar darkness stirred within him. He leaned back onto his heels, eyes clenched shut. When he opened them, they were pools of inky blackness.

A tremor shook his frame as wisps of black smoke curled from his lips, dissipating into the cold night air. He shuddered, fighting to regain control as the tendrils of darkness slowly retreated.

***

"Can't… keep… running," Scott panted, her legs threatening to give out.

Michaels nodded, breathless. "We have to make a stand."

Scott's foot caught on a root hidden beneath the mist, sending her sprawling to the ground. Her Glock flew from her grasp, skidding across the leaves.

"Scott!" Michaels shouted, skidding to a halt. He turned back, helping her scramble to her feet.

She snatched up her weapon, hands trembling. From the shadows ahead, a pair of glowing eyes emerged—cold, unblinking, and fixed directly on them.

Without exchanging a word, both agents raised their pistols and fired. The sharp cracks of gunfire shattered the night, muzzle flashes illuminating twisted trees and swirling mist. The eyes vanished, and silence rushed in to fill the void.

***

Deeper in the woods, the Shadows halted as if sensing a shift. Their heads pivoted unnaturally, empty faces turning toward an unseen force. Suddenly, lances of dark mist burst from the surrounding darkness, impaling each Shadow with lethal precision. They dissolved silently, their forms unraveling into nothingness.

***

Michaels extended a hand to Scott, helping her to her feet. Both were drenched in sweat, their breaths ragged clouds in the frigid air.

"You okay?" he asked, concern etched on his face.

"Yeah," she nodded, swallowing hard. "You?"

"I'll live." He managed a weak smile.

Scott ejected her spent magazine, hands shaking as she loaded a fresh one. "We need to keep moving."

"Agreed." Michaels did the same, the metallic click of his weapon echoing softly.

Their flashlight beams cut through the mist, scanning for any sign of movement. The mist began to thin, revealing a large shape sprawled on the ground ahead.

"Wait," Scott whispered. "What's that?"

They approached cautiously, weapons at the ready. Lying before them was a massive mountain lion, its tawny fur matted and marked with bullet wounds.

"A cougar?" Michaels breathed. "This far north?"

Scott frowned. "Doesn't seem right."

A sudden noise behind them made both agents whirl around, guns aimed. Bryan staggered into view, his face pale and eyes weary. He dropped to his knees, gasping for breath.

"Jensen!" Scott lowered her weapon, rushing to his side.

Michaels joined her. "What are you doing out here?"

"Heard... gunshots," Bryan managed between gulps of air. "Came to... help."

Scott and Michaels exchanged a glance before each took an arm, helping him to his feet.

"You shouldn't be out here," Scott said gently.

Bryan's gaze met hers briefly, a flicker of understanding passing between them. "Couldn't... stay away."

Michaels looked back at the dead mountain lion. "At least we know what was stalking us."

Scott nodded absently, her mind elsewhere. "Let's get back."

Bryan suddenly lurched forward, retching violently. He leaned against a tree for support as he wiped his mouth with the back of his hand. "Sorry... must be coming down with something."

Michaels patted him on the back. "It's okay. Let's get you home."

As they began the slow trek back, Scott kept a watchful eye on Bryan. "You sure you're alright?"

He nodded weakly. "Just need rest."

The trio moved cautiously, the oppressive atmosphere beginning to lift as they left the clearing behind.

***

Once their footsteps faded and the forest fell silent, the lifeless form of the mountain lion stirred. A convulsion rippled through its body, muscles twitching beneath the fur. The creature's eyes snapped open, gleaming unnaturally in the darkness.

With a fluid motion, the form began to change. Fur receded into pale skin, limbs reshaped themselves, and features shifted. In moments, Gee sat up, taking a deep breath as she brushed leaves from her hair.

"Well, that sucked," she muttered, flexing her fingers to shake off the residual numbness.

She stood, stretching to ease the stiffness from her limbs. Casting a glance in the direction Bryan and the agents had gone, a thoughtful expression crossed her face.

"Always cleaning up their messes," she sighed with a hint of amusement.

Her form shimmered subtly as she transformed back into her feline shape. The small cat shook herself briskly, then darted into the underbrush, moving swiftly and silently toward home.

***

As Gee approached Bryan's house, the familiar sights and scents brought a sense of comfort. She leapt gracefully onto the windowsill of Riley's room, nudging the partially open window with her nose. Slipping inside, she found Riley sound asleep, the soft rise and fall of his breathing steady and peaceful.

Gee padded quietly across the floor, curling up against Riley's body. She closed her eyes, allowing herself a moment of rest. The night's events had been taxing, but she was content knowing that, for now, those whom she cared about were safe.

***

The morning light filtered through the curtains of Bryan's house, casting soft beams across the wooden floors. The storm from the previous night had passed, leaving the air crisp and fresh. The house hummed with a quiet energy as Bryan, Anna, and Riley prepared to bid their visitors farewell. The dining table, now clear of the dinner dishes from the night before, held a tray of steaming coffee mugs and a plate of muffins Anna had insisted on making "just in case."

Agent Michaels was the first to come downstairs, his tie slightly askew and his demeanor more relaxed than usual. "Smells good in here," he commented, snagging a muffin and grinning at Anna. "Starting to think you're trying to spoil us."

Anna smirked as she handed him a napkin. "Consider it a parting gift. You won't find this kind of breakfast on the road."

Scott appeared next, her expression as composed as ever, though the faint circles under her eyes suggested she'd had a restless night. She gave Anna a nod of acknowledgment before addressing Bryan. "Thanks for letting us stay. I know this hasn't been easy for any of you."

Bryan leaned against the counter, arms crossed. "It's been a long few days. I'm not sorry to see them end, but thank you for listening. It's not every day someone from the FBI actually tries to understand."

Scott's lips curved into the faintest of smiles. "I just do my job, Mr. Jensen."

Michaels chuckled as he sipped his coffee. "Well, your job includes good instincts and excellent taste in stew." He raised the mug in a mock toast. "Here's to the best dinner I've had on duty in... ever."

Anna rolled her eyes, but her smile was genuine. "Glad we could help. You two have a safe trip back."

Michaels turned to Riley, who was standing by the staircase, looking both eager and hesitant. "And you, little man," Michaels said, crouching slightly to meet Riley's eyes. "Keep being you. The world needs more troublemakers."

Riley grinned. "You're just mad I beat you at checkers."

"Twice," Michaels admitted, holding up two fingers. "But don't get cocky. Next time, I'm coming for you."

Scott stepped forward, her tone softening as she addressed Riley. "Thank you. For being honest and for helping us out. You've got a good head on your shoulders, even if it's a little mischievous."

Riley straightened, clearly proud. "I try."

Scott extended her hand, and Riley shook it firmly, mimicking the formal grip he'd seen adults use. But as she let go, she surprised him by pulling him into a brief hug.

"Stay out of trouble," she murmured, kissing his cheek lightly before stepping back.

Riley's face turned bright red, and he stammered, "I—I will. Maybe."

The adults laughed, the tension in the room easing. Scott and Michaels finished their coffee and stepped toward the door, ready to leave.

*** 

Michaels paused on the porch, turning back to Anna and Bryan. "Thanks again. If you ever decide to write a book about all this, I'd love to read it."

Bryan smirked faintly. "I'll keep that in mind."

Scott stepped down to the gravel path leading to their car but hesitated, glancing back one last time. "Take care of each other," she said, her voice carrying an unexpected warmth. "And if anything changes… You know how to find us."

Anna nodded. "Same to you."

***

As the sedan pulled onto the winding road out of Havenwood, Michaels turned the radio to a classic rock station, the low hum of guitars filling the space. "Well," he said, drumming his fingers on the steering wheel. "That went better than expected."

Scott leaned back in her seat; her expression thoughtful. "They're good people. Tough, but good."

"Yeah, and that kid's got some serious potential," Michaels added with a chuckle. "I bet he grows up to be something special."

Scott didn't respond immediately. Instead, she reached into her jacket pocket, her fingers brushing against something unfamiliar. Frowning slightly, she pulled out a folded piece of paper. Curious, she unfolded it and read:

Agent Samantha Scott,

11 May. Seven years from now. The Plaza Hotel. Drinks at 8. Dessert at 9. On me.

Riley

For a moment, Scott stared at the note, her mind replaying the confident smirk Riley had flashed her earlier.

Of course, he didn't know what he was writing—it was the kind of note a boy cobbled together from movies he shouldn't have been watching. And yet... she knew she'd never forget it.

Then, much to Michaels' surprise, she laughed—a soft, genuine sound that filled the car.

"What's so funny?" he asked, glancing over at her.

Scott folded the note carefully and slipped it back into her pocket. "Nothing. Just... thinking about the future."

Michaels raised an eyebrow but didn't press. Instead, he focused on the road ahead, the quiet beauty of the Havenwood forest giving way to the open highway.

In Scott's pocket, the note felt like a secret she'd carry with her for years, a reminder that even in the strangest places, there were moments that made her believe in the unexpected twists of life.

***

The slam of the front door reverberated through the house, cutting through the lingering quiet of the morning. Riley froze mid-step in the hallway, his sneakers leaving faint smudges on the polished floor. The weight of Anna and Bryan's combined stares bore down on him like a freight train.

"Riley." Anna's voice was sharp, a warning in her tone. "We need to talk. Now!"

Riley glanced at Bryan for backup, but his dad—well, Bryan—offered no refuge. Bryan leaned against the counter, arms crossed, his expression unreadable but unrelenting. The quiet intensity in his gaze was louder than any lecture.

Riley gulped. "Uh-oh," he muttered, his feet dragging him toward the kitchen table like a condemned man approaching the gallows.

Anna followed close behind, her presence crackling with restrained fury. Bryan stayed by the counter, his casual stance betrayed by the sharpness in his eyes, which pinned Riley in place like a butterfly under glass.

"Do you want to explain why we had to hear from the FBI that you took Agent Scott for a stroll through the woods—to that house?" Bryan began, his voice low but firm.

Riley fidgeted, his fingers toying with the hem of his sweatshirt. "She asked," he mumbled, looking away. "I didn't think it was a big deal."

"You didn't think it was a big deal?" Anna snapped, her voice rising. "Do you have any idea how reckless that was? How dangerous?"

"I didn't think anything bad would happen!" Riley's voice rose in defense, a mix of defiance and desperation. "I just wanted to help!"

"And that's the problem," Bryan interjected, his tone deceptively calm. "You didn't think."

Riley opened his mouth to retort, but a soft thud on the table cut through the argument. All three turned toward the sound.

Gee sat perfectly poised on the edge of the table. Her fiery orange fur gleamed in the sunlight streaming through the kitchen window, and her emerald eyes sparkled with unnerving clarity.

The silence was broken by two words, precise and deliberate, spoken directly into their minds: "Excuse me."

"Gee?" Bryan said cautiously, his brows knitting.

Anna staggered back, her hand flying to her chest. "What the—" she gasped.

Gee's feline form shimmered, a faint ripple of light cascading over her like a wave. Fur gave way to smooth skin, and limbs elongated with hypnotic fluidity within moments; where the cat had perched, now sat a striking, radiant woman. Her hair, now fiery red, tumbled in loose waves over her shoulders, framing the same luminous green eyes.

Bryan blinked, his expression caught between shock and a hint of familiarity. "Gee?"

"Yes," she said smoothly, her voice as melodic as a songbird's call. "I believe it's time we had a proper conversation."

The kitchen fell silent, save for the ticking of the wall clock. Anna's mouth opened and closed, searching for words that refused to come.

Gee's fiery hair gleamed in the light as she adjusted the oversized flannel shirt that hung loosely on her frame. It was clearly Bryan's, and Anna's stomach dropped as recognition dawned.

"Wait a minute," Anna hissed, her voice cracking with disbelief. "Is that Bryan's shirt?"

Bryan immediately raised his hands. "Don't look at me!" he said quickly, as though anticipating the accusation.

Gee's lips curved into a mischievous smile. "It was comfortable," she said lightly. Then, as if to underline her point, she closed her eyes and inhaled deeply. The motion was slow, deliberate, and disarmingly sensual. When she reopened them, her gaze fixed on Anna with a playful glint. "Ummmm... Old Spice."

Anna's jaw dropped, her eyes darting between Bryan, who was beginning to look increasingly uncomfortable, and Gee, whose grin widened with amusement.

"Oh, you have got to be kidding me," Anna finally managed, throwing her hands into the air.

"It's a very... pleasing scent," Gee added with an innocent shrug, her gaze lingering on Bryan for just a moment too long. If she noticed the flush creeping up his neck, she didn't let on.

Anna's shock turned swiftly to exasperation. "You're enjoying this, aren't you?"

"Only a little," Gee admitted with a serene smile.

Bryan cleared his throat, stepping in as Anna's face turned an alarming shade of red. "Anna," he said cautiously, "maybe we should—"

—Bryan Jensen, don't you dare tell me to calm down!" Anna snapped, pointing an accusatory finger at him. Then, whirling on Gee, she jabbed the air in the witch's direction. "You—you—have been sleeping in my son's bed, wearing Bryan's shirt, and now you're sniffing it like some kind of—of—aphrodisiac!?"

Gee didn't miss a beat. "It's not just comfortable; it's... intoxicating," she said evenly, her tone entirely too composed. "You should try it."

Gee tilted her head, her feline expression the picture of serenity. "By the way," she said calmly, "I have chosen Riley as my life partner."

Anna's face turned crimson. "You've chosen—what? He's eleven years old! He's a child!"

Gee's playful expression softened as she glanced at Riley, who had been watching the exchange with wide eyes and an increasingly sheepish grin. "Riley," she said gently, her voice losing its teasing edge. "You understand, don't you?"

Riley nodded earnestly. "Yeah, Gee. You're just... you."

Gee hopped down from the table gracefully. "Anna," she said gently, her voice soothing but firm. "My bond with Riley is spiritual, not physical... yet. He is unique. Extraordinary. It is my duty—and my privilege—to protect him."

Anna's glare didn't soften. "Your duty? He's a boy! He doesn't even know what he's getting into!"

Riley finally found his voice. "Mom, Gee's not like other people—or cats. She's my friend. She's helped me."

"And yet," Anna said, her voice trembling with anger, "she's been hiding the truth from us."

Gee exhaled softly, her feline frame shimmering with an ethereal glow. Once again, Gee pulls the shirt up and inhales deeply. "It smells... so good."

Anna said, throwing her hands in the air. "This is insane."

"Anna," Bryan said, his voice calm but firm, "this is how it works. It's a Coven tradition... law... whatever. Gee has every right to choose her life partner... her mate."

"Tradition?" Anna snapped, whirling on him. "We're talking about my son. Don't you dare compare this to what happened with Ashley?"

Riley stepped forward, his voice breaking through the rising tension. "Mom, it's okay. Gee's not trying to hurt anyone. She's just... part of our family now."

Gee's expression softened as she knelt to meet Riley's eye level. "Thank you, Riley. I am honored by your trust."

Anna's chest heaved as she fought to process the overwhelming cascade of revelations. "This is going to take time," she said finally, her voice strained.

"I understand," Gee replied, her tone gentle. "And I will prove myself to you, Anna. For Riley's sake—and yours."

Anna pressed a hand to her forehead, the weight of the morning crashing down on her. "I need coffee."

As she turned toward the counter, Bryan met Gee's gaze, his own filled with a mix of exasperation and grudging acceptance. "You could've picked a less dramatic moment for this, you know."

Gee's lips curved into a small, mischievous smile. "Where would the fun be in that?"

The kitchen was thick with tension, Anna's fury still crackling in the air. Gee's emerald eyes sparkled with their unnerving clarity as she slowly extended her hand to Riley. Her fingers were long and elegant, a faint shimmer playing across her skin as if she were not entirely of this world.

"Come here, husband," Gee purred softly, her voice a low, melodic hum that sent shivers through the room.

Riley blinked in surprise but didn't hesitate. He stepped forward, placing his smaller hand into hers. His face lit up with a sheepish but unmistakable smile.

Anna froze mid-step, her hand gripping the coffee mug as if it were the last tether to her sanity. Her eyes widened in disbelief, darting between Gee's arm wrapped protectively around Riley and the boy's utterly oblivious grin.

"Husband?" Anna repeated her voice, a low growl that matched Gee's purr in intensity.

Bryan instinctively took a step back, sensing the storm was about to erupt. "Anna—"

"—Not now, Bryan!" she snapped, her eyes locked on Gee. The tall, auburn-haired woman met Anna's gaze unflinchingly, her serene expression only serving to stoke Anna's ire.

"Wasn't her hair...?" asks Anna.

Riley shrugs and smiles.

The coffee mug trembled slightly in Anna's grasp as she pivoted toward the counter. Setting the mug down with exaggerated care, she reached up to a high cupboard. Her movements were slow, deliberate, and dangerous.

Bryan's brow furrowed. "Anna, what are you—?"

The clink of glass cut him off as she pulled down a familiar, green-labeled bottle of Jameson's. She unscrewed the cap with a sharp twist and tipped the bottle over her coffee, pouring generously. The liquid swirled into the mug, the comforting smell of whiskey cutting through the tension.

She replaced the cap and turned slowly, her gaze icy as it flicked to Gee, who now stood with her arm draped gently over Riley's shoulders. Riley, for his part, beamed as if nothing in the world was wrong.

Anna lifted the mug halfway to her lips, then seemed to reconsider. Instead, she set it back down, grabbed the bottle by the neck, opened it, and tipped it to her mouth, taking a long slow swig.

Bryan's jaw dropped. "Anna—"

She held up a single finger, silencing him, and exhaled deeply, her shoulders finally relaxing. "Nope," she muttered, her voice tight. "I am not ready for this." She lowered the bottle and wiped her mouth with the back of her hand before pointing it toward Gee. "You, wife, or whatever you want to call yourself—Stay. Right. There."

Gee tilted her head, her feline grace evident even in human form. "I have no intention of leaving," she said smoothly, her arm tightening slightly around Riley.

Anna's gaze narrowed. "Oh, that's comforting," she said flatly. She took another pull from the bottle before setting it firmly on the counter. "Because I have a lot of questions."

"Understandable," Gee replied, her tone as calm as ever. "And I'll answer them. But for now..." She glanced down at Riley, her expression softening. "It's been a long morning. Riley, why don't you grab a snack?"

Riley looked up at her, his grin widening. "Okay, Gee!" He darted out of the kitchen, blissfully unaware of the emotional storm he was leaving behind.

The moment he was gone, Anna rounded on Gee. "Listen here, you—"

Bryan held up both hands, stepping between them. "—Anna, let's just—"

"—I swear to God, Bryan," Anna growled, "if you tell me to calm down one more time, you're sleeping in the truck."

Gee, her hands on the slick hips, says, "You know, I just took five bullets for this family. Doesn't that count for anything?"

Bryan sighed, glancing between the two women. "This day just keeps getting better."

Anna's eye twitched. "I need coffee," she muttered, pivoting toward the counter.

Gee's playful expression softened as she glanced at Riley, who had been watching the exchange with wide eyes and an increasingly sheepish grin. "Riley," she said gently, her voice losing its teasing edge. "You understand, don't you?"

Riley nodded earnestly. "Yeah, Gee. You're just... you."

Anna, clutching her coffee mug like a lifeline, shot him a look of utter disbelief. "Of course he gets it," her hand paused halfway to her mug, her eyes narrowing as if weighing the truth in Gee's words before pouring a very generous amount of Jameson's into her cup. "This is my life now. Shirt-stealing, scent-sniffing witches."

Gee, her gaze meeting Anna's directly now, said softly, "Anna, I don't expect you to trust me. But I promise you'll see—Riley will always come first."

Anna froze mid-sip. The sincerity in Gee's voice hit her like a wave, chipping away at her anger and leaving only uncertainty and the faintest glimmer of understanding.

For now, Anna took another long drink and sighed. "We'll see," she muttered, her voice grudging but no longer icy. "We'll see."

## CHAPTER 14 - FALL

The kitchen felt colder, the sharp warmth of summer replaced by the crisp bite of autumn. Outside the window, trees blazed with fiery reds, oranges, and yellows, their leaves swirling to the ground in restless gusts. The light was softer now, dimmer as the days grew shorter.

Bryan sat at the table, his cane resting against the edge of a nearby chair. His shoulders were slightly hunched, and his hand absently traced the grain of the wood. His beard was fuller than it had been for a while, and while his face had regained some color, his eyes still carried a hollow, distant look.

Browning stood across from him, leaning over the table with his hands braced against the edge. A map lay spread out between them, marked with circles and hastily scribbled notes. He tapped one area with his finger; his brow furrowed.

"This is where the lead on the hospital assault dried up," Browning said. "It's too clean. Nobody saw anything, and the one witness we had was gone. Just like that."

Bryan shifted in his chair, his fingers tightening slightly around the mug in front of him. He stared at the map but didn't speak, his gaze unfocused.

"And the accident?" He asked finally, his voice low and rough.

Browning hesitated, then shook his head. "Same story. Dead ends everywhere. There are no records and no traceable connections. Whoever did this—if they did this—covered their tracks better than anyone I've ever seen."

Bryan's jaw tightened, and his gaze flicked to the window. The swirling leaves outside seemed to echo his restless frustration. He exhaled slowly, his grip on the mug loosening.

Anna entered, carrying a basket of folded laundry. Her hair hung loose, streaked with gray at the temples, and her movements were precise, almost mechanical. She set the basket on the armchair by the window and began folding a towel, her hands moving methodically.

Browning glanced at her. "Anna," he said, his voice softer, "how are you holding up?"

She paused, smoothing the fabric between her hands. "I'm fine," she murmured without looking up. Her tone was distant, and she focused entirely on the task at hand.

Bryan glanced at her briefly, his lips parting as though to speak, but he hesitated. The unspoken words hung in the air, heavy and unresolved.

Browning cleared his throat, his voice returning to a more professional tone. "Look, Jensen, I'm following a lead. It's thin, but it's something. I'll head out tomorrow and see if it takes us anywhere."

Bryan's fingers drummed against the table, his eyes narrowing slightly. "Do it," he said simply.

Anna paused mid-fold, her hands trembling for a moment before she resumed. She turned her head slightly, her gaze lingering on Bryan, but when he didn't look at her, she picked up the basket and walked out of the room.

Riley was sitting in the hallway just outside, his legs crossed, and his sketchpad balanced on his knees. As Anna walked past without so much as a glance, Riley looked up, his smile faltering. He stood, clutching the pad to his chest, and hesitated.

He stepped to the doorway, his small frame filling the space as he watched the two men at the table. Concern flickered across his face as his eyes shifted from Bryan's distant expression to Browning's tense posture.

Riley glanced down at his drawing pad; the image of a family scene was sketched in rough pencil lines. His smile faded entirely, and his shoulders slumped. Without a word, he turned and walked down the hall, his footsteps soft and hesitant.

Back in the kitchen, Browning gathered his things, sliding the map into his satchel. "I'll get in touch as soon as I have news. Don't let this break you, Jensen," he said, pausing by the door. His voice carried a weight that seemed to linger even after he was gone.

Bryan remained at the table, his cane resting nearby, as the leaves continued to swirl outside the window.

***

The first snow of the season had fallen, turning the world outside into a blanket of white, a thick layer of snow muffling the sounds of Havenwood. The bare branches of the trees were outlined in frost, and the sky hung low and gray, threatening with more snow to come. The light that filtered through the windows was pale and cold, casting long, stark shadows across the floor.

A chill settled into the mornings, turning dew on the grass into frost that melted slowly under a pale sun. Inside

Bryan's home, the atmosphere mirrored the season—quiet, subdued, and filled with unspoken tension.

The house seemed to breathe with the changing season, its old wooden floors creaking louder in the silence, the occasional groan of the wind slipping through drafty windows, a ghostly reminder of its age. The quiet was oppressive, a fragile peace waiting to be broken.

Anna moved through the kitchen with a quiet purpose, the soft clink of dishes her only companion. She glanced at Bryan, seated at the kitchen table with a book resting in his hands. His fingers brushed the spine absently, his eyes distant and unfocused, fixed on a page he wasn't reading.

"I made some coffee. Do you want some?" Anna asked, keeping her tone casual.

Bryan looked up, startled, as though he'd forgotten she was there. "Uh… sure. Thanks."

Anna poured the coffee with deliberate care, and her movements were measured to avoid disturbing the fragile equilibrium of the room. She placed the mug in front of him and returned to wiping the counter, her eyes lingering on him for a moment longer than necessary.

The clatter of footsteps broke the stillness. Riley bounded down the stairs, his energy an unintentional contrast to the subdued mood. "Morning!"

Bryan offered a faint smile. "Morning, kiddo."

Riley slid into the seat next to Bryan, snatching a slice of toast from the plate on the table. As he reached for the butter, Gee, in her feline form, padded silently into the room and leapt onto Riley's lap, curling up with a contented purr.

Anna leaned against the counter, watching them. The sight of Riley and Bryan together brought a small smile to her face, but beneath it was a weight she couldn't shake—a tension that lingered in the air like the promise of an oncoming storm.

***

Later that morning, the knock at the door echoed through the house. Bryan answered the door only to find Detective Browning standing on the porch, his expression unreadable but carrying the weight of something significant.

"Matt," Bryan said, stepping aside to let him in.

"Sorry to drop by unannounced," Browning said, shrugging off his coat. "I found something in the case files I thought you needed to see."

Bryan led him to the living room, where both men sat on the couch. Anna, her unease mounting, followed at a distance, her footsteps light but deliberate.

Browning pulled a folder from his briefcase, flipped it open, and handed a photograph to Bryan. It was Bryan's car, which was taken after the accident.

Bryan's jaw tightened as he stared at the image, his breath catching in his chest. The wreckage was all too familiar, a scene burned into his memory. Ashley's charred skull, frozen in an eternal scream, leaned back and away from the vehicle's mangled frame. Tendrils of smoke rose like ghostly fingers into the air, captured mid-dance, while the scars from the inferno were still etched into the asphalt. The truck was a tangled heap of metal, grotesque and unrecognizable violent testament to the tragedy that had unraveled his life.

Bryan sat frozen, his fingers brushing against the photograph as though touching it might burn. His gaze locked onto the image, its stark details pulling him into the abyss of memory and regret.

Anna's presence barely registered as the room around him faded, his mind replaying that fateful morning like a cursed reel of film.

He'd been in his writing room, hunched over his desk...

The light from the monitor cast a soft glow on his face, highlighting the intensity of his focus.

The words flowed easily on the screen: "The creature turns quickly, and then..." But as Ashley approached, Bryan didn't look up, his attention fully captured by the scene unfolding in his mind.

"Hun, Brianne, and I are going to the store," Ashley said in a light and playful voice.

"Uh-huh," Bryan murmured, his fingers pausing briefly on the keyboard before continuing their rhythm.

Ashley's smile widened as an idea formed in her mind. She loved teasing him, especially when he was caught up in his work. Leaning against the doorframe, she tilted her head slightly and said, "And then to Ed Jones' place. He's going to ravish me while Brianne watches."

Bryan's head snapped up, his eyes wide with shock. "Wait, what did you say?"

Ashley laughed, the sound light and musical. "Just kidding, we're going to the store."

Bryan's face was relieved as he spun his chair around to face her. Before he could respond, Ashley straddled his lap, her smile turning seductive as she wrapped her arms around his neck. Bryan's hands instinctively found her hips, and he pulled her closer, their connection electric.

She kissed him softly and nibbled on his ear, her breath warm against his skin. Bryan closed his eyes, savoring the moment as the stress of his work faded away in her embrace.

"What's that fragrance?" he asked, his voice low and appreciative.

"La Chocolat," Ashley replied with a grin.

"As in chips?" Bryan teased, his hands tracing the curve of her waist.

"Exactly," she purred, her eyes twinkling with mischief.

Bryan chuckled, pulling her closer. "And is this Chocolat for me or someone else?"

"Why shouldn't others enjoy such a treat?" Ashley quipped, her tone playful but tinged with affection.

Bryan's brow furrowed slightly, playing along. "Who is this someone else? Describe this man so I can face him."

Ashley's grin grew as she leaned closer, her lips brushing against his ear. "Who said it was a man?" she whispered, her voice sultry.

Bryan's eyes widened in mock surprise. "Jeez, how can I compete with that?"

Ashley laughed softly, resting her forehead against his. "I'm taking her shopping. Need anything?"

Bryan smiled, his heart swelling with love for the woman in his arms. "To be your husband and her dad."

"You got it," Ashley whispered, kissing his lips softly.

"Be safe. Love you," Bryan said as she stood up, reluctantly letting her go.

"Always," Ashley replied, smiling as she headed toward the door. Just before she left, she turned back, their eyes meeting one last time.

"Forever," Bryan added, watching as she disappeared down the hallway.

"I'm taking your car... your car... your car..."

He'd been staring at the monitor, his fingers hovering above the keyboard, when the doorbell rang.

DING-DONG.

The sound of the doorbell jolted Bryan from his thoughts. He closed his eyes as if admitting defeat, unable to will the words to return, before leaning back in his chair with a sigh.

"Sweetheart, can you get that?" he called out.

DING-DONG.

The doorbell rang again, more insistent this time. Bryan's brow furrowed in annoyance. "Ash! Can you get the door, please?"

When no response came, Bryan sighed, running a hand through his hair as he stood up. His muscles ached from sitting for so long, and he stretched briefly before heading down the stairs toward the foyer.

DING-DONG.

Just as Bryan reached the bottom of the stairs, the doorbell rang for a third time. He opened the door, expecting to see Ashley standing there, hands full of groceries, or maybe a neighbor with a friendly request. But when the door swung open, Bryan's heart sank.

A police officer and a priest stood on the porch, their expressions solemn and unreadable. The sight of them sent a cold shock of fear through Bryan's body, rooting him to the spot.

"Mr. Jensen?" Officer Edwards asked, almost quizzically, his voice gentle but firm.

Bryan nodded slowly, the sense of dread growing in his chest.

"May we come in?"

Little did he know that mundane moment would be the last time he'd hear Ashley's voice.

If he hadn't been so consumed by the novel...

If he'd gone with them, he'd have driven the car himself…

If Ashley hadn't been behind the wheel that day…

Bryan's chest tightened, his breath catching in his throat. The weight of those "if only" thoughts was suffocating, crushing him under their relentless pressure.

"Bryan…"

Bryan squeezed his eyes closed, only opening them when he heard Anna's voice.

Anna took a step closer, her heart aching at the sight of his anguish. "Bryan," she said softly, her voice a lifeline against the tide of silence.

A sharp gasp broke the silence, yanking Bryan back to the present.

Both Bryan and Browning turned to find Anna standing behind them at the edge of the kitchen, her hand pressed to her mouth, her eyes wide with horror. Her gaze lingered on the photo for only a second before she turned away, her body trembling as she covered her face with her hands.

"A-Anna," Bryan said, rising to his feet, his voice gentle but urgent. He stood, the photo slipping from his hand, forgotten for the moment. He crossed the room in a few quick strides, placing a steady hand on her shoulder.

"I—I'm sorry," she stammered, her voice barely audible. "I didn't mean to—"

Browning stood silently, watching the interplay between Bryan and Anna.

"—It's okay," Bryan interrupted softly. "You don't have to apologize." He guided her back toward the kitchen, his hand still on her shoulder, his voice low and calming. "Come on. Let's get you a coffee."

*** 

Bryan poured her a cup, his movements deliberate.

Anna stood frozen, her back pressed against the counter as though it could hold her upright against the weight of what she had just seen. Her breathing was shallow, almost trembling, as her mind reeled, trying to piece together the image of the wreckage, the unimaginable loss, and the man now sitting mere feet from her.

That photo—just a photo, she told herself, but it wasn't. It wasn't just a photograph. It was a fragment of eternity, a moment of devastation frozen in time. A cruel relic of the day that had destroyed Bryan's life. Her chest ached as if the air itself had turned heavy, suffocating. She closed her eyes, but the image was seared into her mind: the twisted metal, the smoke curling into the air, the promise of life reduced to ash and ruin.

She risked a glance toward Bryan. His shoulders had been hunched, his back to her, as he leaned forward on the couch. His head hung low, the photograph clutched in his hands like a talisman of grief and guilt. He wasn't crying, she wasn't even sure if Bryan cried anymore—but the weight of his sorrow was palpable, radiating from him in waves.

Anna's fingers curled around the edge of the counter, her knuckles white. She thought of that night—the night she'd seen him standing broken in the doorway of the haunted house, leaning against the doorframe. His body shattered, his

278

face battered and pale, and yet he'd stood there. Barely alive but standing. Protecting her. Protecting Riley. Even then, with death reaching for him, he had made a choice: to shield them.

Her gaze drifted to the stairs leading to the second floor of the house, and her breath hitched. The house... this house. The one that a dead wife's fury had ravaged. By the wrath of a woman whose love for Bryan had transcended death. Ashley's ghost—her rage—had shredded this place, leaving scars in its wake. The walls had been rebuilt, the furniture had been replaced, but Anna knew those marks weren't gone. They lingered, unseen but felt, in every creak of the floorboards, in every shadow that stretched a little too long at night.

And Bryan. God, Bryan. How did he do it? How did he live here, day after day, surrounded by the echoes of his pain? How did he endure the weight of everything he had lost—his wife, his daughter, his very life—and still find the strength to take in her and Riley? To protect them as fiercely as he did.

Her chest tightened as her thoughts turned inward. What if it had been Riley? The thought was a knife slicing through her composure. What if it had been her son's charred body in that wreckage? What if she were the one left behind, the one trying to breathe through the suffocating grief, the one clutching at fragments of a life stolen too soon? Could she even survive it? She didn't think so. And yet, Bryan had.

Her gaze flicked back to him. Mere feet away, feet that felt like miles. She had seen the tension in his hands, the way his fingers curled around the photograph as though it might shatter in his grip. He was a man held together by sheer willpower, and she wondered if even that was starting to fray.

Anna swallowed hard, forcing herself to move. She couldn't just stand there, couldn't let him shoulder this alone. Hand shaking, she grabbed the coffee pot and poured a fresh cup, the sound of the liquid filling the mug grounding her, giving her something to focus on. With measured steps, she crossed the room and set the cup on the table in front of him.

Bryan's eyes met hers, and for a moment, she saw it—the raw, unfiltered agony he usually kept hidden. It took her breath away.

"I thought you might need this," she said softly, her voice and hands trembling despite her efforts to keep them steady.

Bryan nodded, his lips pressing into a thin line. He didn't speak, but he reached for the cup, his hand brushing hers for the briefest of moments. It was enough to send a shiver down her spine—a reminder that this man, who seemed so unbreakable, was holding himself together by the thinnest of threads.

Bryan led her to a chair, and she sat down beside, kneeling in front of her. Her hands clasped tightly in her lap. "Bryan," she began, hesitating. "I... I don't know how you do it."

He frowned, his eyes holding hers. "Do what?"

"Survive this." Her voice broke, and she blinked rapidly, trying to hold back the tears threatening to spill. "If it were Riley... if it were me in your place, I don't think I could. I don't think I'd even want to."

Bryan's jaw tightened, his throat working as he swallowed hard. "You would," he said quietly. "You'd find a way. For him."

Anna shook her head, tears slipping down her cheeks. "But at what cost? Bryan, I've seen what this has done to you. You've given so much of yourself, and there's so little left. I just..." She trailed off, her voice choked with emotion. "I don't want to lose you, too."

Bryan exhaled slowly. He reached for her hand, his grip firm but gentle. "You're not going to," he said, his voice steady despite the storm in his eyes. "I promise you, Anna. I'll figure this out. I'll make it right. For Ashley. For Brianne. For us."

Anna nodded, but the fear in her chest didn't dissipate. She wanted to believe him, she needed to feel him—but the shadows of his past loomed too large, too dark.

And as they sat there, hand in hand, the photograph, sitting a scant fifteen feet away, lay on the coffee table—a silent reminder of everything he'd lost and everything they still stood to lose.

For a moment, the tension between them softened, a quiet understanding passing between them. Anna offered a faint, almost apologetic smile. "I'm okay," she said after a moment. "Go. Talk to him. I just... I needed a minute."

Bryan studied her carefully, then nodded back toward the living room. "If you need me, I'm right here."

Anna nodded, her hands still gripping the mug as if it were a lifeline. Bryan stood, hesitating briefly, before returning to the living room.

Bryan and Browning exchange a knowing look before Bryan picks up the conversation.

"Go on. What about it?" Bryan asked, his voice low.

Both men sat down. Browning pointed to a shadowy figure barely visible in the background near the treeline. "I had it enhanced. It doesn't tell us much, but it raises questions."

Bryan's chest tightened as he leaned closer to study the image. His fingers brushed against the edge of the photograph; his breath slow but heavy. The figure was indistinct, more a suggestion than a certainty, yet it was enough to make his stomach churn.

"Now, take a closer look at the rest of the picture. Notice anything… unusual?" Browning asked.

Bryan frowned but kept focusing on the photo.

Bryan's stomach twisted. He set the photograph on the coffee table, but its image remained burned into his mind.

"Doesn't it seem a little strange? Officer Edwards took this picture. Just like any other traffic accident resulting in a fatality would require. And it isn't like this happens every day."

"So?"

"I've been a cop my entire adult life. I've seen hundreds of accidents, a lot of them involving fatalities, and one thing about this photo stands out. One thing missing!"

Bryan glances at Browning.

'Where are all the lookie-loos? The rubber-neckers? The Nosy-Rosie?" Browning waits for an answer that doesn't come. He finally continues.

'Edwards is taking the photo, and there isn't anyone else in the area except one: our mystery man. What was so special that this guy happened to take a stroll, stop just inside the treeline, and gawk at this?"

Bryan leans back in his chair and waits for Browning to say his peace. It's as if he knew it was going to happen. "This guy knew it was going to happen. Right here, this is your 'Grassy Knoll.'"

Browning taps the photo. "Right at the exact moment... which leads me to believe this guy's clairvoyant or..." Browning pauses to let it sink in. "He knew it was going to happen."

Bryan finally broke the silence, his voice measured but tinged with bitterness. "I've always had this compulsion for routine—same time, same route, same everything. It's something I've tried to manage, but I know it makes me predictable. Hell, if someone wanted to set me up—"

"—They'd only have to watch you for a couple of weeks to know exactly where you'd be and when," says Browning. "Establish a pattern... and wait."

Bryan nods grimly, "I handed them the playbook. Week after week, I drove on that same stretch of road, stopped at the same store, parked in the same damn spot. I thought it was harmless, comforting, even. But it was a map straight to me, and Ashley..."

"And your family paid the price," Browning softly says.

"The bastard stood there, watching it happen." Bryan gestures to the photo on the table, his voice tight with restrained fury. "Who does that? Who waits like that unless they're there to confirm the job is done?"

"Someone meticulous," says Browning, studying the photo. "Patient. Someone who knows how to exploit a pattern. That's not random, Bryan. It's methodical."

Bryan, leaning forward, his voice hardening, says, "Methodical, sure. But it's personal. You don't go to those lengths unless you want someone to suffer. And I think it's time we find out why."

Bryan looked up, meeting Browning's gaze with an intensity that left no room for doubt. "I've always believed I was the target. Whoever 'this guy' is. At least this proves it."

Browning leaned back slightly; his brow furrowed. "But why did he do it?"

Bryan huffed a short, humorless laugh and shook his head. "That's the million-dollar question, isn't it?"

"More importantly, what are you going to do about it?" Browning said softly. He paused, studying Bryan with a mixture of empathy and expectation. "You're not just some guy, not just Bryan Jensen. You're freakin' Alan Hoyle. The 'Alan Hoyle.' You've spent years writing about killers, con men, and criminals who exploit patterns like this."

Bryan tensed, his hands clenching into fists. "So what? I'm not that man. I just made up stories, Matt. That doesn't mean I know how to stop someone like this."

284

"Doesn't it?" Browning countered. His voice hardened, almost a challenge. "You wrote dozens of novels where guys like this are the bad guys. Hell, half the time, they're the puppet masters. You've studied the underworld, and you've dissected their methods—even if they were 'fiction.' You know better than most how someone like this operates."

Bryan leaned back; his gaze distant. "I wrote those books sitting in my study, Matt. I wasn't out there living it."

"No, but you did your homework," Browning pressed. "Your readers believed it because you got the details right. You're familiar with the hierarchy, the strategies, and the 'why.' If anyone can make sense of this…" He gestured toward the photo on the table. "It's you."

Bryan picked up the photo, studying the shadowy figure with a newfound intensity. "So, you think this guy… what? Works for someone?"

Browning shrugged but didn't back down. "It's possible. Or someone works for him. Think about it: if this were random, if this guy were just some loner with a vendetta, why not pull the trigger himself? Why orchestrate an 'accident' that leaves so much to chance? No, this feels bigger, Bryan. Coordinated. Methodical."

Bryan set the photo down with a sharp exhale, his frustration mounting. "And you think it's organized crime?"

Browning leaned forward, his voice low and deliberate. "I think someone like that—someone who's patient enough to exploit your routines, to stand there and watch it all unfold—they're not working alone. They've got resources. Connections. Hell, they might not even be the mastermind. This could be someone else pulling the strings."

Bryan ran a hand over his face, the weight of the conversation settled on him. "You're talking about a hit. A professional hit."

"Maybe not professional," Browning conceded. "But hired. Organized crime has a long history of making problems disappear through 'accidents.' And you know better than most how these things play out. Someone hires the right guy, the guy does the job, and the client keeps their hands clean."

Bryan nods slowly.

"And what is the first rule of 'assassination?'" asks Browning.

Bryan's eyes fix on the old cop. "Kill the assassin."

Bryan's laugh was bitter, almost hollow. "So now you want me to think like one of my villains? Great. That's just what I need."

"I'm not saying you have to become 'Hoyle,'" Browning said, his tone softening. "But you've got a mind for this, Bryan. You see connections other people miss. And I think, deep down, you know this wasn't just bad luck. This was planned."

Bryan leaned forward, resting his elbows on his knees. His voice was quiet, almost a whisper. "Planned or not, it doesn't change what happened, Matt. It doesn't bring them back."

"No, it doesn't," Browning agreed. "But it might stop it from happening again. And if it was planned—if someone orchestrated this—don't you want to know why? Don't you want to make sure they pay for what they did?"

Bryan's eyes flickered with a spark of something—anger, determination, or maybe both. He reached for the photo again, his jaw tightening as he studied the shadowy figure in the treeline.

Browning watched him closely, his voice quieter now but no less firm. "You're the best shot at figuring this out. I can follow the evidence, but I don't have your insight. You know how these people think. You know the lengths they'll go to."

Bryan didn't respond immediately; his thoughts were a whirlwind of guilt, grief, and reluctant acceptance. Finally, he set the photo back on the table, his voice tight with restrained fury. "If this guy's connected to organized crime, if someone paid for this…" He looked up, meeting Browning's gaze. "We need to find out who. And why?"

"And we will," Browning promised. "But we do it together. I'm not letting you shoulder this alone."

Browning tapped the photo on the table, his finger lingering over the blurred figure. "If only…" he muttered, his voice trailing off.

Bryan glanced up; his brows furrowed. "If only what?"

"If only we could sharpen this. I mean, really sharpen it," Browning said. "We might have something—an ID, a lead, anything. But this?" He shook his head. "This is like chasing a ghost."

Bryan leaned back; his gaze fixed on the photograph. The frustration in Browning's voice mirrored his own. The shadowy figure was so close to revealing the truth, yet just out of reach. "There's got to be a way," Bryan said quietly.

"Where there's a will, there's a way. There must be," Browning replied, his tone heavy with doubt. "But not through me. I'm a detective, not a magician. This photo's already been enhanced as far as my resources can take it. What we need..." He paused, looking at Bryan with a mix of hesitation and hope. "What we need is someone with access to tools I don't have. Someone who can extract details from this that we can't even see.

Bryan's mind turned over the possibilities, his fingers brushing against the edge of the photograph. And then it hit him. A name. A face. A possibility. "Scott," he said softly.

Browning raised an eyebrow. "Scott? Who's Scott?"

"FBI," Bryan replied, his voice gaining strength. "Agent Scott. I worked with her... indirectly. She's sharp and resourceful. If anyone can help with this, it's her."

Browning frowned, clearly skeptical. "And you think she's just going to drop whatever she's doing to work on this? She's an FBI agent, Bryan. They don't exactly have a lot of downtime."

Bryan leaned forward, his gaze steady and unwavering. "She owes someone I know."

"If this 'Scott' can get us a clear image... who knows? It might just tell us more than we bargained for," Browning says.

"More's the point, Matt. The question is: are we ready to face what it tells us?"

The light in the kitchen had changed. The golden rays of afternoon had long since given way to a dim orange hue as the sun dipped below the horizon. Shadows stretched across the room, creeping along the walls like silent spectators. The faint hum of the refrigerator seemed louder in the growing quiet, a stark contrast to the earlier buzz of the day.

Outside the window, the world was bathed in twilight. The soft glow of the setting sun painted the sky in streaks of amber and violet, bleeding into deepening shades of blue. Streetlights flickered to life in the distance, their warm halos piercing the encroaching darkness. Somewhere beyond the trees, the faint chirping of crickets announced the arrival of evening, their rhythmic song filling the stillness.

Inside, the kitchen light was warm but subdued, casting a soft glow over the table where Bryan and Riley sat. The overhead fixture flickered briefly, an almost imperceptible reminder of the house's age. The air carried the faint scent of coffee grounds and toasted bread, remnants of a day slipping into memory. Bryan's fingers tapped against the tabletop, the sound sharp against the quiet, as if marking the seconds of the waning day.

Riley, seated across from him, was half-illuminated by the glow of the kitchen light, his expression curious but tinged with the seriousness of the moment. The photograph between them caught the light, its glossy surface reflecting a distorted image of the room as the evening shadows deepened.

"What'd I do this time?" Riley finally asked.

Bryan hesitated, then leaned forward, lowering his voice. "Riley, I need your help with something. Something important. I don't like asking you to do this," he admitted. "You're a kid. You shouldn't have to worry about stuff like this."

Riley tilted his head, his expression both curious and determined. "You once said that if you ever had a son, you wished he'd be like me. Well, this sounds to me like something a kid would do for his 'Dad,' right? And dads and sons are supposed to be a team."

Bryan's chest tightened at the words. "Yeah, we are. But this... this is different. It's not a game, Riley. It's—"

"—Serious. I get it," Riley interrupted, his young voice steady. "But you need me. And if it's to help you, or Mom, or Gee... I'll do it."

Bryan smiled faintly, ruffling Riley's hair. "You're a good kid. A better kid than I deserve."

Riley grinned. "Well, duh. Let's do this." Riley's eyes lit up with a mix of excitement and apprehension. "So, 'Dad.' What is it?"

Bryan smiled faintly at the word "Dad," his chest tightening with a mix of pride and guilt. "I need to get a message to someone. Someone I trust."

"Why can't you just call them?" Riley asked, tilting his head.

Bryan shook his head. "It's not that simple. You remember Agent Scott?" Riley grins. "She works for the FBI.

And we can't use phones or email for this. It has to be…
discreet."

Riley's brow furrowed. "Discreet? You mean, like,
sneaky?"

"Exactly," Bryan said, sliding a piece of paper and a pen
across the table. "You're going to write her a letter. In your
own handwriting. That way, if anyone sees it, they'll think it's
just a kid asking for help."

Riley grinned. "You want me to play spy?"

Bryan's smile widened slightly. "Something like that."

***

The next evening, Riley sat at his desk, his tongue poking
out as he concentrated on writing the letter. His handwriting
was messy, with uneven letters, but that was part of the plan.
Bryan sat beside him, watching over his shoulder.

Bryan watched Riley scribble with fierce concentration,
his tongue poking out slightly as he worked. A pang of guilt
twisted in Bryan's chest. He could almost hear Ashley's voice,
sharp and protective, chastising him for letting their child—
any child—be part of this. But Riley wasn't just any kid. He
was resilient, loyal, and, above all, willing. That alone made
Bryan feel undeserving of the boy's trust.

"Okay," Riley said, putting the pen down and reading
aloud what he'd written:

Hi Agent Scott,

I hope you're doing okay. I'm not sure how to write a
letter, so I'll just get straight to the point. My dad needs your

help. He's trying to figure something out, and he says you're the only person he can trust with this. He didn't want to ask you himself because he knows you're busy and probably don't want to hear from him. But I think it's really important, and I don't want him to be sad anymore.

I'm sending you a photo. It's blurry, but Dad says it's important. He says if anyone can make it better, it's you.

Please don't bother Dad about this. He's already reviewed everything, and he told me to write to you because I'm better at this kind of stuff than he is. (That's a joke, but not really.)

Thanks for helping my dad. He won't say it, but he really needs you. And I guess I do, too.

Sincerely, Riley

Bryan chuckled softly. "That's perfect. She'll know it's from me." Riley grinned. "You think she'll figure it out?"

Bryan nodded. "She's smart. Almost as smart as me, sometimes."

***

The following day, Bryan handed Riley a thick envelope. It contained the letter, the photograph, and a folded sheet of paper with a hastily scribbled note in Bryan's handwriting: Scott, I'm counting on you. Jensen.

Bryan knelt down, looking Riley in the eye. "Now, listen carefully. You're going to give this to Detective Browning. He'll drop it off for us near the Boston FBI field office. No one in Havenwood can know about this. Not your mom, not Gee—no one. Do you understand?"

Riley nodded solemnly. "I got it, Dad. Spy stuff."

Bryan ruffled his hair. "Thanks, kid."

TO BE CONTINUED...

**Next time...**

Eclipse - Book Three of the Shadows Series

I should have known things would go to hell the moment Bryan got that look in his eye — the one that says, "I have a terrible idea, but I'm going to do it anyway." The guy jumps headfirst into insanity like it's his damn job. And, surprise, surprise, it nearly got him killed. Again.

Where do I even start? Oh, right. My life went from mildly chaotic to full-blown apocalyptic when we decided to take on Ed Jones and his cult of creeps. Turns out, Jones wasn't just some shady power-hungry weirdo — he had a whole agenda, and that agenda involved taking control of the Coven. Bad news? He saw Brianne as his golden ticket.

Ashley — yes, Brianne's dear, loving mother — finally had her big "I'm still alive and terrifying" reveal. But did that mean she suddenly developed a heart? No. Instead, she managed to shatter Brianne's world by basically confirming what Brianne had always feared: that she was nothing more than a tool. You know, for all her ancient wisdom, Ashley really sucks at parenting.

Brianne lost it. And by "lost it," I mean she unleashed a power so devastating that it turned Shadows into ash before they could even scream, which would have been awesome if she hadn't been absolutely horrified by it. Lucky for me, my handy-dandy Ward of Protection kept me from becoming crispy bacon.

Meanwhile, Bryan did what Bryan does best — put himself in the line of fire. He and Jones went toe-to-toe, and let's say it was the kind of brawl that left entire city blocks questioning their existence. Bryan made it out — barely — but not before making a few enemies in the process. And Jones? He didn't slink away defeated. No, that smug bastard saw exactly what Brianne could do and decided he wanted her. Great. Fantastic. No notes.

So where does that leave us? Ashley's playing her own game, Jones is about to make his next move, and Brianne — oh, Brianne—is on the edge of something huge. She just doesn't know whether to embrace it or be afraid of it. And me? Well, I get to keep everyone from falling apart while dodging homicidal Shadows and trying not to get set on fire.

Yeah. No pressure.

# ABOUT THE AUTHOR

**Thomas D. Rudd**

Tom is a retired Army warrant officer and a UCLA graduate in screenwriting. He lives in the Pacific Northwest, where his lifelong passion for science fiction fuels his writing. He is the author of Shadows (2025) and the upcoming sequel to Outcast, titled Eclipse. His work blends cinematic storytelling with supernatural intrigue, reflecting his military background and his training as a screenwriter.

www.ingramcontent.com/pod-product-compliance
Lightning Source LLC
Chambersburg PA
CBHW020915200626
46814CB00001BA/343